A savage cry made Hawkes turn—just as the Wolf Chief hurled himself at the mountain man. The Indian's weight bore Hawkes facedown into the deep, churned snow. Hawkes groped for the knife in his belt, drew it from his sheath, and plunged it into the Wolf Chief's thigh.

The Cheyenne roared at the pain and struck with his own knife, aiming for a spot in the middle of the mountain man's back. But Hawkes was twisting his body violently, trying to throw off his adversary, and the Indian's blade merely cut a deep gash in the mountain man's arm. Try as he might, Hawkes could not gain an advantage—the Wolf Chief was too strong, too agile.

The warrior raised his knife again. This time Hawkes knew he would find his mark, and there was nothing he could do about it. . . .

MOUNTAIN
HONOR

Jason Manning

15 3 6   0 2 1 5 1 3

A SIGNET BOOK

SIGNET
Published by New American Library, a division of
Penguin Putnam Inc., 375 Hudson Street,
New York, New York 10014, U.S.A.
Penguin Books Ltd, 80 Strand,
London WC2R ORL, England
Penguin Books Australia Ltd, Ringwood,
Victoria, Australia
Penguin Books Canada Ltd, 10 Alcorn Avenue,
Toronto, Ontario, Canada M4V 3B2
Penguin Books (N.Z.) Ltd, 182–190 Wairau Road,
Auckland 10, New Zealand

Penguin Books Ltd, Registered Offices:
Harmondsworth, Middlesex, England

First published by Signet, an imprint of New American Library,
a division of Penguin Putnam Inc.

First Printing, December 2001
10 9 8 7 6 5 4 3 2 1

 REGISTERED TRADEMARK—MARCA REGISTRADA

Printed in the United States of America

PUBLISHER'S NOTE
This is a work of fiction. Names, characters, places, and incidents either
are the product of the author's imagination or are used fictitiously,
and any resemblance to actual persons, living or dead, business
establishments, events, or locales is entirely coincidental.

Chapter One

Loud Talker was sitting with a few of the Cheyenne chiefs, listening to their excited talk and picking up bits and pieces of what passed between them. He was an Omaha Indian, and the Cheyenne tongue was rather different from his own. Fortunately, he had a knack for picking up languages. He could spend a fortnight with a strange-tongued people, and by the end of that time he could fluently converse in their talk. For two days he had been among the Southern Cheyenne, an honored guest of the great chief Motavato, or Black Kettle, and already he was able to make some sense of what these Cheyenne men were saying. Which meant in turn that he had to rely less and less on sign language.

Not that he minded using sign, at which he was quite proficient. But in his travels—and he had traveled widely—Loud Talker had discovered that one could learn as much about another person by the way he spoke as by the words that passed his lips. Learning about people was what Loud Talker did. He liked to think of it as his profession. He told those who asked him that he was an emissary from the Omaha tribe, what the white man might call an ambassador-at-large. Most of those to whom he told this were either too polite or too indifferent to ask why the Omahas needed a roving diplomat. The Omahas were by no means a powerful or very influential tribe, and they lived on the banks of the Missouri River, many days' ride to the east of the high sagebrush plains where Loud Talker now found himself.

Loud Talker did not make treaties. He could not really speak for the Omaha people, at least not in any official capacity, even though sometimes he said he did if it was necessary to magnify his importance in order to get where he wanted to go. What Loud Talker really did was range far and wide in order to witness with his own eyes as many things as he could. Then he carried the news of the world back to his people. This was a job of his own invention, and one that actually was of some use to the Omaha tribe, because Loud Talker was a keen observer, a man who noticed the smallest detail even while he kept the grand scheme of things in sharp focus.

Had he been a white man, Loud Talker would have excelled as a correspondent for one of the major newspapers back East. He was well educated, perhaps the most educated person in his tribe by the standards of the white man. And that held true whether you measured education on the basis of book-learning or by the yardstick of life experience. He had attended a missionary school as a child and to this day had a fondness for the white man's books, though he seldom got his hands on one. He had spent time among many different tribes—the Pawnee, the Osage, the Delaware, the Seneca, the Arikara, the Sioux, the Kansa, and now the Cheyenne. He had also spent a lot of time among the whites. He even dressed a little like a white man. For instance, today he wore an old frock coat that was gray with dust and frayed at the cuffs, dirty old yellow stroud trousers, and a stovepipe hat that was not only badly bent but also lacked a crown. A drunken teamster had snatched it off Loud Talker's head one night in a camp on the old Santa Fe Trail and driven his fist through it. Loud Talker wasn't sure to this day why the mule skinner had done that. There had been no animosity between them, either before or after that errant act of vandalism. Though he often did not understand why people did the things they did, Loud Talker was seldom surprised these days. No one who spent most of his life watching people could be very much surprised by sudden and irrational behavior. It seemed to be an attribute that was becoming more and more widespread throughout the species.

Loud Talker eschewed boots. He preferred moccasins, but as he had only one pair to his name he often went barefoot, saving the moccasins for special occasions. Today he wore them. He was, after all, among chiefs of the Cheyenne, who were all wearing their finest clothes. In fact, Loud Talker felt a little self-conscious about the shabby state of his own attire in their presence. He worried that his appearance might reflect poorly upon the Omaha tribe he represented, albeit in an unofficial capacity. But there was no help for it—his clothes were as well-traveled as he, and far less durable.

The Cheyenne chiefs Black Kettle, White Antelope

and Lean Bear were looking splendid, thought Loud Talker. They clearly took this meeting with a representative from the President of the United States very seriously. They were clad in their ceremonial regalia: buckskin tunics and leggings adorned with fur piping and intricate and colorful bead– and quill–work, and they wore their war bonnets—even though they were here not for war but to make an agreement with Colonel Greenwood, Commissioner of Indian Affairs, that would hopefully facilitate the keeping of the peace between the whites and the Cheyenne Nation. More and more white people were coming west, invading the traditional hunting grounds of the Cheyenne, and this was cause for concern. For twenty years they had been coming—at first just an occasional train of prairie schooners, but now they came like a roaring river, a constant flood of emigrants. How many white people were there, anyway? This the Cheyenne chiefs had wanted to know from Loud Talker. He had come, after all, from the East, just like the whites had. He dressed like them, he spoke their language—certainly he had to know them better than any Cheyenne did, as the Cheyenne had tried their best to keep their distance from the white interlopers. Avoiding the whites, however, was becoming increasingly difficult.

Loud Talker did know the white people well. The lands of the Omaha were directly in the path of the white flood—and in Loud Talker's opinion it was no small miracle that his people had been able to hold on to their land this long. That was so, he believed, because the Omaha had never posed much of a threat to the whites. Unlike their neighbors, the Sak and

Fox, they had never waged war against the whites. In fact, they had witnessed the fate that befell the Sak and Fox—and learned a most valuable lesson. There were many whites, as many as the blades of grass upon the prairie, and to war against such overwhelming numbers was worse than futile—it was suicidal. So the Omaha, by and large, had managed to maintain peaceful relations with the whites, and so far their presence in the newly settled land had been tolerated.

So Loud Talker had told these leaders of the Cheyenne that there were at least a hundred whites for every person in the tribe, and that was a conservative estimate. They were therefore wise to try getting along with the white man. The trio of chiefs with whom he now sat had been grateful to Loud Talker for this information. Much debate had raged among the chiefs of the Cheyenne bands regarding this treaty they had been asked to sign. Some strongly opposed the agreement because it would require the Cheyenne to live on a strip of land between Sand Creek and the Arkansas River. They wanted to resist the encroachment of the whites, the way the Sioux were doing to the north. But Black Kettle and White Antelope and Lean Bear had disagreed with them, and what Loud Talker had told them about the size of the white tribe confirmed that they had made the right decision. It was better to appease the whites and tolerate their presence, rather than raise a hand against them. This way, perhaps, the Cheyenne would survive.

Still, the devil was in the details, and though he could not understand every word that passed between the Cheyenne chiefs, Loud Talker could get the gist of the conversation. Of the three, Lean Bear was the most ambivalent about this treaty-making.

"We can agree to keep ourselves on this land that the white man says will be ours for all time," he said. "But we cannot make the buffalo stay. The buffalo moves from one place to another when he wants to, and we must be able to follow him wherever he goes. Without the buffalo, the Cheyenne cannot live."

"They will let us go where the buffalo go when we hunt," said Black Kettle. "We can go anywhere we want. It has always been so, and so it will remain. We will not be prisoners on our own land."

"We can go," said Lean Bear, nodding. "But when we sign the treaty paper we say that wherever we go, we will always come back to live on this piece of land. We can live only here, and nowhere else."

White Antelope shrugged his indifference. "We have always lived here. What harm is there in agreeing to do what we are going to do, anyway?"

"If by signing this treaty we are not agreeing to do something besides what we have always done, why sign it at all?" asked Lean Bear, his doubts making him an earnest devil's advocate.

"Because the treaty paper is the White Father's promise that his people will not try to take our land from us," answered Black Kettle.

"Then the White Father should have his people sign the treaty paper, not us." Lean Bear turned to Loud Talker. As he spoke he made sign language, since he had no idea how quickly the Omaha observer could master a language.

"You know the white man well," said the Cheyenne chief. "Is the word of the White Father to be trusted?"

Loud Talker was very happy to be a witness to this historic event, and he was keenly interested in the debate going on between the Cheyenne leaders— but he had no desire to become involved and wanted in no way to influence the outcome. Besides, Lean Bear's question was a difficult one to answer. It was true Loud Talker was acquainted with many white people. And like all people, some whites could be relied upon to keep their word and some could not. Others would keep their word only so long as it was in their best interests to do so. Loud Talker decided that the best thing to do in this situation was equivocate.

"The white people are like a river at flood, driving all things before it. Many wars have been fought, and many ghosts have been made, because tribes leave their homelands as the whites come, and try to find new homes on the lands of other tribes. I think that this is what the White Father is trying to stop with this treaty. He wants your promise that you will stay here, no matter what."

Lean Bear squinted suspiciously at Loud Talker. "Why do the tribes leave their lands? Is it not true that the whites take it from them, even though they make treaty papers promising not to do that, so that the tribes have no choice but to find another place to live?"

Loud Talker shrugged. "I know that this has sometimes happened."

"The whites did not drive Loud Talker's people from their land," White Antelope pointed out.

"That is true," said Loud Talker, with a nod.

"Maybe that is because their land is not very good land, and the whites have no use for it," said Lean Bear.

Loud Talker took a look around. It was summer, the middle of the day. Heat shimmered off the arid sagebrush flats that extended to the horizon in every direction. He was too circumspect to give voice to his sentiments, but this land that the Cheyenne called home was about as desolate as any he had ever laid eyes on. It was certainly poorer than the land of his own people, which was located in the rolling prairie of the Missouri River valley. Loud Talker could not imagine why the whites would ever covet Cheyenne land. They could not grow crops here. It was true that the Mormons had made the desert bloom in the wasteland they called Deseret, many days' ride to the west. Loud Talker had himself seen this miracle. But the Mormons were not ordinary people. Most other whites could not have accomplished what the Mormons had done. Most would not have even tried.

"The land of my people is not poor," he replied, "and as for trusting the white man, there are some whose word is their bond. The same is true among our own people. Some of them have honor. Some do not."

Lean Bear nodded. "I have come here to sign the treaty paper and I will do so. I hope the White Father is not without honor, and that he will keep his word. Because the Cheyenne *will* keep their land."

Loud Talker saw a man coming out of the main gate of Fort Wise, the new fort the bluecoats had built on the banks of the Arkansas River. This person was well known to the Omaha. The Cheyenne called him Little White Man. His other name was William Bent. Many years ago Bent and his brothers had come to this country and built a trading post on the Arkansas, which had come to be known as Bent's Fort. This had been back in the days when only a hardy handful of white men had ventured into these parts, most of them fur trappers. William Bent had married a Cheyenne named Owl Woman, and after she died he had married her sister, Yellow Woman. He had three sons and two daughters who lived among the Cheyenne, while Bent himself moved back and forth between the white man's world and the world of the Indian. In spite of this, few of the Cheyenne doubted that he had their best interests at heart. Bent wore buckskins and had an old trade blanket draped over his shoulder. To look at him, mused Loud Talker, one would never suspect that he was a prosperous man by frontier standards. He could be mistaken for a Cheyenne with his dark broad face, coarse features and horse-bowed walk. His black hair was long in the back and graying at the temples.

"The commissioner is ready to see you," he informed the Cheyenne chiefs, squatting on his heels so that he did not stand over them and in so doing show disrespect.

"What gifts has he brought?" asked White Antelope.

Black Kettle gave White Antelope a stern look, while Loud Talker tried to suppress a smile. White Antelope thought this treaty-signing business was much ado about nothing. In his opinion, it wasn't at all important. It wouldn't change anything. He didn't really understand why the whites put so much stock in words written on a piece of paper, anyway. In White Antelope's world, a man's word that he would do something was sufficient guarantee. Why put a promise on a piece of paper? If the paper grew brittle and then crumbled into dust, did the promises written upon it become as dust, too? Surely not. So why was it so important that promises be written down? Did the white man have such a poor memory that he easily forgot the promises he made to others? It did not make any sense to White Antelope. But he would make his mark on the treaty paper if that would make the White Father happy. It was, after all, necessary to keep the peace with the whites, and that sometimes meant humoring them.

"Tobacco, blankets and medals bearing the likeness of the president on them," replied Bent.

"Tobacco is good," said White Antelope, pleased with the prospect of a good smoke. "And one cannot have too many blankets. As one grows older the winters seem to get colder. But this medal . . ." He shook his head dubiously. "Is it worth anything, Little White Man?"

"Reckon that would depend on how you look at it," said Bent. "I'm guessing it's supposed to symbolize the friendship between the United States and the Cheyenne Nation. On the other hand it's made of bronze, so it wouldn't bring much in trade. Maybe a jug of snakehead whiskey."

"The commissioner knows that we do not speak for all the Cheyenne?" asked Black Kettle.

Bent nodded. "I explained that the Cheyenne have

forty chiefs. No one man can speak for all the people. Commissioner Greenwood said he understood, and that this was all right with him, that the other chiefs could sign the treaty later."

"Have you seen this treaty paper?" asked Lean Bear. "Have you read the words that are written on it, Little White Man?"

Bent shook his head. "All I know about it is what they tell me. Now we should go. The commissioner does not like to be kept waiting."

As he and the Cheyenne chiefs got to their feet, Loud Talker pondered the irony of Bent's last remark. The commissioner had let the chiefs wait for hours. Sadly, the whites did not treat Indians with the respect that they deserved. Precious few white men considered the red man his equal. And all too often whites treated Indians like unruly children. This was a tragic mistake, in the Omaha's opinion. Indians were very proud and had every right to be— they did not like be treated cavalierly, though they often tolerated it for the sake of maintaining good relations. Black Kettle and the other two Cheyenne chiefs were no doubt a little insulted by what amounted to a peremptory summons from Colonel Greenwood. If so, they did not betray their true feelings as they picked up their blankets, shook the dust out of them, and followed William Bent into Fort Wise.

Once inside they found that the chiefs of the Arapaho were already present and accounted for. There was Little Raven, Big Mouth and Storm. A tarpaulin lashed to poles provided some shade from the ruthless sun for the commissioner and his entourage. Colonel A.B. Greenwood was a tall, slender man with stern, hawkish features and a shock of gray-white hair. Resplendent in his dress uniform, he sat in an upholstered armchair that Loud Talker assumed had been carried out of the post commandant's office. It was, guessed the Omaha, the only genuine chair in the fort. In front of Greenwood was a wooden table and at his side was a wooden trunk. Behind him stood a pair of cavalry officers, while a third sat at the table to his left. William Bent took his place to one side of the table—he would act as an interpreter for both parties. The Cheyenne and Arapaho chiefs stood before the table in the hot sun while Loud Talker stayed behind them.

"Tell them that they may sit," Greenwood said to William Bent.

"That would put you above them, Colonel. And that just wouldn't do. Unless of course you're willing to sit on the ground right along with them."

"Never mind," said Greenwood curtly. He stood up, adjusting the dress sword at his side. "For the record, let me introduce the officers present." He gestured at the two who stood behind him. "Lieutenant John Sedgwick and Lieutenant J.E.B. Stuart." Indicating the officer seated at the table with paper, pen and ink bottle before him, Greenwood added, "Lieutenant Brandon Gunnison, who is recording all that is said today relevant to the occasion."

After translating Greenwood's words for the benefit of the chiefs, William Bent switched to English and introduced the Cheyenne and Arapaho leaders. While these formalities were being attended to, Loud Talker surveyed the interior of the adobe fort. Soldiers from the garrison mingled with scouts and traders to watch the goings on.

Greenwood spoke first—about the treaty, the necessity for it and his confidence in it. He assured the chiefs that the Great Father in Washington had the best interests of the tribes at heart, and sought only to prevent bloodshed on the frontier. He praised the Cheyenne and the Arapaho for keeping the peace. And he asked the chiefs if any of them had something to add before they proceeded to the signing of the treaty.

"I would talk," said Little Raven of the Arapaho. "Nine winters ago I was at Laramie to sign a treaty. That paper promised us that we would never have to give up any of our land. Since then I have seen many of the whites in their wagons. I have seen more and more forts like this one. I have seen the white man's talking wire spread from horizon to horizon. I saw many white men come to dig yellow metal out of the ground. These men built a town which they call Denver, and which I once went to see. The white men there treated me well. They gave me cigars to smoke. I told them I hoped they found all the yellow metal they wanted so that they could then go home. But they never went home. They stayed, and more white men came to join them. Your forts, your towns, your camps, your trails and your talking wires— these are all on Arapaho and Cheyenne land. But we have not gone to war against the whites because of this. We have remained at peace because we promised to do so at Laramie."

"This has not always been easy to do," said Black Kettle, after Bent had translated Little Raven's words into English. "Many of our young men are angry because there are so many white men on our land, and they kill so many of our buffalo."

After Bent's translation Lieutenant Stuart drawled, "I wasn't aware that these Indians *owned* the buffalo herds."

"That's enough, Lieutenant," said Greenwood. "Bent, don't translate that. And Lieutenant Gunnison, there is no need to transcribe Stuart's remark."

"I had already decided not to, Colonel," replied Gunnison, with what Loud Talker thought was a less than friendly glance in Stuart's direction.

"We kill buffalo, that's true," said Greenwood. "We have to eat, same as the tribes."

"But some of your people kill many buffalo—many more than they can eat—to take the hide, leaving the rest to rot in the sun," said Lean Bear.

"There are millions of buffalo," replied Greenwood stiffly. Clearly the conversation had taken a turn of which he did not approve. "Nonetheless, we will do what we can to keep the buffalo runners off Cheyenne and Arapaho land."

In Loud Talker's opinion that was an empty promise, made simply to move the proceedings along, and he wondered if Black Kettle and the other chiefs felt the same way.

"The important thing," continued Greenwood, "is that you sign this treaty and keep the promise you thereby make—namely, to remain on your lands. It is the fervent wish of the president—the Great Father—to end the age-old conflicts between the Plains tribes. He wants everyone to live in peace. If the Cheyenne stay on their land, and the Arapaho on

theirs and the Crow on theirs—well, there should be
no reason for discord."

Loud Talker nodded. That same logic, imperfect
though it was, had been the driving force behind the
Fort Laramie Treaty some years ago. It hadn't worked
very well up until now, and the Omaha wondered
why Greenwood thought that this time would be any
different. The problem wasn't with the tribes; with
but a few exceptions, not least being the warlike
Sioux, the tribes had kept their end of the bargain
struck at Laramie as best they could. The problem
was that as more and more whites moved west, they
pushed the Indians off their lands. And they killed
far too many buffalo, which forced the Indians to
send their hunting parties farther afield. That, in
turn, increased the risks of tribal conflict—not to
mention conflict between whites and hotheaded
young braves, many of whom did not agree with
their leaders, who by and large deemed discretion
to be the better part of valor when it came to tan-
gling with the white man. Why was it, mused Loud
Talker, that the white man expected all the tribes to
remain on their allotted lands, and yet held himself
to no such restriction?

The chiefs did not have much more to say. Loud
Talker sensed their fatalism as they gravely took up
the pen and made their mark on the treaty paper. He
wasn't sure that any of them—even Black Kettle—put
much faith in this paper and the words inscribed
upon it. They merely hoped for the best. And what
else could they do, after all?

After signing the treaty himself, Greenwood
turned to the trunk, opened it, and began distributing

the gifts that were contained within. As Bent had said, there were tobacco and blankets and medals. And there was a flag—a garrison flag with thirty-four big white stars on it, representing the states in the Union. A Union, Loud Talker had heard, that was on the verge of being torn asunder by civil war. He glanced at Lieutenant Stuart, who by his drawl had betrayed himself as a Southerner—just as surely as Gunnison's Midwestern twang proved he was from north of the Mason-Dixon Line. Maybe that was why there seemed to be more than a hint of animosity between the two bluecoat officers.

Greenwood presented the flag to Black Kettle. Though Bent had tried explaining to the commissioner that the Cheyenne had no single supreme leader, Greenwood persisted in the erroneous assumption that Black Kettle was the head chief. To many whites, Indian society was completely incomprehensible—and that included the Indian Commissioner of the United States. So the flag went to Black Kettle who, though perplexed, accepted it graciously. Tobacco and blankets and perhaps even the medals had some practical value. But what was he to do with a flag?

"The Great Father wanted me to present this to you," said Greenwood. "As long as you fly this flag all white men will know that your people are our friends and not our enemies. They will not fire upon you, or do harm to your people in any way, as long as this flag flies over your lodge."

Black Kettle solemnly thanked the commissioner, though he continued to look at the carefully folded flag in his hands as though it were an infant—something he could scarcely wait to hand off to someone who knew better what to do with it.

With the ceremony of the treaty signing concluded, the Cheyenne and Arapaho chiefs returned to their lodges. On the following day they would depart to rejoin their various bands.

Colonel Greenwood returned to the post headquarters of Fort Wise, accompanied by the trio of lieutenants who had been present during the ceremony. The post commander, Captain Howard, was presently at Fort Laramie sitting on a court martial, and in his absence the commissioner had appropriated not only his office but also his adjacent quarters. Greenwood brandished a bottle of brandy and four glasses, inviting the junior officers to join him in a toast.

"Gentlemen," he said, "I think that went fairly well, all things considered. I am confident that the president will be pleased with what we have accomplished here today." It was obvious that at least Greenwood was immensely pleased, particularly with himself.

"Will an effort be made to get the rest of the chiefs to sign the treaty, Colonel?" asked Sedgwick.

"I really don't believe that will be necessary, Lieutenant."

"If I may, sir," said Stuart, in his slow Southern drawl, "what obligates the other chiefs to honor the terms of this treaty if they do not themselves sign it?"

"Honor, of course," replied Greenwood, as though the answer was an obvious one. "The Indians place great store by it."

"Well, I hope they keep their word—and we can keep the peace out on the frontier," said Sedgwick. "Considering the trouble that is brewing back East, the last thing we need is an Indian war."

"Lieutenant Sedgwick seems certain we will have war between the southern states and the northern," said Stuart coolly.

"That I do," acknowledged Sedgwick, even more coolly, "since a nation founded on the concepts of freedom and equality can hardly be expected to tolerate the expansion of the peculiar institution called slavery—an expansion that you and your fellow Southerners seem determined to press."

"The nation, sir, was founded on the concept that those powers and responsibilities not expressly given the federal government by the Constitution are reserved to the states. So if you and your abolitionist friends will acknowledge the sovereignty of the southern states with regard to the institution you call peculiar but which stands as a cornerstone of not only our economy but also our society, we will not have war."

"Gentlemen, gentlemen, please," said Greenwood, exasperated. "Let us remember that we are all officers in the United States Army, and conduct ourselves accordingly. Lieutenant Gunnison."

"Sir."

"Be so kind as to make a copy of the record you have just made. Tomorrow you will ride to Denver and present the copy, along with a letter from me, to the territorial governor."

"Yes, sir." Gunnison finished his brandy and gratefully took his leave. He had been subjected for some time now to the constant bickering that went on be-

tween Sedgwick and Stuart, the commissioner's
aides. He was relieved that the treaty had been concluded because it meant Greenwood would soon be
heading back to Washington, taking the two lieutenants with him. And, after he had run this one last
errand for the colonel, he could return to his regi-
mental posting. His commanding officer had se-
conded him to Greenwood because he'd had some
experience with the Arapaho Indians, with whose
Dog Soldiers he had clashed on more than one occasion. Being on the trail of an Arapaho war party was,
in Gunnison's opinion, a much less onerous duty
than having to tolerate Sedgwick and Stuart's verbal
skirmishing about slavery and states' rights.

Out on the parade ground, Gunnison spotted Loud
Talker. He had seen the Omaha with the Cheyenne
chiefs over the past couple of days. Though he didn't
know the Indian's name or where he came from,
Gunnison knew enough about the Plains tribes to
know that the man was certainly no Cheyenne. Loud
Talker was sitting on his heels in a strip of shade at
the corner of the headquarters building. He scooped
up a handful of dirt and let it trickle out between his
fingers. Every now and then he would glance in the
direction of the post's main gate, which was open,
providing a glimpse of the nearby lodges of the
Cheyenne and Arapaho delegations.

Curiosity got the better of Gunnison, and he bent
his steps in Loud Talker's direction.

"What are you doing still here?" asked the officer.
"The show is over."

Loud Talker stood up. "Yes, I know. But I do not
want to pass through that gate just yet, Lieutenant."

Gunnison was surprised by how fluently the Indian spoke English. "You're not a Cheyenne, are you? Where do you come from?"

Loud Talker introduced himself. "I have come to see what is going on with my own eyes. Soon I will return to my people and tell them all that I have seen."

"You're an observer."

"That is what I am, yes."

Gunnison glanced at the gate. "Why don't you want to go through that gate?"

Loud Talker sighed. "You cannot see them, but there are many ghosts that have gathered there."

"What? Ghosts? Are you joking?" Gunnison peered suspiciously at Loud Talker, wondering if the Omaha was having a little fun at his expense.

"I am very serious. Many spirits walk the land, Lieutenant. I have had a gift for many years—I can see them. Not all of the time. But more often than I really want to. I knew I had this gift at an early age. I was only twelve summers old when my father fell ill. There was a long vigil as he lay dying. On the night that he died, I was standing in the lodge, and after he drew his last breath I saw his spirit rise up out of his body. His spirit smiled at me and told me not to grieve, and asked me to look after my mother and my sister."

"Your father's spirit spoke to you," said Gunnison, barely trying to mask his skepticism.

Loud Talker nodded. "I heard his words in here," he said, tapping his temple with a finger.

Gunnison again looked toward the gate. "What ghosts do you see now?"

Loud Talker glanced at the gate and quickly looked away. "I think they are Cheyenne, from many generations past. Men and women, children, too. There are many of them. They appeared just as the treaty was being signed. They have watched what went on here today and they are not happy."

"Why not? The Cheyenne aren't any worse off now because of this treaty."

"The living cannot see past today. A spirit knows what the future holds."

"Do they talk to you, these spirits at the gate?"

"I do not want to hear what they have to say. They speak among themselves with solemn voices."

Gunnison studied the Omaha. It was clear to him that Loud Talker was cold sober—and dead serious. It was also clear that he was afraid. Either the man was demented or there really were spirits and he really could see them. And he didn't appear to be loco.

"Lieutenant, I would like to ride to Denver with you."

"And just how did you know I was going to Denver?"

Loud Talker smiled. "I listened."

Gunnison realized then that the window near the corner of the building where they stood was to the room where he had just been with Colonel Greenwood and the commissioner's two bickering aides. He considered chastising Loud Talker for eavesdropping on Army business. But he refrained, because he found the Omaha to be an intriguing character—all this talk about restless spirits notwithstanding.

"But why do you want to ride with me?" he asked.

"I have seen all that there is to see here."

"I'm thinking maybe Black Kettle wants to send you along as a spy."

"I am not a spy. I am just an observer."

In spite of himself Gunnison cracked a smile. "Well, I could use the company, I guess. Be ready to leave tomorrow at first light." He started to turn away, then thought of something. "But one thing. I'd rather not hear any more about these ghosts you see, okay?"

Chapter Two

Four years passed.

Though he had not been particularly happy to receive it as a gift, Black Kettle had over time become proud of the fact that he possessed the garrison flag Colonel Greenwood had presented to him during the treaty signing at Fort Wise. The Cheyenne chief always flew the flag on a pole erected in front of his skin lodge. And every morning, when he emerged from his teepee for the first time, he would glance up at the flag and hope that today it would protect his people, as the Indian commissioner had said it would.

So far, the flag had been strong medicine. Since the Fort Wise meeting, each passing year bore witness to more and more trouble arising between the Cheyenne and the white people. Hunting parties of young braves from other bands had clashed with bluecoat patrols. Sometimes it was the soldiers who provoked the violence. But at other times the young Cheyenne men were responsible. They were hotheaded, and they resented the fact that the whites were killing off the buffalo just for their hides. They were angry because the soldiers patrolled traditional Cheyenne hunting grounds between the Republican and Smoky Hill rivers to protect the white buffalo runners from Indian attack—to defend white men who had no right to be there in the first place.

Far to the south the Navajos had recently waged war against the whites—and paid a terrible price. To the northeast the Santees had resisted white encroachment and lost not only their lands but their leaders—to the hangman's noose. Arapaho Dog Soldiers continued to make trouble for emigrant trains passing through their land, and on several occasions had skirmished with the United States Army.

Through all this Black Kettle had managed to keep his own people at peace. It hadn't been easy. Many of the young men wanted to go to war against the whites. Now was the time, they said, while the white men were fighting amongst themselves. The garrisons of the frontier forts had been reduced to skeletons crews, as every able-bodied soldier who could be spared was sent to the battlefields in the east. But Black Kettle would not be swayed from his conviction that the warpath led to disaster.

It was a warm and windy spring morning when Black Kettle emerged from his lodge, looked up at the flag flapping heavily at the top of the pole, and then spotted Lean Bear coming toward him. Black Kettle grimaced. He knew what Lean Bear wanted. A decision from him to move north across the Platte, to join with other bands of Cheyenne. News had come that soldiers had attacked a Cheyenne hunting party on the South Platte, and Lean Bear was spokesman for those who thought it would be safer to combine with other bands that had gone north for better hunting in the Powder River country of their Northern Cheyenne cousins. In years past Black Kettle had kept his band south of the Platte, well away from the white man's forts and the emigrant trails. Now, though, it seemed that even the Platte River country was unsafe.

"What have you decided?" asked Lean Bear. "Are we to begin to take down our lodges?"

Black Kettle drew a long and discouraged breath. He felt like a fugitive on his own land, and he couldn't imagine a worse feeling. "Yes. We will go north."

"Good! I will send out a hunting party. We will need food for the journey."

Black Kettle nodded. "We would be wise to travel swiftly until we reach the Powder River."

Lean Bear left him then, and Black Kettle turned back inside his lodge, where his wife and daughter had prepared a morning meal of pemmican and buffalo broth. The women could sense his mood and remained quiet so as not to interrupt his brooding reverie. As he ate, so preoccupied with his thoughts that he did not taste the food, Black Kettle felt the earth tremble beneath him—the horse thunder of the hunters as they rode out in search of buffalo. When he had finished eating, the Cheyenne chief went to the sweat lodge, and after some time spent there, emerged to sit before the sun-bleached skull of a bull buffalo. Lighting a pipe, he offered it to the skull, asking the buffalo's spirit to rise up from the earth with flesh on its bones so that the hunting party would meet with success.

*   *   *

Wolf Chief was among the twenty braves who rode out to find the buffalo. Despite his name, he was not a chief but rather a young warrior who had not yet had an opportunity to display his prowess in battle. He was an able hunter, a superb marksman with the bow and arrow. Handsome, he was the object of considerable attention from the maidens in the village. But while he was old enough to marry he had not earned the right to do so. A member of the Wolf Soldiers, the most militant of all the Cheyenne warrior clans, he was forbidden to take a wife until he had counted coup—struck a blow against an enemy. One performed a coup when he managed to get close enough to an adversary to strike him with something held in hand. It was not necessary to kill the enemy—in fact, to count coup without doing so was considered an especially audacious exploit. And if the brave captured the enemy's horse and weapons he would be held in even higher regard by his peers.

Many years earlier a warrior named Owl Friend had established the Wolf Soldier society. Owl Friend had been a Northern Cheyenne who became lost in a snowstorm on a journey to visit the Southern Cheyenne. He stumbled upon a skin lodge occupied by four young men. Though Owl Friend had never seen them before, they seemed to have been expecting him. Owl Friend stayed for four days. On the evening of the fourth day the four men donned wolf hides adorned with eagle feathers. They performed a ceremony of dancing and singing through the night, telling Owl Friend to pay careful attention to every detail of the ritual. At the end they gave the wolf hides to Owl Friend and told him that they now belonged to him. When Owl

Friend woke in the morning he found himself laying under the open sky on the prairie, with four wolves standing nearby. He knew then that the young men had been wolves. He returned to his band and created the Wolf Soldiers clan.

Wolf Chief had resolved long ago that he would be remembered for his first coup and until such time as he had performed it he would not even think about women. This, of course, was no easy task for a virile young man who was so much admired by the women of the band. The fact that Black Kettle was committed to peace at any cost and kept his band as far removed as possible from the white man was a source of great frustration for Wolf Chief. Like so many of his brothers, he resented the white man's presence and ached for an opportunity to strike a blow against the interlopers. He was of the opinion that sooner or later his chance would come, regardless of Black Kettle's efforts.

As he left the village that morning with the other hunters, Wolf Chief had no idea that his long wait was over.

The hunting party had gone but two miles from the village when they topped a rise and saw a column of bluecoats coming straight at them.

The Cheyenne braves did not doubt for a moment that the soldiers' destination was their village. And at the rear of the column were a pair of giant guns on wheels. Like his brothers, Wolf Chief realized immediately that the bluecoats would not have brought those giant guns if their intentions were peaceable.

No words passed between the braves. As one they whipped their ponies around and rode hard for the village. They could not be certain whether the soldiers had seen them. Wolf Chief presumed that they had. But it didn't matter. The ponies of the hunting party were fresh, and they were swift. The soldiers would not be able to catch them.

When the village was in sight, Wolf Chief abruptly checked his pony. He knew that his people needed to be warned. But he could taste bitter bile, so repugnant was the idea of running like scared dogs from the soldiers. He uttered an incoherent cry of rage and almost as one the other braves halted their ponies and turned to look back at him.

"Red Horse," he said, "go and tell the others that the bluecoats are coming."

Though he held no rank over any of the others, no one questioned his giving a command. Red Horse kicked his pony into a gallop and headed for the village. Wolf Chief could see that people were gathering among the skin lodges, wondering why the hunting party had returned so soon. He turned his pony so that he would be facing the soldiers when they came. The others formed a line to either side of him.

Lean Bear arrived at Black Kettle's skin lodge just as Red Horse rode up to give the chief the news.

"I will go out and meet these soldiers," said Black Kettle. "I will learn why they have come."

"No." Lean Bear placed a hand on Black Kettle's arm. "I will go. If they have come to make war and killed you the people would lose hope."

"They have not come for war. As long as the flag flies above our heads we are safe from the soldiers."

Lean Bear glanced up at the flag. He had never

put much faith in it, but he had too much respect for Black Kettle to tell him so. He looked about him at the people who had gathered round. If the soldiers wanted a fight they would get one. There were nearly five hundred warriors in the village. Perhaps the bluecoats were unaware that he and Black Kettle had merged their bands. If so, they would not be prepared for the large number of Cheyenne braves who would ride against them.

A boy brought him his horse, and Lean Bear mounted up and rode out to join Wolf Chief with an escort of braves. There were many more prepared to ride out with him, but Black Kettle kept them in the village.

When the soldiers drew near enough to see the Cheyenne warriors spread out across their path they halted and formed two lines to either side of the cannons, which were unlimbered from their caissons and aimed at the Indians.

"There are not even a hundred of them," said Lean Bear, watching every move the bluecoats made. "If they wanted war there would be more."

Wolf Chief wasn't so sure. The soldiers had guns, and there weren't a dozen rifles in the entire village—and most of those were old muzzle-loading trade guns. Like the other hunters, Wolf Chief was armed with a lance, a bow, and arrows in a quiver made from the skin of the mountain lion. Were such weapons any match for the giant guns that the soldiers had brought?

"I will go talk with their chief," announced Lean Bear.

"We will go with you," said Wolf Chief.

"No, I go alone. You will all stay here. We do not want to frighten them into shooting at us if they have come in peace."

"And if they have come to make war they will kill you."

Lean Bear smiled tautly, and reached up to touch the bronze medal—the one Commissioner Greenwood had presented to him at the Fort Wise treaty signing—that hung around his neck by a rawhide thong.

"Then we will know what these are really worth," he replied.

He rode forward, holding his pony to a walk, his head held high in proud defiance of . . . of what, wondered Wolf Chief. Of the risks involved? Or was it of some fateful premonition? Wolf Chief thought there had been more than a tinge of resignation in Lean Bear's final words to him. It was as though he knew what was going to happen—something he had been expecting for some time now, perhaps since the treaty signing at Fort Wise. Something called betrayal.

When Lean Bear was a hundred yards from the soldiers, an officer shouted a command and several rifles spoke at once. The bullets that struck Lean Bear hurled him backward off the pony. He was dead before he hit the ground.

Another of the bluecoats' bullets hit a brave in the line immediately to Wolf Chief's left. The Cheyenne slid off his horse and sat down hard in the grass, clutching at his midsection, bright red blood leaking out between his fingers.

Uttering a war cry filled with rage, Wolf Chief

kicked his horse into a gallop. He had already hung
his lance on his saddle by a thong loop and removed
his bow from its carrying case. Now he fit an arrow
to the bow and let fly, guiding the responsive pony
beneath him with his knees. All along the line of
soldiers, rifles were being discharged, and the cannons crashed in unison, sending grapeshot whistling
through the air. The bluecoats were obscured by a
cloud of powdersmoke and dust, but Wolf Chief let
loose another arrow, and then another—all three in
under a minute, and all the while riding for the flank
of the enemy's position. Behind him a great roar rose
up, fury welling up in the throats of hundreds of
Cheyenne braves who had seen Lean Bear fall, and
they surged forward, some on horseback, others on
foot, charging the bluecoats, heedless now of Black
Kettle's remonstrations, which were drowned out by
the din of battle.

Wolf Chief did not look back to see if others followed him. They were—about a dozen braves in all,
but Wolf Chief didn't care. As he neared the end of
the soldiers' line he saw clearly several of the bluecoats, all of them dismounted, and all of them firing
at him, and though he heard the hornet sound of
bullets passing very close by, he was seized by an
icy calm. He fired another arrow, and with grim satisfaction saw one of the soldiers go down. The other
bluecoats turned to their horses and leaped into the
saddles, and for an instant Wolf Chief thought that
their intention was to ride out to do battle with him,
and he was elated. Instead, they turned and rode
away. The whole bluecoat line seemed to disintegrate
at once. A group of soldiers lingered, shooting at

the Indians as they covered the withdrawal of their comrades and the retiring of the cannons. Their steady fire dropped several Cheyenne warriors and blunted the Indian onslaught. The retreat of the soldiers caused many of the Cheyenne to hesitate, but Wolf Chief rushed heedlessly on, intent on but one thing—killing the enemy. Then his horse stumbled and fell, struck by a bullet. Wolf Chief leaped nimbly from the dying horse and landed on his feet. He let loose one more arrow and then the soldiers were out of range, and he shook his fist at them, shouting obscenities. Within a few moments all he could see was a curtain of pale dust that veiled the enemy's retreat. The burning rage bled out of him then, leaving him feeling listless and dissatisfied as he turned back toward the village.

Several warriors had been killed, as had a handful of soldiers. Some of the Cheyenne braves proceeded to strip the bluecoat corpses of weapons and even some articles of clothing—spoils of war, mementos of a day that none would ever forget. Scalps were taken, and a couple of bodies were mutilated by angry braves. Though he knew he had taken the life of at least one of the soldiers, Wolf Chief spurned the taking of any trophy, scalp or otherwise. His only regret was that he had not gotten close enough to a soldier to count coup. They had run away like dogs before he'd had the chance. Even so, Wolf Chief disapproved of his brothers who mutilated the dead. Every mutilation inflicted would mark the soul of the dead forever. It was enough for him that the whites had been killed, were no longer of this world, and no longer in a position to inflict further suffering upon his peo-

ple. He did not particularly care if they were forever
tormented in the afterlife. He wasn't even sure if
white men went to another hunting ground after
death.

Instead, Wolf Chief busied himself with the Cheyenne dead. Aided by several others, he carried Lean
Bear's body back to the village. The other bodies
were also retrieved. The wives and mothers of the
dead braves wailed their anguish. This very day they
would demonstrate the full measure of their loss by
cutting their hair short, making cuts on the calves of
their legs and in some cases even chopping off a
finger joint. For weeks, perhaps even months, they
would sing mourning songs, trying to communicate
with the deceased.

The dead were turned over to their families. The
bodies would be watched over within the skin lodges
for at least one day, just in case the spirit—and life—
returned to it. Meanwhile Black Kettle presided over
a council attended by many of the men in the village,
including Wolf Chief.

There was no question that the band would move.
The dead had to be attended to first, and there was
still a crying need for provisions. A hunting party
would venture out on the following day. This time
it would be much larger; fifty braves would go, and
they would ride prepared for war as well as for the
hunt, just in case. Scouts were dispatched at once to
make sure that adequate warnings would be given
in the event the soldiers returned. In a few days' time
the band would embark on the journey northward
to join the other bands of the Southern Cheyenne
who were encamped in the vicinity of the Powder

River. Nearly everyone present at the council agreed that this was the correct course of action. No one argued for staying, least of all Wolf Chief, who had no quarrel with this decision.

What did bother him was Black Kettle's persistence in speaking out for peace. Even after everything that had happened, Black Kettle insisted that taking the warpath would be a disastrous mistake. Many of those present disagreed. Horse Catcher said that the whites had made war against them and it would bring dishonor to the Cheyenne if they did not retaliate. How could Black Kettle talk of peace when the peace had already been broken?

Black Kettle would not budge from his commitment to the Fort Wise treaty. He would go, he said, to the White Father himself and find out why this tragedy had occurred. Surely it was just a mistake, a big misunderstanding. The White Father could not control all of his people, any more than a chief could always count on restraining his hotheaded braves from committing acts of aggression against other tribes, or the whites. Maybe the bluecoats had mistaken them for the Arapaho, who had lately been preying on the wagon trains.

Shaking his head, Wolf Chief could keep silent no longer. As did all the adult men in the village, he had a right to be heard.

"I say that to fly the white man's flag after what happened today is wrong," he said, when Black Kettle had spoken his piece. "It shows disrespect for our brothers who died today. Take down that flag and throw it into the fire."

Voices rose in hearty agreement.

"No," said Black Kettle curtly. "Keep always in your mind the memory of what happened to the Navajo when they made war against the whites. For four winters that flag has shielded us, just as the wing of the mother hawk shelters her young within the nest."

"We were not sheltered today," said Wolf Chief. "The White Father is not trying to protect us. He is trying to keep us from the warpath and protect his own kind because he knows that his soldiers are no match for the Cheyenne. We saw that this day, with our own eyes. They came because they had talked among themselves about how the Cheyenne were cowards. And why shouldn't they believe that? For many summers we have stood by while the whites grow stronger and take more and more of the land for their own, and kill more and more of the buffalo. And what have we done? Nothing. But they are wrong. The Cheyenne are not afraid."

This time an even larger number of the men gathered around the council circle shouted their accord.

Alarmed by the effects Wolf Chief's inflammatory rhetoric was having on the others, Black Kettle rose up and held out his arms to silence the assembly.

"We are not cowards. We have no need to prove our courage by dying on the field of battle. What would we gain from doing that? We are angry, and we should be. But we cannot let our anger blind us to the truth. We must learn to live with the white man, for we cannot drive him away. We cannot destroy him. The true test of courage is in accepting the truth even though we do not want to. Many of you remember the Omaha whose name was Loud

Talker, who came to stay among us for a while. His people learned to live with the whites. They have not made war. And they still live on the land of their forefathers. Lift up your eyes from the blood that was spilled here today and look around you. Look at the Omaha. Then look at the Navajo. The one prospers. For the other, the wailing of the women who grieve for their dead still fills the sky."

Some of those present were swayed by Black Kettle's heartfelt oratory. But Wolf Chief was not one of them. He disagreed, yet he had already spoken and would not argue. His heart cried out for vengeance, but beyond that he believed that the survival of his people depended on fighting to keep what was theirs. The Cheyenne would not survive without the buffalo, without a safe place to make their home. He was angry at Black Kettle. *He* was the one who was blind. But he was also a chief, and while Wolf Chief had little respect for the man at this point, he had great respect for the position Black Kettle held. So Wolf Chief held his tongue, his face a stony mask concealing the fury that seethed within him.

The following day, as a large hunting party left the village in search of the buffalo, the dead were prepared for their passage to the next life. The bodies were cleansed. Their faces were painted. They were dressed in their finest clothing. Their weapons were placed alongside them, as was a pipe and some tobacco, along with provisions enough to last for a few days, in the event that the journey to the new hunting grounds in the spirit world was a long one.

When the hunters returned they brought with

them fresh buffalo skins that were used as shrouds, tightly wrapped around the bodies and tied with rawhide. More hides were soaked in water, wrapped around the bodies, and then allowed to dry, shrinking to securely encase the corpses. Each dead man's best horse was painted with red splotches. The horse would lead the burial procession, with the body secured to a travois for the trip to a scaffold consisting of four poles holding up a platform made from entwined branches. The four bodies were placed on four scaffolds not far from where the men had fallen. Their feet pointed to the east. The horses were killed, the carcasses left at the foot of each scaffold. They then became spirit animals, available to the dead for their journey. After the mourners turned their backs on the scaffolds no one was permitted to utter aloud the names of the departed.

The disposition of the dead, the buffalo hunt and the preparation for the move took several days. All during that time scouts kept a watchful eye on the horizons. Many—Wolf Chief among them—expected the soldiers to return, this time in much greater numbers. But there was no sign of the bluecoats. Nonetheless, the Wolf Soldiers prepared themselves for war. Meticulous attention was paid to these preparations. Items such as awls and sinew, extra moccasins, war paint and cups made from shells in which the paint was mixed, flint and steel or bows for fire-making and extra bowstrings—all this and more was placed in hide carrying cases. As for weapons, the warriors readied their bows and quivers filled with arrows, their hide shields, elaborately painted and adorned with fur and feathers, war clubs and tomahawks and lances and knives. Water would be carried in buffalo stomachs, tied together at the top with drawstrings, while enough pemmican for several days was placed in a saddle pouch; this in case the warriors became separated from the rest of the band, either to attack a distant enemy or pursue a fleeing foe.

Prior to the departure each Wolf Soldier purified himself in the sweat lodge, and each contributed something of value to the society medicine bundle, which would be carried at all times by the pipe-holder, or leader. This was Horse Catcher, and the others had great confidence in his abilities. During the journey he would be provided with food. His horses and equipment would be tended to. This was because he would be too busy summoning visions that would acquaint him with the location and number of any enemy force. On the morning of the departure, the Wolf Soldiers gathered in front of Horse Catcher's skin lodge, and as women proceeded to disassemble the teepee, the braves smoked the sacred pipe that Horse Catcher passed among them.

The village was large, but it did not take long for the Cheyenne to dismantle it. Personal belongings were placed in parfleche bags and bundles of buffalo robes or deer hides. Teepee coverings were wrapped around lodge poles and lashed tightly together. Everything was loaded onto travois, large ones secured to horses and smaller ones harnessed to camp dogs. The Wolf Soldiers led the way, spreading out to form a protective screen around the column that stretched for more than two miles across the dusty plain. Bringing up the rear was the horse herd, watched over by boys who were not yet old enough to serve as warriors.

In this manner, Black Kettle's band and that of Lean Bear left the Platte River and headed north. Their principal chief prayed for a safe and uneventful journey. But Wolf Chief, while he believed that the spirits sometimes heeded a prayer made in earnest, preferred to rely on his prowess and that of his fellow Wolf Soldiers to ensure the safe passage of his people. And he knew he was not alone in hoping for another chance to show the white men that they had committed a colossal blunder in breaking the peace the Cheyenne had tried so hard to keep.

Chapter Three

In a few short years Denver had grown from a ramshackle frontier outpost to a bustling entrepot. Six hundred miles west of the Missouri River and in the shadow of the southern ranges of the Rockies, it had sprung into being in a mere half-dozen years before William Bent went there to speak to the governor on behalf of the Cheyenne people. Back then, gold seekers had flocked to the area, drawn by news of a rich strike at Pike's Peak. At first just a collection of tents and log structures, Denver had served the prospectors as a supply base. Nowadays the gold fever had subsided—so far, the Colorado gold fields had not compared to the ones found in California, and many gold hunters had since moved on, though some did remain, convinced that rich veins lay hidden among the rugged peaks.

The fading of gold fever had no effect on Denver. It had already developed into a rustic metropolis inhabited by several thousand people. Ben Holladay had put a stagecoach route through Denver, and there was talk that a railroad would be coming through, too, a transcontinental railroad project that awaited only the conclusion of the bloody war between the states still raging in the East. Emigrants, buffalo hunters, trappers, traders, wolfers and soldiers filled the wide rutted streets that Bent negotiated on his way to the governor's residence. Having been in Denver before, Bent was already cognizant of the pride its inhabitants had for their city. They never hesitated to point out that Chicago was a thousand miles from New York City, Denver was a thousand miles west from Chicago, and San Francisco was a thousand miles west of Denver. It was therefore obvious (at least to Denverites) that their city would soon rival those other great cities in size, wealth and importance, as though the fact that Denver just happened to fit so neatly into the Thousand-Mile Theory virtually guaranteed its success.

The governor's residence was where the territory's business was usually conducted, and Bent knew his way there. He was not swayed from his purpose by the enticements Denver had to offer—whiskey of dubious quality and women of easy virtue being the two principal temptations. Neither held much attraction for Bent. He did not drink nor did he dally with calico queens. Even if he'd been so inclined, he was far too focused on his mission to allow distractions. He didn't much care for towns—in fact, he didn't much care for his own kind, whether they were in a town or not, which was why he had come west in the first place, and also why he got along so well with the Indians, whom he considered a far superior race to his own in all the ways that truly mattered—loyalty, virtue, honor and discretion chief among them. Only a serious and urgent matter could have compelled him to come to Denver in the first place, and he could scarcely wait to put the place behind him and return to the plains where he could breathe clean and hear only the sighing of the wind and the howling of wolves.

A sizable one-story structure built of square-cut logs hauled in from nearby forests to the west housed the home and office of Governor John Evans. It sported a wide covered gallery running the entire width of the building. The front door was guarded by a blue-coated member of the Colorado Volunteers. About a dozen civilians stood on or about the gallery, and a few sat on rough-hewn wooden benches in the shade of the overhang. The latter included a pair of women. As he approached, Bent thought the older woman looked familiar. But try as he might he could not remember where he had seen her before. She was slender and pale-haired and pretty, and the last was all the more remarkable because she appeared to be at least forty years old, and it had been Bent's experience that the frontier was unkind to most white women, sapping them of their looks if not their lives at a fairly rapid pace. The woman wore a plain blue gingham dress, and the girl sitting close beside her, watching everything with wide-eyed wonder, wore a dress probably cut from the same bolt of cloth. The older woman was obviously the mother of the younger. The girl had the same willowy figure, delicate features, big light blue eyes and pale yellow hair.

Bent was curious about the two women and why he had the feeling that he had met the older one before, but he had much more important matters to attend to, and after swinging out of the saddle he made straight for the front door. The civilians loitering about the gallery watched him, for he seemed intent on going straight in. The guard, however, had other ideas. He blocked Bent's path, rifle raised at chest level and hooded eyes fastened in an unfriendly way on Bent.

"Just where do you think you're going?" asked the soldier.

"I have to see Governor Evans right away."

"Oh yeah? Well, you're just gonna have to wait your time like everybody else."

Bent glanced at the other civilians, then turned his attention back to the soldier. He was angry—the cold fury that had settled like an anvil in the pit of his stomach during the journey to Denver now flared hot. His was a terrible, wrathful temper when he was provoked. That seemed to be a trait shared by all the Bents. It was particularly infuriating because this man was a Colorado Volunteer, and Bent knew that it had been the Volunteers who'd attacked Black Kettle's village a fortnight ago. He had seen the uniforms stripped from the bodies of the dead soldiers.

"Let me tell you something, mister," rasped Bent, pushing the words through clenched teeth. "There's likely going to be an Indian war in these parts before too much longer, and Governor Evans may be the only man who can stop it. So you had better get in there and tell him that William Bent wants to talk to him—now!"

"Did he say an Indian war?" asked one of the men farther down the gallery, speaking to another man who stood at his shoulder.

"I don't have to take orders from you," said the guard. "I don't care who you are. You could be the king of goddamn England and you still would have to wait your turn."

Bent grimaced, half turned as though to leave— and then whirled back around to plow his fist into the soldier's jaw. The blow caught the guard by surprise, and he went down. Two of the men on the gallery lunged at Bent as he started to step over the guard and enter the house. They bore him back against an upright. Bent was on the verge of laying into them both when an officer he recognized emerged from the house.

"That'll be enough!" snapped the officer. "Release that man."

The two men who had accosted Bent let go of him and stepped back, watching him warily.

"I know you," said Bent. "You were with Colonel Greenwood at the signing of the Fort Wise treaty."

"That I was. Lieutenant Brand Gunnison, at your service, Mr. Bent."

"Is the governor inside?"

"Yes he is."

"I must see him at once. We could have a full blown war . . ."

"I heard what you said a moment ago," interrupted Gunnison, taking a quick look at the faces of the people on the gallery, and reading the varying degrees of alarm registered on them. "It does not bear repeating—especially in public."

"If I don't get in to see the governor I'll make sure everyone in Denver hears it."

"There's no need to resort to blackmail," said Gunnison dryly. "I took you for a better man than that, Bent."

"In desperate times a man does what he must."

"Apparently," said Gunnison, as though he had never been *that* desperate and could only take Bent's word for it. "Wait here." He glanced again at the two men who had attacked Bent, and then at the soldier Bent had knocked down. The latter was picking himself up, a trickle of blood leaking from the corner of his mouth. "Better yet, come with me," said the lieutenant, and turned to go inside.

Bent followed Gunnison into a hallway that ran the length of the house, separating the governor's living quarters—two rooms on the right—from the two rooms on the left that had been turned into his office. Bent heard voices through the second door on the left, and one belonged to Evans, the smooth bull-horn voice of an orator. It sounded to Bent like Evans was excited about something, but he could not make out the words that were being spoken.

Gunnison motioned for him to wait and entered the first room on the left without bothering to knock. As he waited, pacing like a caged tiger up and down the hall, Bent wondered what Gunnison was doing here. The lieutenant was regular Army, not of the Colorado Volunteers. Most of the regular Army stationed at frontier outposts before the war had been called East to fight once hostilities had broken out between North and South. That was the main reason Governor Evans had seen fit to organize and equip the Colorado Volunteers. How had Gunnison managed to avoid reassignment to the battlefront? He was a West Point graduate, and by all accounts a very capable officer. Perhaps "avoid" wasn't the right word—maybe Gunnison had wanted to go back East; a battlefield commission was a quick way up through the ranks. All you had to do was stay alive.

Bent was kept waiting only a handful of minutes, but those minutes passed like hours, and the trader was running out of patience when the second door on the left swung open and Gunnison stepped out to tell him that the governor had consented to see him.

As he entered the room, Bent saw Governor Evans, stocky and bearded and attired in a black frock coat, trousers, white linen shirt beneath a gold vest, polished half boots and a shamrock-green cravat that contrasted sharply with his ruddy face. He was standing behind a handsome desk, at the corner of which stood a man in uniform, lanky and narrow-shouldered, with a moon-shaped face sporting a goatee that didn't do much to conceal a weak chin. His uniform was adorned with scarlet piping and gold braid, and all in all rivaled the positively garish dress uniform preferred by the former commander in chief of the United States Army, General Winfield Scott.

"Ah, Bent," said Evans, coming forward with hand outstretched. "How have you been, my friend? Well, I hope. How is your lovely wife and your children?"

Bent wasn't fooled by all this hale and hearty bonhomie—he knew Evans, the consummate politician, greeted everyone as though they were long-lost kin, and he didn't take it to heart.

"They are well. Fortunately, my sons were hunting with Roman Nose and his band a few weeks ago, and weren't with Black Kettle's people down along the Platte when your Volunteers attacked."

Evans was still smiling, though it looked to be a

more fragile smile than previously. "I take it that's why you've come, then."

"You're damned right it is, Governor."

"Did you want me to remain, sir?" asked Gunnison, poised at the door—and Bent got the impression that the lieutenant was disappointed when Evans nodded and told him to stay.

"Allow me to introduce you to Colonel John Chivington," said Evans, addressing Bent but gesturing at the thin soldier in the gaudy uniform. "The colonel is commanding officer of the Colorado Volunteers. Colonel, this is William Bent. He is—"

"So you ordered your men to attack Black Kettle's village?" Bent asked Chivington, heedlessly interrupting the governor.

Chivington didn't answer. "Not to worry, Governor. I know who this man is. He lives with the Cheyenne most of the time, and he's a spokesman for them."

"I want to know who gave the order to attack Black Kettle's village," snapped Bent. "Was it you, Colonel? Or maybe it was you, Governor."

"I don't think I like your tone, Bent," said Chivington stiffly.

"We've only just met, Colonel, and I don't like anything about you."

"Bent, I think you had better calm down," warned Evans. "You obviously don't have all the facts."

"I know what Black Kettle told me. These are his exact words, Governor. 'We had a fight with the soldiers and killed some of them. We do not know what the fight was about, or why the soldiers marched against us.' "

"That's what *he* says," commented Chivington.

"Black Kettle has never lied in his life. I met him a week ago at Coon Creek. By then I'd already heard that a bunch of the colonel's men had attacked a party of Cheyenne Wolf Soldiers at Fremont's Orchard."

"My men were out looking for stolen horses—and found them, in the possession of the Indians," said Chivington.

"Those Cheyenne were out to retrieve some of their own ponies."

"They had our horses, not Indian ponies."

"I kind of doubt that," said Bent dryly. "But regardless, you had no call to attack a Cheyenne village near Cedar Bluffs."

"Those men were attacked while on patrol. They were merely defending themselvcs."

"Defending themselves? Against the two women and two children that they shot down?"

"The Cheyenne have been on a rampage. It is my duty to keep the territory safe."

"Did you or did you not order the attack on Black Kettle's village, Colonel?"

"I did. Captain George Eayre had orders from me to attack and kill Cheyenne whenever and wherever found."

Bent stared at Chivington in disgust. He could hardly refrain from launching himself at the man and beating him to a bloody pulp. But as much as he would have relished that task, he realized it would avail him nothing in the end—and certainly would be of no help to the Cheyenne people he so loved and admired.

"Well, Colonel," he said, when at last he could trust himself to speak calmly, "had my sons been there, as they very well could have been, I would kill you where you stand."

"I'll brook none of that kind of talk," snapped Evans.

"And by the way," added Bent, "Black Kettle's village was in *Kansas*, not the Colorado Territory, Colonel. Your men had no right to be there."

"I don't care where they were camped. They posed a threat to the people of this territory."

Bent shook his head and turned to Gunnison. "Lieutenant, I know you have a brain—and a great deal of experience with the Indians in these parts. Tell this—this *man* that the Southern Cheyenne have never lifted a hand in anger against whites."

Still standing near the door, which he had closed, Gunnison studiously ignored Governor Evans's stare.

"As far as I know," he said flatly, "that's the case."

"Well, sir, I happen to know different," said Chivington defensively. "And I know that you, Lieutenant, are a notorious Indian lover."

"Me?" Gunnison was startled—and had to laugh. "I've been fighting and killing Indians for five years, Colonel. I have not, however, fought or killed any Cheyenne."

"Governor, all I got to say is you had better keep the colonel here and his Volunteers on a short rein," Bent advised Evans. "Or else you're going to have an all-out war on your hands—and I doubt that President Lincoln would be too happy about that, considering all the problems he has already, back East."

"That sounds like a threat," said Evans darkly.

"It's just good advice," said Bent, realizing that the governor was acting as guilty as Chivington. And of course he had good reason to act that way; Evans was responsible for the very existence of the Volunteers.

"I'm sure the governor is not concerned about your friends the Cheyenne," Chivington told Bent. "And if anyone needs advice it would be the Indians. You had better tell them to lay down their weapons and submit to our authority. Otherwise they will suffer the consequences. I am confident that my men can make short work of the Cheyenne if given the word." He glanced at Evans, clearly hoping that the word would be forthcoming.

Bent stared at Chivington in disbelief. Never had he met quite so pompous an ass.

"I have it on good authority that your men fled the field when Black Kettle's braves rode out to meet them."

Chivington's face reddened. "They rode into an ambush. The Cheyenne were waiting for them and had amassed a considerable force."

"That's utter nonsense," protested Bent. "Those were just the men from Black Kettle's and Lean Bear's band. The Cheyenne can put at least two thousand warriors in the field. And with them will ride the Arapaho. There have long been close ties between the two tribes, and as all of you know, the Arapahos have already lost faith in the empty promises of white men. Arapaho Dog Soldiers have been playing hell with your wagon trains for some time now. Throw the Cheyenne into the mix and you will have a lot of dead folks strewn from one end of the Colorado Territory to the other."

"The emigrants will have to look out for themselves," said Chivington. "I do not have enough men in my command to provide safe passage for every wagon train."

"Which is precisely Mr. Bent's point, I believe," ventured Gunnison.

Governor Evans fired a perturbed glance in the lieutenant's direction. He now regretted having told Gunnison to stay in the room. It hadn't occurred to him that the officer would side with Bent.

"Since you have spoken recently with Black Kettle, Mr. Bent," said Evans, "perhaps you can tell us what his intentions are."

"His intentions are to keep the goddamn peace," replied Bent. "He promised me he would try to keep his braves from making raids. But that won't be easy to do. His young men want revenge. They feel betrayed. It's not natural for an Indian to turn the other cheek."

"Naturally not," sneered Chivington. "They are heathens, not Christians, after all."

Bent had the urge to ask Evans where in God's name he had found a man as ignorant of the realities of the frontier as Chivington—but decided it would be a pointless exercise. Chivington had been the governor's hand-picked man to command the Volunteers, and he would not take kindly to his judgment being called into question. Bent knew he had antagonized both Evans and Chivington quite sufficiently as it was.

"I have heard that Black Kettle's band is on the move," said the governor. "What is his destination?"

"The Powder River country."

"You see, Governor?" asked Chivington. "The South-ern and Northern Cheyenne are joining forces. Once combined they will launch an attack against us."

"Jesus," muttered Bent. "They are joining forces to protect themselves from you, Colonel!"

"Here's what we will do, gentlemen," said Evans. "I will write a proclamation requiring all the Chey-enne and Arapahos who wish to remain at peace with the United States to report at once to the Indian agent, Samuel Colley, at Fort Lyon. That way we will know their true intentions. If they respond and do as I say, they will come to no harm. I will direct that provisions be given them. Those who do not respond will be considered hostiles—and treated accord-ingly."

"You can't just kill all the buffalo and then expect the Indians to accept salt pork as a substitute," said Bent. "And by the way, Sam Colley is as crooked as a dog's hind leg."

"Colley is a personal friend of mine," said Evans stiffly.

"You should pick your friends more carefully, then. He's been selling the annuities the government sends the tribes for years and pocketing the profits."

"Bent, you will see that my proclamation is pre-sented to the Cheyenne. Lieutenant Gunnison, no one is better acquainted than you with the disposition of the various Arapaho bands. You will be in charge of presenting the proclamation to any and all peacefully inclined Arapahos—assuming you can find any. Is that understood?"

"Governor, with all due respect, my orders should come from my commanding officer, Major Merritt."

Evans fumed. "Quite right, Lieutenant. I will tell your major to issue you orders to do what I just told you to do. How is that? Would that be acceptable to you, sir?"

"More than acceptable, Governor."

Evans nodded, a look on his face like he had just bitten into sour fruit. "Well then, if that's all, I have other matters to attend to. It was nice to see you again, Bent." He didn't even bother trying to sound like he meant it. "Lieutenant, be so kind as to show Mr. Bent out. I'll have the proclamation ready before the day is done."

As they headed down the hall, Bent glanced wryly at Gunnison. "I get the feeling he can't wait to be rid of us."

"Can you blame him? You hit them where it hurts."

"That was my intention all along."

"You should know something. I've heard it said that, according to Chivington, Evans formed the Colorado Volunteers for one purpose, and one purpose only. To kill Indians. Kill them or run them out. They won't rest until there are no Indians left in the territory."

"That's insane. There is more than enough room in this country for whites and Indians alike."

"That's not the way Chivington sees it. Or the governor, either, according to some. Though Evans is much too tactful to just come right out and say such a thing. And that's a view shared by many others. It really doesn't have much to do with room, you see. It's all about destroying something you don't understand. If you can't understand something you tend to be afraid it might hurt you, in one way or another.

So you deal with your fear by getting rid of what scares you."

"And do you share this view, Lieutenant?"

"Not really. But then, my point of view really doesn't matter. I just follow orders."

"You would follow orders even if you knew they were wrong?"

"It isn't my place to question the decisions of my superiors."

"It is if you know they are wrong."

Gunnison smiled faintly. "Obviously you never attended West Point."

Bent left it at that. He figured Gunnison was a good, decent man—a man with a clear vision of what was right and what was wrong. But he was a soldier first and foremost, a man with a conscience second. Such men, in Bent's opinion, sometimes hid behind duty to avoid having to make those tough decisions between right and wrong. Only later did they realize that they had forsaken their honor in the name of duty.

As they emerged onto the gallery, Bent remembered the pale-haired woman and approached her.

"I beg your pardon, ma'am," he said.

She smiled up at him. "Hello, Mr. Bent. I was wondering a few moments ago whether you recalled that we had met once before."

"I thought that must be the case. But I'm ashamed to admit that I don't recall your name."

She glanced—a little warily, thought Bent—at Gunnison. "Eliza. Eliza Hawkes. And this is my daughter, Grace."

Gunnison had not been paying all that much attention to her, being struck by the willowy, delicate beauty of the younger woman. Such beauty was exceedingly rare on the frontier. But when he heard the name, Gunnison fastened an intent gaze upon Eliza.

"Hawkes?" he said. "Any relation to Gordon Hawkes?"

"He is my husband," she replied, with just a trace of defiance in her tone and the way she held her head up when she said it.

"I know him," said Gunnison flatly, trying not to betray any emotion despite that the name—and memory—of Gordon Hawks stirred a number of strong emotions within him. He bowed stiffly. "I am Lieutenant Brandon Gunnison, ma'am, at your service." He executed another slight declination for Grace. "My pleasure, miss."

Grace blushed—and Gunnison's gaze lingered.

"How do you happen to know my husband, Lieutenant?" asked Eliza. She sounded to Bent like someone who was afraid she already knew the answer.

"I placed him under arrest in a gold camp called Gilder Gulch a few years ago."

"Oh yes," she said softly. "So you are the officer he spoke so highly of."

"Spoke highly of me?" Gunnison was caught off guard.

"Does that surprise you, Lieutenant?"

"Somewhat."

"He said you were just doing your job. Obeying orders, and doing so quite well."

"Not well enough. He got away. Killed a man. And not his first in Gilder Gulch, I might add."

"He killed the men who took our son's life," said

Eliza, so softly that it was just shy of a whisper. "Can you blame him?"

"My orders were to bring law and order to the gold camp. So that made it my responsibility to bring to justice the man who killed your son. I was in the process of doing that, too. Except your husband killed him first."

"That man you speak of," said Eliza. "He had also escaped your custody."

Gunnison grimaced. The events at Gilder Gulch were the one black mark on his record. He'd been told to bring order to the gold camp, and he had failed. This woman's son, Cameron Hawkes, had been killed by a group of prospectors led by one Chandler Doone, who claimed the younger Hawkes had murdered his brother. Seeking vengeance, Gordon Hawkes had terrorized Gilder Gulch, taking the lives of several men. Eliza Hawkes was correct— Gunnison had apprehended Chandler Doone with the intention of bringing the man out of the mountains so that he could stand trial, but Doone had escaped, and so had Hawkes, and Gunnison had been powerless to prevent the latter from killing the former. It wasn't a question of whether justice had been done—Gunnison had a hunch it had been—but rather *how* it was done.

Sensing an impasse developing between Gunnison and Eliza, Bent spoke up. "I heard that your son was dead, Mrs. Hawkes. I am truly sorry."

"As am I, of course," said Gunnison.

Bent could tell that mention of her lost brother was upsetting Grace, and changed the subject. "What brings you to Denver, then, Mrs. Hawkes?"

"I have come to see the governor. I intend to petition him for a full pardon for my husband."

"A full pardon?" exclaimed Gunnison.

Eliza stiffened perceptively. "I take it you don't believe there is much hope for that, Lieutenant."

"Well, ma'am, I did a little digging into your husband's past. Not only did he kill several men at Gilder Gulch, but he is wanted for two murders back East, one in Louisiana and the other in Missouri. I honestly don't see how you could succeed in your mission considering all of that."

"He was wrongly accused of the murders," she replied. "And we have already discussed his motives for doing what he did at the gold camp."

"Please don't misunderstand, Mrs. Hawkes," said Gunnison. "It is not my place to judge your husband, nor do I have an opinion concerning his innocence or guilt with respect to the crimes they claim he has committed. But I am fairly well acquainted with Governor Evans, and I feel obliged to tell you that in my opinion you are wasting your time."

"And why is that?"

"The governor has some good qualities. But he is not a very forgiving man, or a particularly compassionate one."

"I appreciate your candor," said Eliza. "But I have come a long way and I will not go back without at least making an earnest attempt."

Gunnison got the feeling that Eliza Hawkes didn't have much use for him—and not only because he wasn't being very encouraging with regard to the mission that had brought her to Denver. There was more to it, and he figured it had to be that at one point her husband had been his prisoner, placed in irons and very nearly taken away from her forever. It bothered Gunnison that she didn't like him, and bothered him even more to think that her daughter probably shared Eliza's distaste for him. Though he feared it would be futile, Gunnison decided he had to try to rehabilitate himself in their eyes.

"Personally, I'm relieved that your husband escaped from my custody," he told Eliza. Though he hadn't always felt that way—hadn't until this moment, in fact—it wasn't really a lie. "At the time I did not know about the murder charges against him. Had I succeeded in taking him back to the fort I'm afraid he would have been hanged for sure."

"And that would have bothered you?" asked Grace, gazing at him with an intensity that surprised Gunnison.

"Why yes. Yes, it would have bothered me a great deal."

She smiled, ever so slightly. But the smile vanished, and she looked meekly down as Eliza gave her a stern and disapproving glance.

"We appreciate the sentiment," Eliza told him, with a rather cool courtesy.

"'Do you have a place to stay while you're in Denver, Mrs. Hawkes?" asked Bent.

"I have not yet found a place, no. We only just arrived today."

"I have a few friends hereabouts," he said. "There's one—a widow woman, who lives alone, has plenty of room. She's a good person. I can vouch for her, and I'm sure she'd be happy to put you up."

"I wouldn't want to be a burden to anyone."

"I'm sure she'd be glad to have the company."

"Thank you so much, Mr. Bent."

"It's my pleasure, ma'am."

"If you would allow me," said Gunnison, "I would like to invite you and your daughter to dinner this evening, Mrs. Hawkes."

"Well, I . . ."

"If you would do me the honor, I would be indebted to you, ma'am."

She relented. "Oh, very well, then."

Much relieved, Gunnison smiled broadly. "Then I will call on you at six this evening."

"But . . . how will you find us?" asked Grace, with a hint of anxiety in her voice.

"Don't worry, miss," said Bent, suppressing a grin. "I'll make sure he knows where to find you."

As they walked away, Bent glanced sidelong at Gunnison.

"She is a pretty lass, I'll grant you," he said.

"Yes, I suppose she is," replied the Army officer, feigning indifference.

"A trifle young yet, I think, though. To be wed, I mean. Though Indian girls her age sometimes already have a husband."

Gunnison glowered. "What on earth are you rattling on about, Bent?"

"Oh, nothing," replied the trader. "Nothing at all."

Chapter Four

"Mrs. Hawkes," sighed Governor Evans, "I admire the devotion to your husband that you display. You are obviously a good and decent woman. But the record seems irrefutable—your husband is not the most virtuous of men."

"Gordon Hawkes may not be the most virtuous of men," replied Eliza crisply, "but he is a good man who has tried to do what's right. To suggest, as you do, that he is a bad man in the presence of his sixteen-year-old daughter demonstrates that you lack certain virtues yourself, Governor. Tact, for one."

Evans smiled. Slumped back in the chair behind his desk, he was weary after a long day of dealing with the affairs of the territory, and he had no desire to sit through a long, impassioned plea for amnesty from a misguided wife. Good women ended up with bad men all the time, and often they refused to face the truth. Evans believed that was precisely the case with Mrs. Eliza Hawkes. But he had to admire her spirit. She wasn't intimidated by him. And she was attractive—that was always a plus.

"Perhaps I have been less than tactful," he acknowledged. "If so, please accept my apology. But can you provide me with some solid evidence that Gordon Hawkes did not commit the crimes of which he has been accused? Affidavits from witnesses, for instance?"

"I have nothing like that in my possession," admitted Eliza. "The first incident occurred more than twenty-five years ago, before I had even met my husband. The second was about fifteen years ago. I would not know where to begin to look for witnesses—assuming there were any, and if so that they were still alive."

"Mrs. Hawkes, you must understand, I do not have the authority to pardon your husband for acts *allegedly* committed in another state."

"Then you can at least give him amnesty for the so-called crimes he committed in Gilder Gulch."

Evans nodded. "Well, yes, I *could* do that."

"He was going after the men who killed our son."

"Yes, yes, you've told me. And while what he did was against the law, I suppose one could argue that there were extenuating circumstances."

Eliza leaned forward in her chair—sensing that she had an opening, and wanting to exploit it.

"Gordon has done more than most men to try and keep the Indians at peace with our kind, Governor. He could do a lot more along those lines if he didn't have to lead the life of a fugitive."

"That's worthy of consideration," acknowledged Evans, concentrating more on the prospect of crossing the hall to his private quarters—and a glass of good brandy—than on the plight of this woman's husband. "I will give the matter some thought and give you my answer in the next day or two. You have my word on that, Mrs. Hawkes."

"I will trust that you are a man of your word, Governor—as I have no reason to suspect otherwise."

Evans smiled. "Why thank you. Most kind. If there is nothing further, I hope you will excuse me now. It has been an extremely tiring day and I'm not as young and spry as I used to be."

Eliza and Grace took their leave of the governor. Grace waited until they were outside before speaking her mind.

"Mother, how could you?"

"How could I what, dear?"

"You as much as told that man that Father would help him keep the Indians off the warpath."

"Yes, I realize that's the impression I left."

"But Father wants nothing to do with Governor Evans. He's said on more than one occasion that he doesn't trust the governor, whom he believes wants to drive all the Indians out of the territory—or kill them. Father won't lift a finger to help him."

"I expect you're right," said Eliza.

"Then you lied to the governor?"

"I didn't lie. I said Gordon could do a lot more to keep the Indians at peace. I didn't say he ever *would*."

"Well," said Grace dubiously, "that may not qualify as a lie, but it's certainly dishonest."

Eliza smiled tolerantly at her daughter. "It is for a worthy cause. I would contemplate doing worse than that if I could remove the stigma of those murder charges from your father."

"Oh," said Grace, gasping as she looked beyond Eliza. "Here comes that lieutenant."

Eliza turned to see Gunnison coming along the street with quick long strides as he attempted to intercept them. He was a handsome young man—she would concede that—and she glanced surreptitiously at Grace to see, as she thought that she might, an expression of near rapture on her daughter's face.

"He does cut a fine figure, I admit," Eliza said. "Don't you think so, dear?"

Grace blushed. "I am sure I hadn't noticed," she replied, flustered.

Somehow Eliza managed to keep a straight face.

As he drew near the two women Gunnison swept the hat from his head and belatedly remembered to pay at least a little attention to Eliza.

"Good afternoon, Miss Hawkes—oh, and good afternoon to you, Mrs. Hawkes. How did you fare with the governor?"

"We may know something tomorrow," replied Eliza, trying to sound optimistic.

"I hope tomorrow brings you good news, then." Gunnison glanced at the sun, an orange-yellow globe seemingly balanced on the cobalt-blue peaks to the west. *Will the damned sun never set on this day?* he wondered, frustrated. The last few hours had seemed an eternity to him. "I, um, I am on my way to see the governor myself," he said. "Shall I call on the two of you in, say, a half hour, for dinner?"

"Give us at least an hour, please, Lieutenant," said

Eliza. "We need to pretty up a bit. Otherwise you won't want to be seen out in public with us."

"An hour it is," said Gunnison, with an audible sigh. He glanced at Grace and added, "I can't see why you would feel the need to 'pretty up.' It is impossible to improve on perfection."

Grace blushed furiously and Eliza murmured, "Oh my."

Fearing he had overstepped his bounds, Gunnison hastily mumbled his farewells and hurried away in the direction of the governor's residence.

"No man has ever paid me a compliment like that," gasped Grace.

"Your father always tells you that you're the prettiest thing he's ever seen."

"Next to you," said Grace—and they laughed.

"But there will be a lot more flattery coming your way, dear," said Eliza. "You mustn't let the first man who comes along turn your head. Even if that man is a dashing young cavalry officer."

"Maybe if I got to know him better I could persuade him to help us get the amnesty for Father."

"In my opinion, you already wield a good deal of influence on our young friend. But he's only a lieutenant, remember."

"He is an officer in the United States Army. He must know a lot of important people."

Eliza shook her head in mild dismay. Her daughter was terribly naive in so many ways. There were a lot of things she simply didn't understand, things she would need to know to survive among her own people. All her life Grace had lived deep in the wild country. Once or twice a year she might get to visit a trading post. And before they had relocated farther south, she had been afforded some time, usually during the summer months, with their friends the Absaroka Crow. Sadly, that was no longer possible—they now lived too far from Absaroka country to make the journey.

Though she did not mind the isolation herself, Eliza had always been concerned about what living so far removed from others of their kind would do to her children. She believed that their life in exile had contributed greatly to her son Cameron's fateful decision to explore the gold camp called Gilder Gulch. His curiosity abut the world beyond the mountains had been so strong that for the first time Cam had defied his father's wishes; in that case, Gordon had insisted that his son stay far away from the gold camp. It wasn't just because he was a fugitive and wanted to keep his whereabouts a secret that Gordon tried to distance his children from others. Gordon, too, understood that his children were ill equipped to deal with the so-called civilized world. Now Cam was dead. Eliza didn't want a tragedy to befall Grace just because she was blissfully ignorant of the ways of the world, and she had done her best to educate her daughter. But her own knowledge about the world was limited. The daughter of Methodist missionaries, she had herself been isolated from a society that her parents believed was shot through with wickedness. So Eliza wasn't sure if she was any less naïve about worldly matters than Grace. And besides, there were some things you simply could not teach your children, things they had to learn for themselves.

"Well," she said, putting an arm around her daughter's shoulder. "You're only sixteen, and too young to even think about getting men to do your bidding."

"I still say Lieutenant Gunnison would, if I just asked him," replied Grace smugly.

Eliza laughed. "Come along. The sooner we freshen up the sooner you'll see him again."

"Oh yes, let's hurry," agreed Grace, and hastened her step.

There was really only one good restaurant in Denver—a place run by an Englishman who, according to rumor, was an aristocratic black sheep who had killed a man in Kent—or was it Yorkshire?—over a gambling debt. Or was it over a woman? Whatever the truth of the matter, the Englishman was something of a connoisseur when it came to food and drink. Appalled by the quality (or lack thereof) of frontier fare, he had imported a French cook and a fine wine cellar at considerable expense. Where he got the money was the subject of a whole new set of rumors, but nobody thought he had actually earned it by dint of honest sweat.

In Gunnison's opinion the French cook could work wonders with the limited supplies available on the frontier—venison or buffalo steaks and a few vegetables like potatoes and onions. With Eliza's permission, he ordered a sherry, and Grace was allowed a glass, the first time she had tasted strong spirits.

Eliza felt it wise to find out more about the lieutenant, since one would have to be deaf, dumb and blind not to realize that Grace was infatuated with the young man. So as they dined, she coaxed Gunnison into talking about himself—something the Army officer was not in the habit of doing.

"I was born in Indiana," he told them. "Back then that was still pretty wild country. My father was a lawyer. When I was still very young he joined a company of volunteers and marched off to fight in the war with Mexico. He didn't come back. He died at the Battle of Buena Vista, at the end of a Mexican dragoon's lance."

"I'm so sorry," whispered Grace.

Gunnison smiled. "Thank you. But quite often soldiers are called upon to give their lives for their country. They say he fought gallantly, and died well. He left my mother with five children to raise. She was equal to the task. My older brother became a lawyer and occupied our father's old office. I wanted to be a soldier. Never really thought about becoming anything else. The governor of Indiana at the time was a friend of my father's. He recommended me for the military academy. As my father was a hero, they could hardly turn me down—though in the next four years there were times they might have wished they had. At least that's what the commandant told me." Gunnison laughed ruefully.

"Were you always getting into trouble at West Point?" asked Eliza.

"Oh, occasionally. But I managed to get through."

"Did you graduate at the top of your class?" asked Grace.

"Hardly! But I did graduate—and was immediately assigned to a post out here. I've been here ever since."

"How long now?" asked Grace.

"Six years this coming winter."

"Do you regret not being back East—in the war?" asked Eliza.

"I did, in the beginning. But a few had to stay behind. And now I would not want to go."

"Why not?"

"Because the war is all but over. After Vicksburg fell a year ago, and Lee lost at Gettysburg, the Confederacy was doomed. Its surrender is just a matter of time. Many more good men on both sides will have to die before it's well and truly over, but their sacrifice will be pointless."

"If the outcome is no longer in doubt why does the South fight on?" asked Eliza.

Gunnison shrugged. "Stubborn pride would be my guess. So now, I'm right where I should be. Because the next war will break out right here."

"You think there will be war with the Indians?"

"I do. I feel it coming. I think it is as inevitable as the fall of the Confederate States. Not that I want it to happen. In this war many innocent people will perish. That's the nature of guerrilla warfare—which is the kind of war the Indians wage, and they usually wage it very effectively."

"Is there no hope for peace?" asked Grace.

Gunnison stole a glance around the room to gauge whether any of the restaurant's other customers were within earshot. "There's not much hope, in my opinion. It would take a miracle—because the only thing that would prevent it would be if no more whites came west."

"My father would be all for that," said Grace.

"But it won't happen. And the buffalo will be killed off, and the tribes will be forced to give up more and more of their land. I think every year more of them are beginning to see where this is all leading. The situation is a powderkeg. All it needs is a spark and the territory will go up in flames."

"What kind of spark?"

Gunnison's first thought was of Colonel Chivington and his Colorado Volunteers.

"One more attack by soldiers on a peaceful village might do it," he said. "One more instance of Indian women and children being killed. Then the tribes will likely set aside their differences and take to the warpath together. When that happens we'll be up to our hat brims in trouble."

"You're a soldier," said Grace. "You wouldn't attack a peaceful village of Indians, would you?"

"Regular Army units aren't the problem. It's volunteers like Chivington's Second Colorado."

"But why would they kill innocent women and children?"

"Because too many of them, from their commanding officer on down, consider all Indians to be vermin. Not really human beings, but pests that need to be exterminated."

"I grew up around Indians. They are not vermin," said Grace hotly.

"You almost sound like you're on the side of the Indians, Lieutenant," observed Eliza. "That could be a problem for you out here, if it's true."

"I've been called an Indian lover—and more than once. As for you, Mrs. Hawkes, I'm surprised you're not an Indian hater, seeing as how your parents were murdered by—Flathead Indians, weren't they? William Bent told me about it."

"Yes, that happened. But I do not hate all Indians because of it. I don't even hate the ones who committed the act. Forgiveness is one of the three principal virtues. Honesty and loyalty being the other two. That's what my parents taught me."

"I guess I'm an Indian lover, too," said Grace. "They are decent people. Honest and reliable. And they live cleaner and less noisily than we do."

Gunnison smiled at her last comment. "I take it you haven't been overly impressed by what you've seen—and heard—in Denver."

"Well, I certainly would not want to live here."

"I wouldn't, either," said Gunnison. "I prefer the wide open spaces. Another reason why I'm not sorry I've had to remain out here. I haven't been home since I graduated from West Point, and to be honest with you I have no urge to go back any time soon. I think it would all seem . . . I don't know . . . too *small*. Too crowded."

When they had finished their dinner Gunnison insisted on walking them back to the house where William Bent had arranged for their boarding. Like most frontier towns, Denver was not the kind of place where respectable women could safely walk after sundown.

When they arrived at their destination, Eliza thanked the lieutenant for the dinner and conversation. For his part, Gunnison was wishing he could find some excuse to steal a few minutes alone with Grace. But he was too much the gentleman to come right out and ask her if she would linger with him on the porch for a while.

Grace was too shy to suggest it. And Eliza was too wise to allow it by excusing herself.

"I hope you have good news about the amnesty tomorrow," he told Eliza.

"I hope we do, too," said Grace. "I can't wait to get home. I miss my father so."

"Is it a long journey home for you?" asked Gunnison.

"A week through the mountains," replied Eliza. "But I am well acquainted with the route."

"Still . . . two women alone in the mountains. Are you sure you'll be okay?"

"We will be safer there than we are here. And none of the people we'd be likely to meet along the way would do us harm."

"People aren't the only danger. There are grizzlies, panthers . . ."

"My mother is an excellent shot with both rifle and pistol," said Grace proudly. "And I'm better than fair myself."

"Lieutenant, you're not to worry," said Eliza. "I've lived a quarter of a century with a mountain man, and Grace has lived her entire life in the high country. We've learned a thing or two."

"Of course," he said. "Well, I—I wish I could say we would meet again. But tomorrow I must leave Denver."

The forlorn look he gave Grace did not escape Eliza's notice—and she suddenly relented.

"Lieutenant, you have been most kind to us. I wonder if you would tell me where I might be able to write to you. It would please me if we could correspond."

"Yes, that would be wonderful," agreed Grace. "And I might even feel compelled to write to you as well—that is, if you wouldn't object."

Gunnison felt nearly as giddy as a schoolboy who had stolen a kiss from his sweetheart. "That would please me very much!" he said. "I am posted at Fort Lyon. Send your letters to me there. But where would I send a reply?"

"To Bent's Fort," said Eliza. "We would get them, though it might take some time."

Gunnison beamed. "Mrs. Hawkes, it has been a real honor to make your acquaintance." He turned to Grace, his gaze lingering on her beautiful face as he tried to commit it to memory. "And I hope I am not being too forward, Miss Hawkes, in saying that I find your company most pleasurable. I hope the fates will be kind and we meet again someday."

"I hope so, too," she said, a little breathlessly.

Gunnison bade them both good night and walked away. Grace stared after him. Eliza gave her a moment before softly saying, "Come along, dear."

Grace followed her mother inside, stealing one more glance along the night-shadowed street in hopes of a final glimpse of the cavalryman.

The next morning, as Eliza made her way back to the governor's residence, she was hoping for the best but trying to prepare herself for the worst. She was nervous, and she could tell that Grace was, too, though both tried gamely to conceal their anxiety for the other's sake.

This time there was no long wait on the porch bench, much to Eliza's surprise. A man who introduced himself as Colonel John Chivington of the Colorado Volunteers escorted them right in. Eliza was an outstanding judge of character, and her first impression of Chivington was not a good one. He struck her as a man who was very full of himself, and all the gold braid on his immaculate uniform seemed to bear this out. No man except one who was greatly impressed by his own importance would outfit himself in such a garish fashion. She could not, however, find fault with his manners. Those were impeccable. Chivington treated her and her daughter as though they were royalty—and only belatedly, as they entered the governor's office, did Eliza begin to wonder if there was an ulterior motive behind all this chivalry. After all, who was she? A nobody. The wife of a reclusive mountain man. The wife of a man wanted by the law, too. Hardly someone due such unflagging courtesy.

Governor Evans rose from behind his desk as they were ushered into his office, and came forward to greet them with a cheery bonhomie that had been entirely lacking during the course of their previous meeting.

"Mrs. Hawkes, Miss Hawkes—I hope you had a restful night."

"And I hope you did as well, Governor," replied Eliza. "Have you reached a decision regarding my husband?"

Evans was a bit taken aback by her directness. Clearly she had no desire to engage in small talk.

"Right to the point, I see," he said, forcing a chuckle.

"Well, I know you are a busy man, Governor."

"Yes, quite right. That I am. Indeed, I gave your petition a great deal of thought, Mrs. Hawkes. A great deal of thought. And I have decided to grant your husband a full amnesty."

"That's wonderful!" exclaimed Grace.

"But I only have the authority to grant amnesty for acts committed within the Territory of Colorado. That means your husband will no longer have to fear prosecution for the killing of several men at Gilder Gulch. Obviously one could make a good argument that he was justified in his actions, considering the fate that befell your son. Others might argue that while he may have committed murder there were extenuating circumstances. Still others would say that there can be no justification whatsoever for taking the law into one's own hands. But I am willing to err on the side of mercy in this case, and give your husband the benefit of the doubt."

"So that means my father will still be wanted for murder in Louisiana and Missouri," said Grace, crestfallen.

"I simply do not have the authority to pardon him for committing those crimes, miss."

"He didn't do them!" said Grace angrily.

"Be that as it may, my hands are tied. The best I can do is offer you the amnesty for all crimes committed within this territory. I have a paper drawn up. It only awaits my signature."

"Then please sign it, Governor," said Eliza. "Forgive my daughter for her outburst, and accept our most profound gratitude."

Evans beamed. "Think nothing of it." He went to his desk, sat down behind it, and with a flourish dipped pen into inkwell and scrawled his signature on the document in question. Then he blotted the wet ink and very neatly folded the vellum once, then again, and placed his seal in wax upon it to secure its closure. This done, he rose and proffered the document to Eliza.

"There you are, ma'am."

"Thank you, Governor."

"Mrs. Hawkes," said Chivington, "the governor tells me that your husband may be able to assist us in keeping the Indians off the warpath."

"He has always tried to keep the peace—though it is as much for the sake of the Indians as for his own kind that he did so."

"We want to keep the peace for the sake of all concerned, as well," said Evans. "I have asked that all the tribes with peaceful intent send envoys to Fort Lyon. If your husband could use his influence among the Indians to aid us in the accomplishment of that goal—well, let me just say that his service would not go unnoticed."

"I can only promise that I will speak to him about it."

"And do your utmost to persuade him, I trust."

Eliza smiled. "My husband knows his own mind. He is not an easy one to talk into something unless he's already willing to go along."

"But you are his wife of many years. Surely you have some sway over him."

"I don't know about that. He will listen to me. Governor—is this amnesty conditional on my husband helping you?"

"No, of course not."

"I can tell you that if my husband feels he can do something to save lives, I expect he will do it."

Evans nodded. "That's all we ask, Mrs. Hawkes."

"Where is your husband now, ma'am?" asked Chivington.

"In the high country," she replied, with a disarming smile. "And we have been absent from him for far too long. So, if you gentlemen will excuse us . . ."

"Of course," said Evans. "It has been a pleasure to meet you, Mrs. Hawkes. The same goes for you, Miss Hawkes."

Chivington escorted them out. He was surprised to find William Bent waiting on the porch.

"I thought you would be on your way back to the Cheyenne," said Chivington. "The governor is depending on you to deliver his proclamation."

"Don't you worry, Colonel. I'll be on my way, soon as I have a few words with Mrs. Hawkes." Bent extended an arm to Eliza. She took it, and they headed up the street with Grace coming along behind.

"Did you get what you came for?" asked Bent.

"Some of it. Gordon has been granted an amnesty for all that he did at Gilder Gulch."

"Well, frankly, I'm surprised Evans gave you that much. He's not one to go to any trouble on someone's account, unless he thinks there might be something in it for him."

"Perhaps you're being a little harsh on him."

Bent thought about it, then adamantly shook his head. "Nope."

"The governor says he wants my husband's help in keeping the peace with the Indians."

Bent laughed cynically. "Evans doesn't want peace. His aim is to drive every last Indian out of the territory."

"How can you be certain of that? He seemed sincere enough to me."

"Of course he comes across as sincere. He's a politician, isn't he? The more sincere they seem, the less likely it is that they're telling you the truth."

"Then why would he be so eager to have Gordon's help?"

Bent frowned. "He wants my help, too—with the Cheyenne. And for some reason I feel like I'm being used."

"Used, in what way?"

The trader shook his head. "I wish I knew what the governor and that glory-seeking colonel of his are planning. But I can tell you one thing. Whatever it is, it does not bode well for the Indians. Of that I'm sure."

"I do hope you're wrong."

"I hope so, too, Mrs. Hawkes."

"Please, call me Eliza."

Bent grinned. "Only if you'll call me Bill. So tell me, are you going home now?"

"We'll leave at once."

"I know a certain army officer who will be sorry to hear that," said Bent, glancing at Grace and smiling as she blushed. "Your husband—he's not far away, is he?" he asked Eliza.

Eliza laughed. "Now, Bill, why would you think that?"

"Because I think I know what kind of man Gordon

Hawkes is. And I don't believe he would let his wife and daughter make a long journey alone if he didn't have to."

"Grace and I are perfectly capable of looking out for ourselves."

Bent held up a hand. "I know, I know. I don't doubt that for a moment. My guess is your husband came with you, and set up camp not more than a day's ride from here."

"I don't think you'd believe me if I denied that, now would you, Bill?"

"I don't think you'll bother denying it, Eliza."

"He didn't want me to come at all. Thought I was wasting my time. Won't he be surprised when I show him the amnesty . . . tonight?"

Bent nodded. "Good. Then I can rest easy—and go on about my business, or should I say, the governor's business—knowing you will be safely reunited with your husband before the day is out."

"I appreciate your concern, I really do."

Bent shrugged. "These are unsafe times, Eliza. If I could I would advise your husband to stay deep within the mountains and keep his family out of danger."

"Then you're convinced that there will be war."

"I feel it in my bones," said Bent grimly. "I hate to say this, but I think we're in for one hell of a bloody scrape."

Chapter Five

From his vantage point on a rocky ledge that girdled a partially wooded hill, Gordon Hawkes watched the pair of riders on the trail below. It was his wife and daughter, returning from Denver on the trail that led to Dead Horse Pass, and he was very relieved to see them. Word was that Denver had become a good bit more civilized of late, growing out of its rough-and-tumble-frontier-outpost stage into a bona fide town, with at least as many respectable citizens as there were scoundrels and cutthroats. But as far as Hawkes was concerned, any place where his own people congregated, be it large or small, was a dangerous place, and for the past two days he had been fretting about Eliza and Grace. His wife had insisted on going to Denver and he had eventually caved in, but it was against his better judgment. Particularly since he was convinced that she was wasting her time with a petition to the territorial governor on his behalf.

As much as he wanted to go down and meet them, Hawkes lingered on the rocky ledge and carefully scanned the trail to the north. He had spent a quarter of a century as a fugitive from the law, and caution was deeply ingrained in him. The mountain man figured he was still a wanted man, so he had to consider the possibility that Eliza and Grace had been followed by a man, or men, who had in mind profiting from the capture of a criminal. This was why he had remained in the camp. He wasn't one to get caught with his guard down. So he let his wife and daughter ride on, and patiently maintained his vigil.

Gordon Hawkes was nearly fifty years of age, and though they had been hard years for the most part, he carried them well. There was a hint of gray in his hair and beard, and the creases in his sun-darkened face deepened with each passing winter. Though not as agile as he had been twenty or even ten years earlier, he was still lean and strong. His eyesight was unimpaired and his nerves were steady. Hawkes figured he was lucky. The life of a mountain man was a tough one, and many of his counterparts suffered from debilitating chronic illnesses or crippling permanent injuries. Many looked much older than their years. He knew more that had died before reaching the half-century mark than had surpassed it. Hawkes had two things going for him—an iron constitution and a wife who had devoted most of her life to looking out for him.

After a half hour of watching Eliza's back trail, Hawkes was reasonably satisfied that his wife had not been followed. Rising, he went to his horse, a dun mountain mustang, tied his sheathed Hawken Plains rifle to the saddle, and mounted up. Letting the surefooted horse pick its way down the slope, he cut Eliza's trail and turned to follow it.

He caught up with them a few miles on. When

they heard him coming, Eliza and Grace stopped their horses to look back. Identifying the mountain mustang and then its rider, they hurried back to meet him. Before she could check her horse and dismount, Eliza found herself swept from the saddle by her husband's strong arm. Pressing her to him, Hawkes kissed her—a kiss so passionate that it took her breath away. Grace laughed to see her parents behaving like a pair of lovestruck kids, and Eliza actually blushed, something she hadn't done in years.

"Gordon!" she exclaimed, embarrassed. She had never felt comfortable engaging in displays of affection in front of others, especially her own child, and particularly an exhibition as exuberant as this one. Usually her husband had been as inhibited as she. "Gordon, put me down before you drop me!"

He laughed. "I'd never drop you, darlin'." But he heeded her wishes and set her down on the ground, dismounting to reach up for Grace. His big hands nearly encircled her tiny waist as he helped her out of the saddle and into an embrace. "I missed you, girl," he said, and she hugged him as tightly as she was able. "So tell me, what did you bring me?"

Grace had to laugh at that. It was their own little private joke. *What did you bring me* always seemed to be the first words to pass her lips when her father returned from some foray or another. It had always been so, ever since she'd been a little girl. And Hawkes had turned the tables on her; he had warned her before she and her mother had departed for Denver that he intended to pose the question upon their return.

"As a matter of fact," she said coyly, "we did bring you something. Tell him what we brought, Mother."

Hawkes turned to Eliza, eyebrows raised quizzically.

Smiling broadly, Eliza produced the sealed amnesty paper that Evans had given her that very morning.

"What's this?" asked Hawkes, not daring to hope.

"The governor saw his way clear to give you an amnesty for everything that happened at Gilder Gulch."

"Well, I'll be." It was all Hawkes could think to say.

"You didn't think she could do it, did you?" asked Grace. "Come on, admit it."

"I admit it." He stared at Eliza in admiration and awe. "How did you talk him into it?"

"I appealed to his better nature."

"I'd heard Evans didn't have one of those."

"Everybody has one, Gordon."

Hawkes grinned, shaking his head. "You have a lot more faith in people than I do," he said.

"I've had an easier time with other people than you have, too. That's why."

Hawkes took the amnesty paper. He looked at it for a long time, and then up at his wife. Eliza just smiled; she understood just how grateful he was— and she also understood that it was often difficult for him to express his feelings.

"I think we should get moving," she said. "It will be dark soon and we're still a few miles from the camp."

Hawkes nodded. He slipped the amnesty paper under his buckskin tunic and turned to help his daughter back aboard her horse. As Eliza was about to climb into the saddle she felt her husband's hand on her arm.

"Thanks," he said.

She placed her hand on his. Then they mounted up and, with Grace riding between them, headed down the trail.

But even with the amnesty paper under his hunting shirt, Gordon Hawkes couldn't help checking their back trail.

They left their camp the following morning at first light. It would take the better part of a week to reach home—a comfortable cabin in a remote valley about seventy-five miles due west of Dead Horse Pass. Once through the pass the going would be rough. Hawkes told Eliza that they would do well to stop at Alonzo Burn's trading post located near the foot of the pass. Eliza wasn't happy with the prospect. She knew Burn as an unprincipled man who cheated his customers at every opportunity and sold rotgut whiskey to the Indians. But there was no other place near between Denver and Bent's Fort to buy supplies.

By midafternoon they had arrived at the trading post—a dogtrot cabin, stone-walled storehouse and corral hard by a rippling creek lined with birch trees. Hawkes was glad to see only a horse and a couple of mules in the corral. Those belonged to Burn, he knew. And that meant the trader had no customers today. The fewer people he met, the better Hawkes liked it.

As they drew nearer, the trader's Arapaho squaw emerged, a stocky, coarse-featured woman in a blue calico dress and beaded moccasins. She was carrying two empty buckets, and paused to study the trio of riders a moment before turning away, as inscrutable as always, to head for the creek. It didn't surprise Hawkes that she did not speak to them—he had been here several times before and could not recall her ever uttering a word in his presence.

"That poor woman," muttered Grace. "She looks so . . . so miserably unhappy. As though she carries some terrible burden."

"Being married to Alonzo Burn must be an awful burden indeed," said Eliza.

Hawkes glanced wryly at his wife. It was uncommon for Eliza to speak so uncharitably of someone.

"Let's see if we can't find Burn's better nature," he said, dismounting, "so we can appeal to it for a fair price on the provisions we need."

"There is some good in all men, I suppose," said Eliza. "Though if there had to be an exception to the rule it would most certainly be . . ."

At that instant Alonzo Burn stepped out of the cabin onto the dogtrot. He was a big-bellied man with a scruffy beard and beady blue eyes buried in deep sockets above beefy, ruddy jowls. One hand resting on the butt of a pistol stuck under a broad leather belt, he carried a jug of whiskey in the other. Recognizing his visitors, he flashed a yellow-toothed grin and removed his hand from the horse pistol. Even at fifteen feet Eliza could catch a whiff of his unsavory odor—unwashed flesh and sour rotgut.

"I know, I know," said Burn, chuckling. "Speak of the devil—and here he is in the flesh! Mrs. Gordon, it's troubling that you think so poorly of me. As for myself, I hold you in very high regard. Howdy,

Henry, good to see you're still above snakes. And is this Miss Grace? Why, last time I saw you, gal, you was just a bony-kneed little kid. And now aren't you as purty as a picture. I know many a buck who'd trade a hunnerd horses for your favors."

"Shut up, Burn," said Hawkes.

"Just paying your daughter a compliment is all, Henry. Don't be so thin-skinned, hoss."

"I need some supplies."

"I got everything you could possibly want right inside. Come on in." Burn tilted his head toward the doorway through which he had just passed, then led the way into the trading post.

Eliza and Grace dismounted. "I think we'll wait out here," said the former.

"I won't be long," promised Hawkes.

The room was small, almost claustrophobic, with a single window and every square foot of wall covered with shelves stocked with goods. To one side of the door was a counter piled high with furs. On the other was a table with split-log benches. Burn had settled his bulk on one of these, and as Hawkes entered he slid the jug across the rough-hewn surface of the tabletop.

"Have a snort, Henry," offered the trader. "Go ahead and help yourself."

"I'll pass, thanks just the same." Like many others in the high country, Burn knew Hawkes as Henry Gordon. Until recently Hawkes had managed to keep his true identity a secret from all except a handful of people he knew he could trust. The business at Gilder Gulch a few years ago had begun to change all that, though. For now, at least, Burn remained ignorant of the truth, and Hawkes hoped to keep it that way as long as possible.

With a shrug the trader retrieved the jug and indulged in a long pull.

"So what can I do for you today?" he asked, and belched.

"I could use some flour, coffee, sugar, beans. Tobacco, if you have some."

"What are you gonna pay for all that with?"

Hawkes produced a small deerskin pouch and tossed it once, twice, up in the air just so Burn could hear the distinctive jingle of the hard money it contained.

Burn grinned. That was his natural reaction when he knew there was money in the vicinity.

"Soon as my woman gets back from fetching water I'll have her round up your supplies," he said.

Hawkes nodded. Burn never did anything himself that he could have the Arapaho woman do for him—except drink.

"So where you all headed?" asked the trader.

"Home."

"Where is home anyhow, Henry? You ain't never seen fit to tell me."

"That's because I don't want you to know."

Burn barked a laugh. "Then where you all coming from?"

Hawkes looked at him. "You know, you keep sticking your nose into other people's business you're liable to lose it one day."

"Just trying to be sociable is all," replied Burn, pretending that his feelings were hurt. Hawkes knew better. The trader didn't have any feelings, far as he could tell. And he knew Burn wasn't just trying to make idle talk. Information was another precious commodity out here, something that could sometimes be sold for a tidy sum, and Burn made a point of finding out everything he could, based on the premise that you never knew what someone might want to know so badly that they would be willing to pay handsomely for it.

The Arapaho woman appeared in the doorway, filling it with her bulk, and the two buckets she carried were now filled with water from the creek, some of it sloshing over the rims.

"Many horses," she announced.

Burn heaved himself up from the table. "She means there be riders coming."

He headed out onto the dogtrot. Hawkes moved to the single window. A plume of dust marked the passage of the horsemen. They were coming from the south, across the sagebrush plain. Judging by the amount of dust there were a good many of them.

The mountain man's first instinct was to go, to slip away with his family before the riders reached the trading post. But they needed the supplies they had stopped here to get, so he had to take his chances and hope that he wasn't about to find out whether the governor's amnesty was worth the paper it had been written on.

Eliza and Grace entered the trading post to join him at the window. Though Hawkes didn't speak, Eliza could sense the tension within him, and slipped her hand into his.

As the riders drew near, Hawkes could see that most of them were soldiers. And when they were closer still, the mountain man realized that they were not regular Army.

"Colorado Volunteers," said Eliza.

"How do you know?"

"I saw a lot of them in Denver. Including their commanding officer, a Colonel Chivington."

"Those five Indians riding with them—are they scouts?" asked Grace.

"No," said Hawkes grimly. "Looks like they're prisoners."

They watched as the riders checked their horses in front of the trading post. Through the thick drift of dust kicked up by their arrival, Hawkes counted a dozen Colorado Volunteers. All five Indians had their hands tied behind their backs with rope. They were all young Cheyenne braves.

One Volunteer dismounted, handing his reins to another soldier before turning to give Burn and his Arapaho woman a long once-over.

"You run this place?" he asked.

"This is my trading post. Alonzo Burn is the name. And who might you be?"

"Captain Talbot." He was eyeing the Arapaho woman. "Who is she?"

"This is my woman. You couldn't pronounce her Arapaho name. I just call her Willow."

"Can she be trusted?"

"To do what?"

Talbot glanced at Burn. "Just keep her away from my prisoners. We've come a long way today. My men and their horses are tuckered out. We need water and food." The captain surveyed the trading post's setting.

"I reckon we may as well camp here for the night. It's one more long day's ride to Denver."

"You're welcome to the water in the crick. God owns that so I don't charge for it. But a meal will cost you four bits a head."

Talbot squinted at him. "You expect me to pay you to feed my men?"

"You expect me to feed 'em for nothing? I'm running a business here, not a charity house."

"We're Colorado Volunteers. We risk our necks to keep you safe from vermin like this." Talbot made a curt gesture to indicate the five Cheyenne.

"I get along with the Indians just fine. I don't need you to protect me from them."

Talbot glanced at Willow and smirked. "Yeah, I see how you get along. And I bet you sell them whiskey and guns, too."

"You got no proof of that," said Burn, suddenly apprehensive.

"If I did I'd slap you in irons and haul you straight to the gallows. We have enough trouble with these heathens without the likes of you plying 'em with liquid bravemaker and rifles."

"Fine," said Burn. He knew when to fold his tents. "I'll feed you and your men. You can camp down by the crick."

Talbot turned and snapped an order. The soldiers and their captives proceeded past the dogtrot, making for the shade of the creekside birch trees. As he stripped off his buckskin gloves, the captain eyed the three horses tied up in front of the trading post.

"You got company, I see," he said.

"Customers," replied Burn. "And *paying* customers, at that."

"Who are they?"

"You're one suspicious cuss, Captain. Come in and see for yourself."

Burn led the way. As Talbot entered the room he seemed to relax at the sight of Eliza and Grace. He nodded to them. "Hello, ladies. Captain James Talbot, Colorado Volunteers."

"This here's Henry Gordon, his wife Eliza and his purty little daughter Grace," said Burn.

"Indeed," said Talbot, his eyes lingering on Grace. "Where are you from, Mr. Gordon?"

His face a stoic mask betraying not a trace of his unease, Hawkes said, "I live up in the high country west of here."

With a curt nod Talbot glanced around the trading post and said, "Burn, my men are hungry. Get your squaw to cooking."

"Captain," said Eliza, as Talbot turned to go.

"Yes, ma'am?"

"Who are those Indians out there?"

"Cheyenne Wolf Soldiers. We surprised them in camp two days' ride from here. Had to kill a few. Plan to take the rest to Denver." Talbot smiled. "I reckon Colonel Chivington will be glad to have a few in hand, so he can make an example of them, if you know what I mean."

"I don't know what you mean. Please explain."

"My guess is they'll be put on trial—and hanged. It'll be a big event. And a feather in my cap for bringing them in, if I do say so myself."

"Put on trial for what?"

The questions were beginning to annoy Talbot. "Those redskins have been raiding wagon trains. Killing innocent people. Maybe you being high up in the mountains you don't know about all that's been going on down here on the plains."

"Not the Cheyenne," said Eliza. "They have abided by the terms of all the treaties they've been a party to."

"And how would you know that?" asked Talbot skeptically.

"I have it on very good authority," she replied. "William Bent, for one. He happens to be a friend of mine."

Talbot's laugh was scoffing. "Bent! He's a damned Indian himself, or might as well be."

"My wife is right," said Hawkes. "Those Cheyenne prisoners of yours were probably just a hunting party."

"Yeah, sure. Hunting party or not, they killed one of my men."

"You said you jumped them. I expect they were only trying to defend themselves."

"You can think what you want," said Talbot coldly. "Fact remains, they are my prisoners and they are going to Denver and I wouldn't give a plugged nickel for their chances there." He glowered at Burn. "I don't see your squaw cooking our supper yet."

"You'll get it," said Burn.

"Make it quick." With that, Talbot turned and left the trading post.

"Bastard," muttered Burn. He spoke to Willow in her own tongue and then looked at Hawkes. "I'll get your supplies for you now, Henry."

"Come on, Grace," said Eliza.

She led her daughter out onto the dogtrot. They stood at the back and watched the soldiers making camp under the trees beside the creek—just in time to see the Cheyenne braves dragged roughly off their ponies. The captives were set down with their backs to trees and tied securely to the trunks with rope. Several of them were kicked or struck in the process. Some of the Volunteers seemed to delight in tormenting them. The rest were indifferent.

"Mother, can't we do something?" asked Grace angrily. "Look how they're treating those poor men. I wish Lieutenant Gunnison was here. He would put a stop to that."

"Your lieutenant has no authority over the Colorado Volunteers."

"Well, I'm sure he would try, all the same."

"He might try," said Hawkes, coming up behind them, a bag filled with the provisions he had just purchased slung over a shoulder. Eliza had told him all about their meeting Gunnison at the governor's residence—and about the dinner they had taken together. She had failed to mention to her husband that her daughter seemed more than slightly infatuated with the Army officer, and he with her. "But he would likely get himself killed for his trouble if he did."

Grace turned to him. "You've got to do something, Father."

Hawkes looked at Eliza. "Where is William Bent now? Still in Denver?"

"There's no way of knowing. He left Denver yesterday, carrying a message of some kind from the governor to the Cheyenne leaders."

"We must find some way to set those poor men free," insisted Grace.

"I do something like that, you and your mother are put at risk," said Hawkes, shaking his head. "I'm sorry, Grace. I don't see what I *can* do."

"If those Indians are hanged," said Eliza quietly, "what will the Cheyenne do?"

"Go to war, I reckon," said Hawkes. "Even the ones like Black Kettle would take up the war lance."

"Then we must prevent that from happening, Gordon."

Hawkes grimaced. The smart thing to do, as he well knew, would be to take Eliza and Grace home, where they would be safe. But neither of them seemed inclined to do the smart thing. They couldn't simply walk away. When he thought about it, Hawkes figured he couldn't, either.

"Then you two better ride back to Denver," he said. "Wait for me there."

"What will you do?" asked Grace, suddenly worried about her father's well-being, and starting to regret her insistence that he act to save the Cheyenne prisoners.

"I'll stick close to this bunch, look for a chance. But it may not come. If it doesn't we'll have to go see the governor." He grinned lopsidedly at Eliza. "You'll get to appeal to his better nature one more time."

She reached up to touch his bearded cheek. "Be careful, Gordon."

"Always." He handed her the provisions he had bought from Alonzo Burn. "Take these with you."

"Let's go," Eliza told her daughter. Leaving her husband was much too difficult a thing to linger over.

Grace gave her father a big hug and then turned to follow her mother. She didn't want him to see her tears.

As far as Alonzo Burn and Captain Talbot were concerned, Hawkes left shortly after his wife and daughter. To justify lingering while the women went on ahead, he took Burn up on the trader's offer of a jug to share. Burn was drinking a lot, and now and then glanced across the dogtrot, through the doorway into the other part of the cabin, where he could see Willow as she worked to prepare a meal for Talbot's hungry soldiers.

"I don't cotton to being called a squaw man," he said, surly, in between slugs of rotgut. "I ain't no Injun lover, mind you. But I wouldn't trade old Willow in for no white woman, that's for sure. Never met a white woman who could work half as hard as that gal. She ain't much to look at, I'll admit. But then I ain't, either. And she don't talk back. No small thing, that."

Hawkes didn't say much—and he didn't drink much, either, though he gave the appearance of doing so. After a while he abruptly took his leave. Mounting the dun mustang, he rode away in the direction Eliza and Grace had taken. By that time the Volunteers were done setting up camp, and he'd gotten a good look at their disposition under the birch trees.

When he was well out of sight of the trading post

he circled right around, located the creek, and followed it downstream until he was about a quarter of a mile from the Burn place. He left his horse and proceeded on foot until he came to a spot—some debris trapped between several trees right on the creek bank—from which he could watch the camp of the Volunteers without risk of discovery. Talbot had posted a couple of sentries, but they weren't much good as lookouts, and stuck too close to camp. That suited Hawkes just fine.

Shadows lengthened as the day drew to a close, and Hawkes watched as Burn arrived in the camp, presumably to inform Talbot that the meal Willow had prepared was ready. Two soldiers followed Burn back to the trading post and returned with a fire-blackened kettle that they carried on a thick piece of wood between them. Whatever the kettle contained, the ravenous soldiers consumed it quickly. Hawkes noticed that the Indian prisoners were offered no food.

Hawkes heard distant thunder rolling in over the mountains and checked the western sky. Dark storm clouds were moving in over the high peaks and a freshening wind carried the unmistakable scent of rain. Storms came suddenly in this country, and the mountain man calculated that within the hour a deluge would be upon them. He didn't mind at all. In fact, he began to consider an attempt to free the Cheyenne braves this very night. The storm would provide him with the cover he needed.

For now, though, all he could do was wait—wait for night to descend, and the rain to come.

An hour later it was full dark, and the first heavy

drops of rain were beginning to fall. A frantic wind whipped through the tops of the birch trees and made the flames of the soldiers' campfires bend and dance. Jagged bolts of blue-white lightning struck the earth, and thunder shook the ground. The cursing of the soldiers as they broke out their oilskins and canvas was quickly drowned out by the noise of the downpour as the front edge of the storm struck them. Hawkes hunkered down to wait for the initial fury of the storm to pass. Wind-driven sheets of rain soaked him to the skin. He ignored the discomfort and, as he had expected, the violence of the storm soon diminished.

The campfires had been extinguished by that time. Hawkes didn't need them to get his bearings; by now he knew exactly where every soldier and each prisoner had been prior to the storm's arrival. Returning to his horse, he tied his long gun to the saddle and led the mountain mustang closer to the camp. The steady rainfall masked any sound he made. Tethering the horse again, he moved still closer on foot, sticking to the edge of the creek, a pistol in one hand, a knife in the other. It was his fervent hope that there would be no need to use either. But if it happened it would be at close range, and so he had little use for the Plains rifle under such circumstances.

As he neared the place where one of the sentries had been posted, he paused often, straining eyes and ears to locate the enemy. Failing that, he wondered if perhaps the man had gone back to join his comrades in camp. Captain Talbot didn't strike him as the kind of officer who would tolerate a soldier leaving his post, but then these were volunteers, not regular troops. Hawkes had no way of knowing how well they had been trained, but word was that many of them had yet to be battle tested. Chivington had recruited bookkeepers and buffalo hunters, miners and merchants, to fill the ranks of his regiment in a hurry, and only about half of the officers and a mere handful of the enlisted men had any prior military experience to speak of.

Still, the mountain man wasn't going to underestimate his adversaries, and he proceeded with painstaking caution. Then he heard a groan. The sound was unmistakable. And it came from somewhere close by. A moment later he had located the source—a man lay facedown on the ground. It was the sentry. Crouched a few feet away, Hawkes considered all the possible reasons for this unexpected development. The only plausible one that he could come up with was that the sentry had been ambushed and knocked unconscious. If that was so it could mean only one thing—he wasn't the only one on a mission to free the Cheyenne prisoners.

The wisest course of action would have been to turn back to his horse and move off a ways and wait for dawn. Instead, Hawkes pressed on toward the camp. He doubted he would get a better opportunity to accomplish the goal he had set for himself. There was an unknown ingredient thrown into the mix now and that made this venture twice as dangerous as before, but Hawkes had never been one to shy away from taking the big chance.

A moment later he heard a shout, then another, and a gun went off. Hawkes saw the muzzle flash about twenty feet dead ahead. The camp exploded into chaos. Out of the darkness a shape abruptly loomed in his path. Hawkes raised the pistol. At the last second he recognized the man as one of the Cheyenne prisoners. There was something wrong with him. He stumbled, fell, and Hawkes knelt down to reach out and touch the Indian. The latter didn't move, and the mountain man moved his hand across the Cheyenne's shoulders and then down his back. His hand came away covered with blood.

A horse that had gotten loose—or been cut loose—from the picket line galloped right past Hawkes, startling him. Guns were going off throughout the soldiers' camp. In all the shouting and tumult Hawkes could distinguish Captain Talbot's voice. The captain was yelling at his men to kill all the prisoners.

Muttering a curse, Hawkes plunged into the melee. He could barely see ten feet in front of him. Muzzle flashes cast the forms of moving men in momentary sharp relief. The mountain man collided with a soldier. Both men went down. There was a brief struggle until Hawkes slammed the butt of his pistol down hard on the man's skull, knocking him out cold. Looking up just as lightning flashed, Hawkes spotted Talbot, standing over one of the Cheyenne, who sat at the base of a tree still tightly bound. The captain was aiming his pistol at the defenseless man's head, and the expression on his face, though Hawkes saw it for only an instant in the blue blaze of lightning flash, was terrible to behold. In all his years Hawkes had never seen a man who looked so pleased at the prospect of snuffing out a life.

With a shout the mountain man lunged forward. Startled, Talbot turned, momentarily distracted from the job at hand, swinging his pistol around, but Hawkes closed with him before he could get off a clean shot, striking Talbot's gun arm and deflecting the shot into the ground. Plowing full speed into the captain, Hawkes sent him sprawling. Straddling the stunned officer, he brought his knife's edge to the man's throat. Blinking rain out of his eyes, Talbot looked up at Hawkes and recognized him instantly.

"You!"

For an instant Hawkes hesitated, knowing he had to kill Talbot now. There were two good reasons to slit the man's throat. One was that the captain was a butcher, all too willing to kill his prisoners in cold blood. It was a mistake to let such men live. The second was that he knew Hawkes was involved. *If Talbot survives, I'll once again be an outlaw in the Colorado Territory*, Hawkes told himself. The amnesty Eliza had secured for him would become so much worthless paper.

But he couldn't do it.

Only a few years before he had become a killing machine, filled with a terrible rage by the murder of his son, and he had been prepared to wreak a savage and bloody vengeance, to slaughter every man in the gold camp of Gilder Gulch if necessary to have his reckoning. And he *had* killed. Several men had died at his hand, and he had felt no remorse.

Since then, though, he'd found the prospect of taking life repugnant. Not just human life, either. Even hunting game troubled him. Now, at this moment, killing Talbot was an absolute impossibility.

Talbot struck at him with his empty pistol, struggling to throw him off, but Hawkes blocked the blow and brought his own pistol down against the captain's temple, rendering Talbot unconscious just as he had done a few moments before to the other soldier.

Turning to the Cheyenne prisoner, Hawkes used his knife to cut the rope that bound the man to the tree.

"Follow me," rasped the mountain man, wiping the rain from his face.

He ran for the creek. Another soldier appeared suddenly in front of him. The Volunteer had a rifle, but he hesitated a few precious seconds in using it because he was uncertain of Hawkes's identity, thinking that he might be one of his comrades. By the time he'd figured out that wasn't the case, it was too late. Hawkes lowered a shoulder and sent the man spinning off balance. The mountain man kept running, barely missing a stride. The Cheyenne following closely behind him, however, lingered long enough to wrench the rifle from the soldier's grasp and, using it like a club, struck with such force that he heard the man's neck snap. The soldier died on his feet. The warrior ran on, not even waiting to see his victim fall.

Reaching the creek, Hawkes turned upstream and kept running for several hundred yards until he felt sure he was near the spot where he had left the mountain mustang. Only then did he stop, crouching down to listen while he caught his breath. The Cheyenne did as he did. When he was fairly certain that no one was after them, Hawkes let out a low whistle. The mustang tethered nearby answered with a soft whicker, which led Hawkes right to it. Gathering up the reins, he walked the horse a good half mile up the creek before stopping again. Only then did he speak to the Cheyenne.

"I am waiting here until daybreak," he said, in the brave's own tongue. "You're welcome to go your own way. But I'm thinking that in the morning we might be able to catch up a stray horse for you. Someone cut the soldiers' ponies loose."

"It was the Arapaho woman," said the Cheyenne.

"Willow?"

"You did not know this? The two of you were not together?"

"No."

"She set their horses loose and then came into the camp to free us. She cut Wounded Bear loose first. As he ran a soldier shot him in the back. Before she could free another one of us the soldiers killed her."

"I reckon that Captain Talbot will make things rough for Burn, then."

"Why did you not kill their leader? You had a knife to his throat."

"Because I've killed enough men in my time," said Hawkes grimly. "I'm sick and tired of it."

"I will not rest until all the bluecoats are dead."

"One question. Were you hunting buffalo? Or were you on the warpath, like Talbot said, when they captured you?"

Hawkes could tell by the expression on the Cheyenne's face that the memory of his capture at the hands of the Volunteers was a humiliating one.

"We were hunting. But we carried our war lances because the soldiers attack us even though we are not at war with them. But now I, Wolf Chief, am at war." He looked back in the direction of the camp. "I will avenge the deaths of my brothers."

Hawkes nodded wearily. "I know how you feel," he muttered, in English.

Wolf Chief looked intently at the mountain man's face. "Why did you come back to free us?"

"I was trying to do the impossible—stop a war from breaking out."

"You are too late."

"Yeah, I know."

Wolf Chief sat on his heels, his back against a tree trunk, the dead soldier's rifle cradled in his arm. "I will wait with you," he decided. "I need a pony to get back to my people so that I can tell them what has happened here. Maybe then even Black Kettle will see the truth about the white man's empty promises."

Hawkes said nothing. He sat cross-legged in the mud, shoulders hunched against the pelting rain, and the mountain mustang looming over him. Closing his eyes, he tried to sleep, but sleep was long in coming.

Chapter Six

By the time morning came the rain had stopped, but the sky remained overcast, with dark clouds moving low and fast to the east. Through the dripping trees Hawkes and Wolf Chief moved cautiously closer to the soldiers' camp, keeping their eyes peeled for any sign of the Colorado Volunteers or one of their horses. They heard a single gunshot from afar, but that was all. No soldiers. That surprised Hawkes. He had expected Talbot to come looking for them. By the time they had reached the vicinity of the camp, the mountain man was getting a little worried. Talbot hadn't struck him as the type to give up easily, much less make no attempt to track down an escaped prisoner and the man who had put a knife to his throat. But the camp was empty. The soldiers were gone. Gone, but not before they had burned the trading post. The dogtrot cabin was charred and smoking rubble. Four Cheyenne braves and Burn's Arapaho woman lay dead. And Burn was propped up against a stump over near the empty corral, his kneecap shattered by a bullet. He watched Hawkes and Wolf Chief approach with bleak and bloodshot eyes.

"The bastards are gone," he rasped, seeing how Hawkes was warily surveying the scene. It was obvious that the mountain man was leery, half expecting an ambush. "They did all the damage they could do and then rode out. Took their dead with them."

"How many dead?"

"Three. Too bad there was only three." Burn winced, gritting his teeth at the pain that the wound in his leg sent shooting through his entire body at the slightest movement. "God I could use a drink!"

"Who shot you?"

"Who do you think?"

"Talbot. But why?"

" 'Cause I balked when he said he was taking my horse and the mules, that's why. Those sons of bitches. Calling themselves soldiers. Hell, they're no better than thieves. Murdering thieves, that's what they really are." He glanced across the muddy expanse at the sodden corpses that lay beneath the trees. "I never thought I'd live to say it," he muttered. "But I'm gonna miss Willow. She was meaner than Old Scratch, twice as stubborn as a mule, and not much better looking. But she had a good heart. Reckon that's what got her kilt."

Hawkes watched Wolf Chief as the warrior walked away, heading for the creek and the bodies of his Cheyenne brothers.

"Did you know she was going to try to free those braves?" Hawkes asked Burn.

"Hell no. I would've stopped her had I known she'd gotten such a foolish notion into her head. She waited until I was asleep and slipped away. Willow was a hefty gal, but she could move quiet as a whisper when she wanted to. First I knew of it, the shooting woke me and I seen she was gone, and I figured out then that I'd be in the market for a new blanket warmer."

It seemed a callous and uncaring thing to say but Hawkes sensed that Burn was trying very hard to hide his grief behind a gruff facade.

"Reckon it was on account of she's Arapaho and they was Cheyenne," continued Burn. "You know them two tribes have always been right close. I don't know if there's any truth to it, but I hear tell that a long while back they was all one big tribe."

"I wouldn't know about that," said Hawkes. "I better take a look at that leg."

"Leave it alone. Not a damn thing you can do. I'm crippled for life now. I'm not sure why that bastard didn't just kill me. That Talbot is a mean son of a bitch and he likes killing. Reckon he just wanted me to suffer. One thing you *can* do for me—if you have any whiskey I could sure use a drink!"

Hawkes shook his head. "Sorry. I don't have any."

"Damn." Burn glanced forlornly at the pile of blackened timbers which was all that remained of his trading post. "After the ruckus they put me under arrest. Wouldn't even let me go and fetch Willow out of the mud. Made me stand by and watch my place go up in smoke. Talbot said he figured I had been in on it with Willow. That I might even have put her up to it, since I did so much trading with Injuns and all. Said I'd sold my last jug of whiskey and trade rifle to the redskins. Looks like he's right about that."

"Why did he take your horse and mules?"

"Appears that Willow cut their horses loose last

night to create a diversion. They couldn't find 'em all this morning. So they confiscated my stock. That's the word Talbot used. Confiscated. The bastard."

"Still think I should have a look at that leg of yours."

"Forget my goddamn leg. I've already written it off, okay?"

Hawkes nodded. "So are you planning to sit there until you die?"

"Hell no. I'm gonna get up in a day or two. I ain't about to run up the white flag just yet. My woman's been kilt and I've lost everything I owned and now I'm a cripple till the end of my days—but that ain't no reason to give up the ghost. I've been broke and bleeding before and I made do then. Will this time, too."

Hawkes was beginning to think he had misjudged Alonzo Burn. The man had plenty of grit. Sure, he was a foul-mouthed, lecherous, conniving, drunken cheat, but as Eliza was fond of saying, there was some good in every man. With the possible exception of one Captain James Talbot.

"By the way," said Burn, cocking his head to one side and peering suspiciously at Hawkes. "Just what are you doing back here anyhow?"

"I got so partial to your company I decided to come back and jaw with you for a while longer."

That made Burn laugh, but the laugh was short-lived. He winced at the excruciating pain that reminded him of his wound.

"You're a damned poor liar, Henry. You come back to save them Cheyenne lads."

They both glanced across the way at Wolf Chief.

The Cheyenne warrior was on his knees among the trees where his brethren lay, chanting.

"Death song?" asked Burn.

Hawkes shook his head, watching as Wolf Chief scooped up handfuls of soggy earth and raised his arms skyward, as though offering the mud to the heavens. "A prayer," he replied. "Asking that the souls of the dead Cheyenne be permitted into the spirit world."

"Well, that takes care of their souls. But what about their mortal remains?"

"That'll be up to him."

"Henry, before you go, I got a favor to ask you."

"What is it?"

"Bring Willow's body up here close by me. That way I can at least keep the scavengers away from her."

Hawkes went to the mountain mustang to get a blanket before walking down to the creek to retrieve the corpse of the Arapaho woman. He wrapped her in the blanket and carried her back to Burn, laying her gently down beside him. Taking the pistol from his belt, he handed the weapon to the trader. "You might find you need this. I'll leave you some caps and cartridges, too."

Burn was struggling to maintain his composure. "I owe you."

"Don't worry about it."

The mountain man turned away, sensing that Burn wanted to be alone with his grief. He headed back to the site of the soldiers' camp, pondering the trader's news that three Colorado Volunteers had been killed during the previous night's melee. He doubted that Willow had taken any lives, and he did not know that Wolf Chief had broken one soldier's neck during the escape. So he assumed that in the chaos panicked Volunteers had shot and killed some of their own. Of course, Talbot would not report it that way. No, he would say that an Arapaho squaw and a mountain man he knew as Henry Gordon were the responsible parties. And the word would get out that this Henry Gordon had been traveling with a wife and daughter . . . and before long someone would put two and two together and realize that the culprit's real name was Gordon Hawkes. Someone like Colonel Chivington, or Governor Evans. Hawkes shook his head. Once again fate had conspired against him. Once again he would be blamed for killings he did not commit. Seemed it was his lot in life to be a man on the run.

He waited at a respectful distance until Wolf Chief had concluded his prayer ritual. Only when the Cheyenne had gotten to his feet did Hawkes approach.

"I should take them back," said Wolf Chief. "But my people are many days from here."

"You mentioned Black Kettle. I thought he always made summer camp along the Platte River."

"We were attacked by the soldiers. It was decided that we would go north into the Powder River country and join Roman Nose and others who live there."

"What do you want to do?"

"I must go back and tell my people what has happened here."

"And the dead?"

"I will do what I can for them here."

"I'll give you a hand."

Wolf Chief gave him a long look. The Cheyenne brave's heart had hardened against all white men. Until now he had not been required to make distinctions between good whites and bad ones. But this mountain man had saved his life. He wasn't sure why. His instincts told him that Hawkes had no ulterior motives in seeking to help him. That he could be trusted. Wolf Chief nodded, accepting the offer of help. But he would withhold his trust.

They could not give the dead Cheyenne braves a proper burial, but they did the best they could with what they had available. It took them the better part of the day to erect scaffolds about eight feet off the ground. The soldiers hadn't destroyed quite all of Alonzo Burn's belongings; there was an ax jutting from a stump where the trader—or more likely Willow had chopped wood into kindling. And there was some rope in a tack box in the corral. They used the ax to cut poles and lashed them together with the rope. In the creek, Wolf Chief washed the blood and mud off the bodies of his friends. He insisted on doing this himself. When he was finished he redressed them and laid them on the scaffolds. While he performed another ritual chant, Hawkes returned to his horse, got some caps and cartridges out of his provisions bag, and took them to Burn. The trader hadn't moved all day. He just sat there, the body of the Arapaho woman beside him.

"We'll be on our way soon," said Hawkes. "Anything else you need?"

"One clean shot at that Captain Talbot."

"Well, you never know." Hawkes was no more

inclined to preach to Burn about the folly of revenge
than he had been to do the same to Wolf Chief last
night. He knew from personal experience that sometimes hate was all that kept a man going. Right now
hate was all Alonzo Burn had left. It might destroy
him in the end, but at the moment it would serve as
a reason to go on living. It would get him up off the
ground once the shock of the disaster that had be-
fallen him wore off.

When Wolf Chief was finished, he and Hawkes
took their leave. The mountain man offered to let the
Cheyenne warrior ride double, but Wolf Chief refused. They moved north along the creek for a spell,
hoping to find one of Talbot's stray horses in the
timber. But they had no luck. Finally they gave up
on that and struck out across the plain. No words
passed between them. Hawkes was bone tired, and
he figured Wolf Chief had to be, too. Yet the Cheyenne did not falter, maintaining a long, striding lope
to keep up with his mounted traveling companion.
For three hours they journeyed, stopping only when
night had fallen. Camping in a ravine that branched
off from a dry creek bed, Hawkes built a small fire
using buffalo chips and cooked some beans and fried
up some flour cakes. It was all he had left; he had
given the rest of the supplies to Eliza and Grace.
Wolf Chief consented to share the vittles with him.
Hawkes wondered how long it had been since the
Cheyenne had eaten. Talbot sure hadn't gone to any
trouble to feed his prisoners.

"I do not need your help to get back to my people," Wolf Chief told him.

"I know that." In fact, Hawkes had grave doubts

that the Cheyenne could complete the journey. He was on foot, without food or water except for what he could find, and the soldier's rifle he carried was practically worthless. He had one shot, if that—the rifle's load was probably fouled—and Hawkes could not help him there as the rifle was of a smaller caliber than the Hawken the mountain man carried. Having given his pistol to Burn, Hawkes did not have a spare weapon to give Wolf Chief. Besides, the plains were probably crawling with patrols of Colorado Volunteers, as it appeared that Chivington was doing his level best to stir up a conflict with the Indians.

In effect Wolf Chief was urging him to go his own way. Hawkes wasn't the least bit offended. He didn't think it was because the Cheyenne was ungrateful for the help he had already given. No, it had more to do with pride than anything, reckoned the mountain man. Bad enough from Wolf Chief's point of view that he had been captured by the bluecoats. And that he had been unable to save the lives of his Cheyenne brothers. Worse still, he now owed his own life to a white man, a member of the very race that posed such a threat to the continued survival of his people. He did not care to be any more beholden to Hawkes than he was already, and the mountain man understood that.

"Thing of it is," said Hawkes, "I need to talk to William Bent, the one your people call Little White Man."

"The two women I saw you with. Who are they?"

"My wife and daughter."

"You should be with them, not with me."

"That's just it. They went to Denver. I reckon that's

where Captain Talbot was headed, too. So I can't go to them, you see. If I did I'd put them in even more danger. That's why I need to talk to Bent. I need to ask him a favor: to go to Denver and get Eliza and Grace out of there."

Wolf Chief mulled all this over in his mind.

"My wife told me that the governor sent William Bent to your people with a message," continued Hawkes. "So, as luck would have it, you and I are trying to get to the same place. We might as well make the trip together."

Wolf Chief nodded reluctant agreement. He lay down on his side, the rifle within reach, and in a few moments was sound asleep. Hawkes killed the fire and sat there for a spell, listening to coyotes yapping in the distance, and studying the stars. At least the skies had cleared during the day. He figured a person had to look on the bright side, no matter how hard it was to find a bright side sometimes. He had to get to Bent as quickly as possible and more rain would just slow him down. It was Eliza and Grace that he worried about, because Talbot knew them. Question was, what would he do to them?

They traveled without incident for several days in a northeasterly direction. They also traveled without much in the way of conversation passing between them. It was obvious to Hawkes that Wolf Chief was only tolerating his presence, and that just barely. The Cheyenne warrior was consumed by his hatred for whites, and the mountain man had to assume that the only reason Wolf Chief hadn't turned on him already was because it would be a dishonorable thing to do, under the circumstances.

Thanks to the accuracy of the Plains rifle and his sharpshooting skills, Hawkes was able to provide fresh meat for the journey, killing an antelope with a single shot at a range of over five hundred yards. Finding water proved more difficult. Hawkes was unfamiliar with the arid sagebrush plains they were crossing. Rarely had he ventured this far from the high country that had been his home—his sanctuary—for the past twenty-five years. Wolf Chief was better acquainted with this country, but the first water hole he located had gone bad. On the third day—twenty-four hours after the last drop of water in the mountain man's canteen had been consumed—they stumbled across a creek. The creek water was brackish and brown but it was potable. They drank all they could, filled the canteen, and pressed on.

It was that same day, an hour before sundown, when they spotted the telltale dust of horsemen to the north. Wolf Chief put his ear to the ground and listened for a spell. Finally he rose up to calmly inform Hawkes that there were many horses and that they were coming closer. The mountain man surveyed his surroundings and led the way to a ravine. There was no point in taking any chances. The riders might be Cheyenne or Arapaho. Or they might be soldiers.

They turned out to be the latter, ten of them, a patrol of Colorado Volunteers, and they passed too close to the ravine for comfort. Hawkes wondered what mischief they were planning as he watched them gallop by about fifty yards from his hiding place. He was caught unprepared for the fact that it was Wolf Chief who had mischief in mind. The Cheyenne leveled his rifle, drawing a bead on the last horseman, and would have pulled the trigger had Hawkes not reacted so quickly. The mountain man wasn't going to count on the rifle misfiring. He backhanded the Cheyenne, a blow that sent Wolf Chief sprawling to the bottom of the ravine. Before the warrior could get up, Hawkes was on him. The latter had the advantage in weight, but the Indian was young and agile and incredibly strong. Hawkes tried to wrestle the rifle away from him. Wolf Chief threw him off, and as both men scrambled to their feet the Cheyenne swung the rifle up and pulled the trigger.

The rifle misfired.

Hawkes charged, lowering his head and plowing into his adversary, driving him hard into the ravine's steep bank, and then bringing his knee up into the Cheyenne's groin. Wolf Chief doubled over and the mountain man finished the fight by slamming a forearm across the back of the Indian's skull. Wolf Chief collapsed. Retrieving his Plains rifle, Hawkes scrambled back up to the top of the rim. He was relieved to see that the patrol had ridden on past, unaware of the struggle that had taken place a stone's throw away.

The sound of the soldiers' horses dwindling in his ears, Hawkes slid back down to the bottom of the ravine. He rolled Wolf Chief over on his back, and backhanded him. Then he stepped away, biting down hard on his anger and watching warily as the Cheyenne came to.

Wolf Chief got to his feet and gazed impassively at the Plains rifle that Hawkes held at waist level. The weapon wasn't exactly aimed at him, but Hawkes had his finger on the trigger.

"Kill me," said the warrior.

"I've been thinking about it," said Hawkes. "But I reckon I won't. I don't want to have to explain to my wife and daughter why I killed a man I stuck my neck out to save just a few days before."

"I tried to kill you," said Wolf Chief, putting into words the reason that seemed to be sufficient.

"Yes you did," rasped Hawkes. "And that just proves you're a fool. You'd better put a tight rein on that hate of yours. If you don't it will get you killed. And me right along with you."

"I am not afraid to die."

"Of course not," said the mountain man dryly. "But you won't do your people much good if you're dead."

"My people are dead," replied Wolf Chief. "It is only a matter now of how we die. And I will die fighting the bluecoats."

"Fine. You do that. But just wait until I'm not around, if you don't mind."

"I do not want you to be with me."

"Too bad. I've made up my mind that I'm going to get you back to your people."

"Why?"

"Let's just say I'm stubborn and leave it at that. Now you can walk or you can go the rest of the way tied up and draped over the back of my horse. It's your decision."

Wolf Chief glanced at the useless rifle he had taken from the soldier, picked it up, and climbed out of the ravine to continue walking north by west, the direction they had been traveling since leaving Alonzo Burn's trading post. Shaking his head, Hawkes led the mountain mustang out of the ravine, mounted up, and followed in Wolf Chief's tracks. The Cheyenne warrior was a fool all right, but he considered himself an even bigger fool for being in the position in which he now found himself. *One of these days*, he told himself, *you're going to learn to mind your own damned business and stay out of other people's troubles.*

Several days later they spotted two more horsemen. This time, however, the riders were Cheyenne. Better yet, they were scouts from Black Kettle's band. They were happy to see their brother Wolf Chief. The hunting party of which he had been a part was long overdue, a cause for apprehension in the village. When Wolf Chief told the scouts what had happened, and that all of his companions were dead, murdered by the bluecoats, the two Cheyenne braves shouted their outrage. When asked about Hawkes, Wolf Chief reluctantly explained that the mountain man had helped him escape the soldiers. The palpable hostility of the scouts toward Hawkes diminished somewhat. But it didn't go away entirely. They didn't trust the mountain man any more than Wolf Chief did.

Hawkes asked the scouts if Little White Man—William Bent—was with the band, and the Cheyenne answered in the affirmative. He was in the village that had just been raised on the banks of Sand Creek, only a day's ride from the villages of the bands led by Roman Nose and One Eye. The scouts pointed them in the right direction and then proceeded on their way.

A short while later, Hawkes and Wolf Chief topped a low rise to see the Cheyenne encampment spread out before them on the arid flats through which a small creek had carved its serpentine course. Their appearance caused a commotion down below. Several warriors grabbed their weapons, leaped astride their ponies and galloped out to confront them. When they identified Wolf Chief, one raced back to the skin lodges to spread the news, so that by the time Hawkes and his Cheyenne traveling companion reached the village a crowd had gathered. Women called out to Wolf Chief, asking anxiously what had become of the rest of the hunting party. "The soldiers killed them all," he replied grimly, and this unleashed a rising swell of anguished wails mixed with shouts of anger. Wolf Chief walked impassively through the crowd until he spotted Black Kettle. The Cheyenne parted respectfully to give Black Kettle some room, but the way Wolf Chief approached him was more confrontational than respectful. Cold rage twisted Wolf Chief's gaunt face.

"Our brothers are dead, murdered by the bluecoats," he said. "They attacked our camp. They made captives of us. And our brothers died with their hands tied behind their backs. They were not given the chance to die like warriors. The men who did this flew *that* flag!" He jabbed an angry finger at the garrison flag fluttering limply above Black Kettle's lodge. "Why do you fly the flag of the men who take our land and kill our buffalo and murder our brothers, Black Kettle?"

The crowd was hushed. Seldom had they heard Black Kettle addressed in so curt and hostile a manner—and never by someone so young and of relatively low standing in the band as Wolf Chief.

If Black Kettle was offended he hid it behind a stoic mask. "What soldiers were these? The soldiers of Governor Evans? Or the soldiers of the White Father in Washington?"

"What difference does that make?" asked Wolf Chief, exasperated. "They are all the same."

"No. Little White Man has told me what the difference is. The White Father's soldiers are not the ones who attacked us on the Platte. And I think they were not the ones who attacked you."

"He is not our father," said Wolf Chief. "He is our enemy. How many more Cheyenne must die before you see the truth?"

"It is the death of the Cheyenne that I am trying to prevent," replied Black Kettle sternly.

Hawkes, standing a little ways off with the reins of the mountain mustang in hand, was distracted from this conversation by the appearance of William Bent at his side.

"What are you doing here?" asked Bent.

"It's a long story."

"Come to my lodge and tell me."

"I need your help, Bill."

Bent nodded and pushed through the crowd that

was riveted to the clash of words between Black Kettle and Wolf Chief. Hawkes followed him.

"That Wolf Chief is a hothead," remarked Bent as they broke away from the press of Cheyenne.

"Yeah, I know. I'm a little surprised he's getting away with what he's doing."

"Black Kettle tends to be too lenient at times. But he's between a rock and a hard place, you know. Many—maybe most—of the warriors here agree with Wolf Chief, though most wouldn't stand up and say so. He's become something of a hero, even though he's very young. They say he fought like a wildcat down on the Platte when Chivington's boys attacked these people down there. Coming back alive after another scrape with the Volunteers won't hurt his image, either. So Black Kettle has to be careful with him. He comes down too hard on Wolf Chief, this band might split apart. All the ones who want to fight might just pull up stakes and leave. But on the other hand, if he lets Wolf Chief go too far with this, he loses face. So how did you end up with that young brave, anyway? And how can I be of help to you?"

Hawkes told him the whole story about the events that had transpired at Burn's trading post and the details of his journey with Wolf Chief, including the part about how the Cheyenne had tried to kill him.

Bent shook his head. "I would have plugged him right then and there, I think."

"Eliza and Grace went back to Denver just in case those Cheyenne boys ended up there. They were going to try to reason with the governor. But now I expect they're in plenty of hot water, because Chivington and Evans will know I helped Wolf Chief escape. Three Volunteers lost their lives. Not by my hand, but I don't reckon that's a distinction anybody will take the time to make."

"I expect you're right about that. Sounds to me like I had better make tracks for Denver. Was planning to head that way in a few days anyway. Need to let the governor know that Black Kettle has agreed to go to Fort Lyon. See, Evans has ordered all the Indians who desire peace to assemble there. Those that don't show up will be considered hostiles. I'll leave first thing in the morning, Gordon. Meanwhile, you can stay with me tonight. I don't think you've ever met my boys, George and Charlie."

Bent's sons sat around a cook fire tended by their mother, Yellow Woman, outside a skin lodge. George and Charlie Bent looked like Cheyenne braves. Hawkes calculated that they were barely out of their teens. The Bents shared their evening meal with the mountain man, and as he ate the Indian bread and buffalo meat, Hawkes listened to George tell of his own scrapes with the Colorado Volunteers.

"We were hunting along the Solomon River," said George. "Patrols attacked us again and again. They would come at dawn or dusk. We were usually in camp. There were two or three of them for every one of us. We had done nothing wrong. We were only trying to hunt the buffalo. But they would not leave us alone. Finally we decided to strike back. We raided several stage stations. Ran off their horses. We burned one of the stations, too. We didn't kill anybody, though. The soldiers had to protect the stations then, so they were too busy to bother us after that."

"Black Kettle was angry that we raided the stage stations," added Charlie. "But Roman Nose told us that we had done well."

"I don't understand what Black Kettle is trying to do," admitted George. "Some Wolf Soldiers from Roman Nose's village captured several white women and children. There was some talk of holding them hostage so that maybe the soldiers would not attack us anymore. But Black Kettle ransomed them, trading many of his best horses for their freedom, and made sure they got to Denver safely."

William Bent shook his head. "Black Kettle did the right thing. Chivington's boys would not have been stopped by a few white hostages. That would have just made matters worse. And had one of them been killed . . ." He didn't finish, just shook his head again.

"It was a noble gesture on Black Kettle's part," said Hawkes. "But I bet it will go unnoticed by Chivington and the governor. Anyway, no matter how this works out, women and children should not be involved."

"Tell that to the Colorado Volunteers," said Charlie.

"Trying to keep the peace is fast becoming a losing battle for Black Kettle," said Bent. "His own people are on the verge of turning against him."

Hawkes nodded, gazing into the cook fire's flames. He had a strong hunch that all hell was about to break loose, and he had to hurry up and get his wife and daughter back to their mountain sanctuary before that happened.

Later that night he told Bent that maybe he should take his family into the high country, too, until the storm blew over.

"I don't think I can do that," sighed Bent, puffing on a pipe. "The Cheyenne are my people. And my sons would never leave. To do so would be dishonorable. But you—you need to get your family as far away from here as possible. Because we both know that Black Kettle's cause is hopeless. War is coming, Gordon, and it's not your fight."

Hawkes nodded. That was very true. It wasn't his fight. But the injustice of it all still rankled. The Cheyenne were being driven into a war they could not possibly win. By ruthless Indian haters like James Talbot. Hawkes felt no allegiance to the Cheyenne, as he did to the Absaroka Crow, his friends for all his years in the mountains. Still, a great wrong was being done here, and he knew it would not be easy to just turn his back on that. He had to focus on what was best for Eliza and Grace. He kept telling himself that they were his first priority.

Chapter Seven

When Eliza and Grace left their rooms in Denver, they were surprised to find a pair of Colorado Volunteers waiting for them at the foot of the porch steps. It was early in the morning, and golden sunlight slanted across the wide, rutted street that was already bustling with activity. There wasn't a cloud in the sky, or a breath of wind. A pall of pale dust hung like fog over the street. The day promised to be a hot one, and Eliza felt a twinge of homesickness for the mountains. They were there, just to the west, jagged blue peaks, some capped with snow. How she wished she was in them at this moment, safe with her husband, far removed from the din and dirt of "civilization." But she had come here on a mission of mercy and she was compelled to see it through. Even though Governor Evans had managed to avoid giving her an audience for several days now. "He thinks we will just give up and go away eventually," she'd told her daughter. "Well, he's very much mistaken," Grace had replied, with a fervor that made Eliza smile every time she thought about it.

"Mrs. Hawkes?" asked one of the Volunteers.

"I'm Eliza Hawkes."

"You're to come with us, ma'am. Both of you."

"Where are you taking us?"

"The governor wants to see you."

"Oh, good. I want to see him, too. Lead the way."

"After you, ma'am."

"Come along, Grace."

They proceeded down the street with the pair of soldiers in tow.

"Why did the governor send them for us, Mother?" whispered Grace, with a glance over her shoulder at their escort.

"Maybe he finally realized that we weren't going to give up."

"But why *two* soldiers if it was just to deliver a message?"

Eliza gave no answer. She didn't have a good one. Grace was no fool—and neither was she. Something more than just a summons was behind the presence of the soldiers on their stoop. And Eliza had a hunch it had something to do with Gordon. But what? She didn't dare speculate, and she tried her level best to keep her anxiety from showing.

Reaching the governor's residence, they were seen straight into the office where, not too many days earlier, Evans had presented Eliza with her husband's amnesty. Once again the governor was behind his desk. He rose at the entrance of the women, but there was nothing friendly about his expression. Colonel Chivington was present as well, resplendent as always in his gaudy uniform. And there was a third man, a grim, dark-eyed man in the uniform of a captain in the Colorado Volunteers. This man took one look at Eliza and Grace, turned to Evans, and said,

"That's them. These are the two women I saw at the trading post with the man who was introduced to me as Henry Gordon."

Evans leveled a cold gaze upon Eliza. "I presume Henry Gordon is an alias of your husband's."

"Having been wrongly accused of murder he has found it necessary to employ an alias on occasion."

"Personally, I doubt your husband has ever been wrongly accused of anything," said Chivington curtly.

"I'll handle this, Colonel, thank you," said Evans. "Mrs. Hawkes, I find myself burdened with an unpleasant task. I am revoking the amnesty I provided your husband. And I am placing both you and your daughter in custody."

Alarmed, Grace reached out to grip her mother's arm. Eliza coolly placed her hand over her daughter's to give it a reassuring squeeze.

"Do you mind telling us why?" she asked, steadily meeting the governor's gaze.

"I think I will let Captain Talbot explain. Captain?"

"Your husband attempted to free my prisoners the night we camped at the trading post," said Talbot, his tone hard as steel. "He managed to get away with one of them. And in the process, three of my men were killed."

"What happened to your other prisoners?" asked Grace.

Talbot smiled coldly. "I'm happy to report that they have lifted their last white scalp."

"Who killed them?" asked Eliza.

"My soldiers did, on my orders."

"You bastard," breathed Grace.

"That's enough, Grace," said Eliza.

"You should be thanking me," said Talbot. "Might have been your scalp they'd have taken next. Of course I expect they would have taken more than that." He leered, his eyes taking in Grace's slender figure.

"Captain, behave like a gentleman in my presence, if you don't mind," said Evans.

"Yes, sir."

"Are you saying my husband killed those three soldiers?" asked Eliza.

"That's right. That's exactly what I'm saying."

"Then you are a liar, Captain," she said.

Talbot's temper flared. He took a half step toward Eliza, hands balled into fists, and she had no doubt that he would have struck her but for Chivington's intervention.

"As you were, Talbot!" snapped the colonel.

Talbot trembled with the exertion of restraining himself. "Don't be fooled by her innocent act, Governor," he said. "She and that one left Burn's trading post earlier in the day, but I doubt they went far, and I'm sure they knew what Hawkes was going to do."

Eliza wanted to tell them that indeed she had known. That in truth it had been largely because of her and Grace that Gordon had done what he'd done. But she had to think of her daughter. Had to, somehow, get Grace out of this.

"My daughter and I came straightaway to Denver," she said. "In order to see you, Governor. And you are well aware that we've been trying to do just that for several days now."

"See me on what matter?"

"About the Cheyenne prisoners. Captain Talbot told us they were going to hang. I had hoped to reason with you, sir. Make you see how disastrous it would be, for everyone, if you allowed such a thing to happen."

"Well," said Evans, looking at his hands folded on the desk in front of him. "That's all a rather moot point now, is it not?"

"You asked me if my husband would help you keep the peace among the Indians," said Eliza tersely. "That is what he was trying to do. Had those boys been hanged, you would have had a war for sure. Or is that what you want, Governor? In spite of all your protests to the contrary?"

"It is not your place, or your husband's, to determine when, how and upon whom justice will be meted out in this territory, Mrs. Hawkes. Captain Talbot claims he had reason to believe that those Cheyenne were on the warpath."

"It was a hunting party."

"Oh, and you're an expert," said Talbot.

"I know enough to have noticed that their ponies were not painted for war, Captain!"

Talbot glanced at Chivington and Chivington looked at Evans and the governor cleared his throat and grimaced.

"I understand you are staying with that widow woman . . . what is her name, Colonel?"

"Denham, sir."

"Yes, that's right. William Bent's friend. Mrs. Hawkes, you and your daughter will be confined under house arrest at Mrs. Denham's home until it can be determined whether charges shall be made against you."

"What charges were you contemplating, Governor?" she asked.

"Aiding and abetting the escape of a prisoner, for a start," suggested Chivington.

Eliza smirked. "That's as good as any other, I suppose."

"They should be placed in our custody," said Talbot.

"I would not subject them to such an ordeal," said Evans. "Colonel, you will post a guard on the Denham home around the clock. Neither Mrs. Hawkes nor her daughter are to be allowed to leave, under any circumstances, without my written permission. And no one is to be allowed to see them without authority from me. Is that understood?"

"Yes, sir."

"Let my daughter go free," said Eliza. "You don't need her to see your scheme through."

"No," said Grace firmly. "I'm staying with you, Mother."

"And to what scheme are you referring?" asked Evans.

"You're baiting a trap for my husband. Anyone could see that."

Evans smiled thinly. "And do you think it will work?"

"You had better hope it doesn't," said Eliza fiercely.

"What is that supposed to mean?"

"It means my father is the last man you want to cross," snapped Grace.

"That's enough, dear," said Eliza. "Colonel, if you don't mind, we would like to return to our quarters."

"I'll be sure to check in on the two of you from time to time," said Talbot, still staring at Grace.

"No you won't," said Evans. "If any harm comes to either of these women, Captain, I will hold you personally responsible."

If any harm comes to us, thought Eliza, *the captain will be the one who is responsible.*

When Lieutenant Gunnison arrived in Denver he rode straight to the governor's residence. The guard posted at the door informed him that the governor was not seeing anyone else that day. Gunnison toyed with the idea of forcing the issue but remembered his place and decided what he had to say to the governor could wait until tomorrow.

As he walked away along the street, Gunnison saw movement in the night shadow that had already gathered in an alleyway. Instinctively his hand moved to the pistol at his hip. Denver had its fair share of cutthroats, and they tended to come out at night. No one was safe on the streets after the sun went down.

But this was no cutthroat. As the man came out into the open, Gunnison recognized William Bent.

"What are you doing here?" asked the cavalryman. "I figured you'd be with the Cheyenne."

"I'm here to help a friend. What are *you* doing here, Lieutenant?"

"I got back to Fort Lyon yesterday and heard the scuttlebutt."

"Involving Gordon Hawkes?"

Gunnison nodded. "Word is the governor ordered his wife and daughter placed under arrest."

"House arrest," said Bent, looking up and down the street. "That was several days ago. I just got here myself, today."

"So what's this all about? All I've heard is barracks gossip."

"Some of Chivington's volunteers attacked a Cheyenne hunting party, took five of them prisoner. They claimed these braves were on the warpath, but that's not true."

"You're sure about that?"

"They were from Black Kettle's band."

"Just because he wouldn't send them out to make war doesn't mean they weren't looking for trouble."

"It was a hunting party, Lieutenant. You can take my word for it."

Gunnison nodded. "I guess I will. But will the governor?"

"The governor is not the least bit interested in the truth."

"They say Hawkes tried to free the Indians. Killed several Volunteers in the process."

"He tried to free them, that's true. He figured they were as good as dead if they got to Denver, and I reckon he's right on that score. But he only managed to get one away. The rest were killed. And from what Hawkes told me, the Volunteers who were killed were probably shot by their own men in the confusion. It was night, it was storming and there was some panic."

Gunnison knew from experience that it could very well have happened just that way. Especially when you were dealing with inexperienced, poorly trained troops. From what he'd heard and seen, the Colorado Volunteers qualified as both. Even veterans sometimes broke under pressure, and few experiences were more nerve-wracking than being the victim of a night attack.

"So Hawkes is hiding out with the Cheyenne, I take it," he said.

Bent nodded, peering intently at Gunnison through the fast-deepening gloom. "Maybe I made a mistake letting on about that."

"Maybe you did. Thing is, that doesn't bode well for the Cheyenne if the governor or Chivington find out. Is Hawkes the friend you're here to help?"

"He asked me to come here and fetch his family to him. Eliza and Grace came back here to plead with the governor on behalf of the Cheyenne prisoners. Instead, they've become pawns in a dangerous game."

"Pawns? What do you mean?"

"The governor isn't interested in prosecuting them. He wants Hawkes. He's using the man's family as bait."

Gunnison pondered this news. He was ambivalent about Gordon Hawkes, not knowing what to believe where the mountain man was concerned. It seemed to him to be highly unlikely that a man could be falsely accused of killing not once, not even twice, but three times now. That hardly seemed credible. Based on his own experiences with the man, Gunnison could come to no other conclusion than that

Hawkes was a very dangerous individual. And one who made no effort to live by the rules, if the rules did not suit his purpose. He made his own law. That seemed to be the way with many of the men who had lived in the high country as trappers and traders. Up there they had one law: survival of the fittest. Kill, or be killed. You couldn't blame them for living by that law in the wilderness. But Hawkes wasn't the only one of his kind who couldn't adjust to the coming of civilization, and with it the coming of a more civilized body of law. More than a few mountain men had come to a bad end because they refused to submit to man-made laws, couldn't manage to live by society's rules. Gordon Hawkes would also come to a bad end, for the same reason. For Gunnison that was neither an appealing or an appalling prospect. He cared about what happened to Hawkes only to the extent that the man was the father of the young woman he had not been able to stop thinking about since they'd met a week and a half ago.

The idea that Grace Hawkes was being used as bait didn't sit well with Gunnison. And even in the darkness of the Denver street Bent could tell it bothered the lieutenant considerably.

"Will the governor's scheme work?" asked Gunnison. "Will Hawkes take the bait, do you think?"

Bent sighed. "If I go back and tell him what's happened he'll come straight to Denver, you can count on that."

"If you tell him? I don't see that you have any choice, Mr. Bent."

"Well, I'd rather not go back without them."

Gunnison stared at him. "I don't think I want to hear what comes next," he said dryly.

Bent grinned. "If you don't hear what I have in mind, how will you decide whether to help me or not?"

"I don't have to decide. Whatever plan you're cooking up I want no part of it. And I don't want to know about it, either. Because if I knew about it I might be obligated to inform the governor."

Bent shook his head. "It's the man who straddles the fence that gets splinters in the worst places. Damn it to hell, Lieutenant. One of these days you're going to have to stick your neck out and make a stand for what's right."

"Don't preach to me," snapped Gunnison. "You see this uniform I'm wearing? I've spent my entire adult life in it. The Army *is* my life. I don't know anything else, and I don't *want* to know anything else. I swore an oath to serve my country. And that service includes abiding by the laws."

"Even if the law is wrong?"

"Yes, even then. It's not my place to determine the right or wrong of the laws, any more than I am free to decide whether an order I have been given is a good one or a bad one."

"But it is your place to do that," replied Bent earnestly. "You're just too blind to see it. Or maybe you're hiding behind that uniform because you don't have the guts to do what's right."

Fists clenched, Gunnison turned sharply on his heel and walked away, his strides long and angry. It was either walk away or punch William Bent in the mouth.

He marched into the first saloon he came to, went to the bar and growled at the barkeep to bring him a whiskey. He just had time to down the shot before William Bent showed up at his elbow.

"That just proves my point," said Bent. "You would rather walk away from trouble than face it."

"Listen. You're an old man, Bent, so don't push your luck with me."

Bent laughed. "Old man? Well, maybe so. But I can still cut you from collar to crotch in less time than it would take that feller over yonder to pour you another drink."

The saloon suddenly fell silent. All eyes focused on the Army officer and the Indian trader at the bar, and the men in their proximity began to inch away.

Gunnison ran a hand over his face, feeling the beard stubble on his cheeks and feeling very tired. He had been in the saddle continually since leaving Denver over a week ago, carrying the governor's proclamation to several Arapaho villages and then making the long ride back to his post—only to learn upon arrival at Fort Lyon about the arrest of Grace Hawkes and her mother. He'd lingered only long enough to get permission from his commanding officer, Major Merritt, before climbing back into the saddle and riding hell-bent for Denver.

And what if the major hadn't given him permission to come? Gunnison had to ask himself that question because it went to the heart of what Bent was saying. If Merritt had said no, would he have come anyway? Would he have gone absent without leave, on Grace's account? Fortunately, Merritt liked him. Perhaps more importantly, the major didn't like Evans.

Didn't trust the governor. "That man wants one thing," Merritt had once told him. "He wants to be famous. And one way to accomplish that is to become the man who put down a full-blown Indian war. The nation would be forever in his debt. And with that feather in his cap there would be no limit to how far he could go. Maybe as far as the Executive Mansion."

So perhaps it was to be expected that Merritt would approve his request to ride to Denver and—and do what, exactly? Gunnison hadn't really thought his way through that part of it. What had he expected to accomplish? Did he think he could convince the governor to let Grace and her mother go free? Or was he merely going to lodge a complaint and then ride back to Fort Lyon? He had to admit to himself that he had no idea what he'd planned to do once he got there. But one thing he hadn't planned on doing was to get into a scrape with William Bent. He didn't have anything to prove. Backing down didn't bother him. A man who had fought Arapaho Dog Soldiers was a long way past having to prove his manhood in a bucket-of-blood saloon like this.

"Just leave me alone, Bent," he said wearily.

"Okay," said Bent. "I will. Because I don't want to have to kill you, son. See, I know you'll come around, sooner or later. I just hope when you do it's not too late."

"And just how do you know that?"

Bent leaned closer and pitched his voice low so that only Gunnison could hear what he said next.

"Because I've seen the way you look at Miss Hawkes, that's why."

With that, Bent left the saloon.

*   *   *

When he left the governor's residence the following morning, Gunnison went straight back to the saloon. As bad as he had needed a stiff drink after his confrontation with William Bent, he needed one a lot worse now. He was a man who prided himself on his self-control, an attribute he had developed at an early age and honed at West Point. It was therefore disconcerting to him when he lost control of his emotions. That had happened recently on the occasion of his meeting Grace Hawkes—and he had a feeling that he'd never quite been the same since. It had happened again yesterday, in the argument with Bent that had nearly deteriorated into fisticuffs. And it had happened yet again today, in the office of Governor Evans, when he had finally faced facts and come to terms with the truth regarding what the governor was after—and the lengths to which the man would go to get it.

Belly up to the bar, Gunnison knocked back one shot of snakehead and called for a second. He was staring into the glass when he heard William Bent's voice—just about the last thing he wanted to hear at this moment.

"I take it you've seen the governor," said the trader.

"What are you doing here?"

"Waiting for you. I kind of figured you'd drop by."

"You're too clever for your own good."

Bent chuckled. "We'll find out about that soon enough."

"How do you mean?"

"I mean when we get Eliza Hawkes and her daughter out of here."

Gunnison stared at him. "You're loco."

"You could at least hear my plan first."

"I don't want to hear it." Gunnison downed the second shot of whiskey and gasped. "I don't want to be any part of it."

"What about Miss Hawkes?"

"What about her? Maybe she is under house arrest, so what? At least she's safe. You go through with this madness, you might just end up getting her hurt, or worse."

"That won't happen. I'm just wondering when you will stop thinking about yourself and start thinking about what's best for her."

"Don't press your luck, Bent."

"How do you suppose she'll feel when she sees her father gunned down when he comes to try to free her and her mother?"

Gunnison sighed. "If Hawkes is a friend of yours, you need to go back and tell him to just sit tight and do nothing. Once Evans realizes that his scheme won't work, that Hawkes won't take the bait, he'll let Grace and her mother go. He doesn't have any evidence against them."

"You should know better than that. You've dealt with Hawkes before. You really think he's the kind of man who would just sit tight and do nothing? And by now you've got the governor figured out, surely. You know he'll stop at nothing to get what he wants. He won't care who gets hurt."

Gunnison threw a quick look around the room. It was early in the day and the saloon was virtually empty. No one stood near enough to overhear them. The sole barkeep had moved to the other end of the bar once Bent had arrived and started talking to the Army officer. Smart man, thought Gunnison. He makes it a habit to mind his own business. Am I smart enough to do that?

"The governor doesn't want Hawkes that badly," he said.

"Like I said, you just flat out know better. Evans is working very hard to start an Indian uprising, so he can put it down and become the savior of the Colorado Territory. He pulls it off and he'll be able to write his own ticket politically. And he needs to make an example out of Hawkes so that the Volunteers know he's behind them all the way. Hawkes will also be an example to any civilians who see through the governor's scheme, people who might get the notion to do what's right and help the Indians, otherwise." Bent shook his head. "Nope. Evans won't turn loose of Eliza or her daughter. He'll make it so that Hawkes *has* to walk into the trap."

"How would he go about doing that?" asked Gunnison, though he was fairly sure that he didn't really want to know.

"Well, I'm told there's a certain Captain Talbot who really has a bone to pick with Hawkes. He was the one in charge of the Cheyenne prisoner that Hawkes set free."

"Yes, I know. I've heard all about what happened at Burn's trading post."

"Talbot wanted the women put into his custody. Evans wouldn't do it, but he might, if he gets desperate enough. He didn't want to because he wasn't too sure what would happen to Grace if he did. Seems this Captain Talbot is something of a ladies' man. But he's no gentleman about it. That's the word around Denver, anyway."

Gunnison was staring into his glass again. Bent fell silent, watching the lieutenant out of the corner of his eye. He could sense that Gunnison was wavering, and to say anything more might be counterproductive.

"What's your plan?" muttered Gunnison.

"It'll be easier if I just show you."

Gunnison looked at Bent, who motioned toward the street. The cavalryman nodded, and Bent led the way out of the saloon.

They walked through Denver, a half-dozen blocks along the main thoroughfare and then left on another street, then right and to the end of a third, and long before then Gunnison knew where they were headed— to the house where Grace and her mother had been staying on the evening he had taken them out to dinner. Bent turned down a side street before they reached the house, however, and after that cut into an alley. As he neared the end of the alley he motioned for Gunnison to stop. Backed up against a wall, Bent took a quick peek around the corner. Moving away, he gestured at Gunnison to have a look.

"That's the back of Widow Denham's house," said Bent. "As you can see, there's only one guard stationed at the back. One at the front. There are always only the two."

Gunnison shook his head. Something wasn't right and he was about to say so when Bent said it for him.

"I know what you're thinking: This is supposed to be a trap laid out for Gordon Hawkes and there are only two guards?"

Gunnison took a long look around. "There must be others hidden nearby."

"There are. The next house to the west of the Denham home. Governor Evans moved the people who lived there out and put his Volunteers in. Way it looks to me, there are usually about a half-dozen soldiers on watch in there, day and night. And believe me, they are watching. Because Captain Talbot is in charge of this whole business, and he wants Hawkes so bad he can taste it."

"So what do you propose to do?"

Bent grinned. "I propose to give the men in that house a real distraction. And then I'll get the guard there in back to go around to the front. That's where you come in."

"Oh? I never said I'd be a part of this."

Bent acted like he hadn't even heard what Gunnison said. "When that guard leaves his post, you go in through the back door and bring Grace and Eliza out. We'll have horses waiting right here in this alley. And we'll be miles away before they figure out we're gone."

"They'll come after us."

"I've been chased by Utes and Kiowas and got away with my topknot still attached. I can shake off those Colorado Volunteers."

Gunnison thought it over. "You'll do this under cover of darkness, I hope."

"Tonight, in fact. So what do you say, Lieutenant? Are you up for it?"

"Throw away my career? Four years at West Point, eight years of service out here—and you want me to just throw it all away."

"You want to help Grace Hawkes or not?"

"Christ," muttered Gunnison. He was looking at the Denham house, but the image of Grace was in his mind's eye.

"Men have done more for love," observed Bent. "There's many men who have thrown away their lives."

"I might be doing that, too," said Gunnison dryly.

"Well, for one thing, you don't wear that uniform tonight. Like as not no one will ever know you played a hand. Not if everything goes according to plan."

"It never does."

"So you have a better idea? Don't tell me, let me guess. You were going to ride back to Fort Lyon and convince your commanding officer to send a report off to Washington. And even if the folks in Washington decide to do something, by the time they got around to it, Talbot would have killed Hawkes, and probably done worse than that to Grace, and Evans will have his war, and a lot of innocent people—"

"Okay, okay," said Gunnison, exasperated. "I'll help you—if only to shut you the hell up."

"Good. Because I'm tired of talking. Meet me back here at dark."

Gunnison nodded. "Just one thing, Bent. I don't want any killing. Those men may be Colorado Volunteers, but they're still wearing a uniform. They're still soldiers. And so am I, at least for a while yet."

"That suits me," said Bent.

* * *

Gunnison was back in the alley at the appointed time, but with no fewer misgivings than he had had before. He had spent most of the day trying to figure out why he was doing this, why he was jeopardizing his career by getting involved in Bent's scheme. A soldier was all he had ever wanted to be, the only profession he felt he was suited for. The only answer he could come up with was that he was in love. Not that it was a good answer. Love was like temporary insanity. He was in love with a young woman he had only just met, had only spoken to briefly, and who had given him no indication that she reciprocated his feelings for her. A young woman who was in desperate straits, and he was going to play the role of knight in shining armor and rescue her and to hell with the consequences, which would probably be quite severe. It was ludicrous, and Gunnison knew that. But he seemed powerless to restrain himself. He had lost control. He had no willpower where Grace Hawkes was concerned. And he approached the whole endeavor with a sense of fatalism, too, because he knew it would somehow go awry. He would be discovered. Cashiered out of the Army, if not court-martialed. In short he was walking with eyes wide open into certain disaster.

William Bent was there, along with two other men. One looked like an Indian, though he wore a white man's store-bought clothes instead of buckskin, except for beaded moccasins. The other was a white man with a carrot-red beard and a patch over his left eye. Bent introduced them as Big Tom and Rudd Coltrain respectively. Big Tom was a Shawnee who, for a time, had served as a scout for the United States Army, until he'd become too overly fond of rotgut whiskey, so that he had come to be in a state of almost constant inebriation and unable to perform his duties. Since then, according to Bent—Big Tom said nothing—he had tried his hand at this and that: muleskinning, mustanging, wolfing and for a time had even found gainful employment as a bouncer in a house of ill repute. Bent assured Gunnison that Big Tom could be relied upon, when he was sober—and tonight he was stone-cold sober. As for Coltrain, the man had been a fur trapper, lost his eye in a scrape with Blackfoot Indians and had on occasion worked for one or the other Bent brothers as a teamster, hauling furs east and trade goods west.

"Rudd and Big Tom are going to start a ruckus in front of the Denham house," Bent explained. "When they do, the guard in the back will go around to the front to see what's going on. When he does, Lieutenant, you'll go in the back way and bring Eliza and Grace out, as we discussed before."

"And what about the soldiers in the other house?" asked Gunnison.

Bent grinned. "You just leave that to me."

Gunnison glanced at the horses. Including the one he had just brought into the alley with him, there were six mounts.

"So Rudd and Big Tom are coming with us?" he assumed.

"After this they won't be able to stick around here," said Bent.

Gunnison wanted to ask Bent why these men were risking so much and if he was sure they could be trusted. But he figured all he would do in the asking was insult them, and Bent as well. Besides, Rudd and Big Tom were watching him in a way that made it clear that they wondered the same thing about him.

"Okay," said Bent. "We all know what we're supposed to do." He nodded encouragingly at Gunnison, sensing the lieutenant's uncertainty. "I'll be back before it's time for you to go in."

Gunnison still wanted to know how Bent intended to deal with the soldiers holed up in the house next door, but before he could ask the trader was gone, and so were Rudd and Big Tom, leaving Gunnison alone with his doubts. All he could so was watch the house that had become a prison for Grace and her mother from the back of the alley. It was very dark—the moon had yet to rise—so he had no need to worry that he might be spotted. The nearest soldier was the guard at the back of the Denham house, and he was a good two hundred feet away across an empty lot. There was lamplight spilling out of some of the windows of the house, and occasionally the guard would pass through a shaft of light as he listlessly paced back and forth at his post. Gunnison could hear distant laughter and the tinny sound of a piano being indifferently played, but that came from the center of town. This part of Denver was quiet. He doubted it would stay that way much longer.

A half hour passed. Gunnison had a keywinder, and he tried not to check it too frequently, but the minutes crawled by, and his patience was soon exhausted. Waiting was the worst part when you knew action was imminent. So it was with great relief that he spotted Bent coming up the alley toward him.

"We're all set," said the trader. "Get ready."

"First, tell me what you did about the soldiers in the other house."

"Don't you trust me, Lieutenant?"

"Why should I? I hardly know you."

"Fair enough. Two ladies of the evening, each with two bottles of good whiskey laced with a lot of laudanum." Gunnison could see teeth flash as Bent grinned. "I don't think you have to worry about those men, do you?"

"I hope you're right."

Bent grabbed Gunnison's arm. "Listen!"

Gunnison could hear a man shouting angrily from somewhere in the street in front of the Denham house.

"That's Rudd," said Bent, pleased. "He's giving Big Tom a good cussing. I've never met a more talented cusser than Rudd Coltrain in all my born days. Big Tom will lay into him in a minute. It will be a real dustup 'cause they'll both get mad, even though they know it's just an act. I'm almost sorry I have to miss it."

A moment later Gunnison heard another man shouting.

"That must be the guard at the front," said Bent.

Gunnison watched the back guard, who stood in a shaft of lamplight from one of the windows, looking toward the front of the house. Then he caught a glimpse of someone in one of the windows—a woman, silhouetted against a lamplit room. He could make out the golden hair but wasn't sure if it was Grace or Eliza . . .

"There he goes!" said Bent.

Gunnison searched for the guard. The man had disappeared, abandoning his post.

"Get going!" rasped Bent. "The guard just ran to the front of the house."

Gunnison hesitated.

"Damn it, don't freeze up on me now!" exclaimed Bent, horrified. "What the hell—you stay here with the horses and I'll go."

"No," said Gunnison. "I'll go."

"Then go!"

He set off across the empty lot with long strides and was somewhat amazed when he reached the back door of the Denham house without an alarm being raised. For the first time he dared hope that Bent's audacious plan might actually succeed. With one last quick look around, he slipped inside. He found himself at the end of a hallway that ran the full length of the house. There were two doors to the left, three to the right and a narrow staircase leading to rooms upstairs. Victorian in design, the Spartan house was plain by Eastern standards, but still one of the better homes to be found in Denver, proof that this frontier town had come a long way in the short time that had passed since its founding.

Moving quietly down the hallway, Gunnison could hear the commotion in the street out front: two men engaged in a spirited knockdown, drag-out bout of fisticuffs and a pair of soldiers urging them on, happy with any kind of entertainment to break the monotony of guard duty. Passing the staircase, he could also hear a woman's voice, coming from a front room through an open doorway to the left, and he thought it was Eliza Hawkes. Proceeding to the doorway, he paused at the threshold. Eliza and Grace were standing at a front window, peering through the velveteen drapes into the night. Gunnison opened his mouth to speak—but the words died stillborn on his tongue when he heard the unmistakable double click of a pistol being cocked, very loud in his left ear.

"You move and I'll blow your brains out." It was a woman's voice.

Gunnison didn't move. He watched Eliza and Grace turn from the window and said, "Mrs. Hawkes, I sure hope you remember me."

"Lieutenant Gunnison? What on earth are you doing here?"

"I've come to take you and your daughter out, ma'am. William Bent is waiting for us nearby."

"I had to kill a man once," said the woman behind him. "It bothered me some, but I got over it pretty quick. Reckon I could get over it again, too."

"Still," said Gunnison, "I hope you never have to kill another."

"Please, Mrs. Denham," said Grace. "He is a friend."

God knows, mused Gunnison, *I hope I live long enough to be more than just a friend to her.*

"Yes, Mary," said Eliza. "You can put the pistol away. Lieutenant Gunnison is indeed a friend, and I am certain he has come, as he says, to help."

"Lieutenant?" Mary Denham stepped away from Gunnison, lowering the pistol and squinting suspiciously at him. "Not with the Colorado Volunteers."

"No, ma'am," said Gunnison. "Second Cavalry, United States Army, out of Fort Lyon."

"Good. 'Cause were you with the Volunteers I'd

have to say that Miss Grace's faith in you was undoubtedly misplaced."

Gunnison glanced at the widow woman—a long stern face etched deeply by hardship and grief, dark hair pulled back in a severe bun, a stocky figure clad in a plain gingham dress. The horse pistol she held in both hands was a Walker Colt, but Mary Denham looked like she could handle it. She was clearly of sturdy pioneer stock, strong and resilient and well able to fend for herself. It was Gunnison's understanding that her husband had opened the first general store in Denver and prospered nicely, only to die several years ago when his horse threw him. Mary Denham had already lost two children, so she was left alone but well provided for, thanks to her husband's successful business venture. Gunnison had also heard that she and William Bent were more than just friends, though he wasn't sure if he believed that since Bent seemed so devoted to his Cheyenne wife.

"We don't have much time," Gunnison told Eliza. "That fight out front is a decoy. There are horses in an alley nearby. We can slip out the back way."

"There are Volunteers in the house next door," warned Mary Denham.

"I know, but they've been taken care of as well."

"But how?"

"I'll explain everything later. There's no time for that now. We must get going."

Eliza nodded. "One question. Why are you doing this, Lieutenant? Why are you taking such a chance?"

"Because you're being used as bait to lure your husband into a trap."

"Yes, I'm aware of that. Is that the reason?"

"Well, no, ma'am. I'm here because . . ." He glanced at Grace. "Because I believe I am in love with your daughter."

"Oh dear," said Mary Denham.

"And because Bent kept pestering me and wouldn't quit until I agreed to help."

Eliza and he grinned at each other.

"Okay," she said. "I'll accept that. Let's go."

"I'll go upstairs and get our belongings," said Grace, looking for any excuse to escape the room. Gunnison's words had thrilled her as nothing in her whole life had. Her heart had fluttered at his admission. She had lain awake at night thinking about him, thinking forbidden thoughts, of gazing deeply into his eyes as he took her in a strong embrace and possessed her, passionately, totally. But now she could not even bring herself to meet his gaze. And he was watching her, searching for some sign that she was pleased by his words.

"No time for that," said Eliza.

"Get word to me and I will send your things along, wherever you end up," said Mary Denham.

"Thank you so much for everything, Mary," said Eliza fondly, embracing the widow woman. "We will never be able to repay you for your many kindnesses."

"Your friendship and your prayers are payment enough. Now be off with you both."

Gunnison led the way down the hall. At the back door he gestured for them to wait and stepped cautiously outside to make sure the coast was clear. It sounded like Big Tom and Rudd Coltrain were still mixing it up in front of the Denham house. He motioned for the women to join him, and together they hurried across the empty lot to the alley where Bent waited with the horses. As Bent helped Eliza aboard her horse, Gunnison lent Grace a hand to climb into the saddle of another.

"Should we wait for the others?" Gunnison asked the trader.

"They'll go their own way," said Bent. "No call to worry about them. Besides, they're having too much fun right now to call it quits."

Gunnison shook his head and mounted up. Bent led the way out of town, followed by Eliza and Grace, and the cavalryman brought up the rear. He could hardly believe Bent's plan had come off without a hitch. But as they left Denver behind them he knew better than to relax. They had won the first round, but he doubted that Chivington and Evans would throw in the towel just yet. By morning he figured the Colorado Volunteers would be hot on their trail.

Chapter Eight

When they reached the Cheyenne village at Sand Creek, Gunnison knew the Colorado Volunteers were hot on their trail. He had seen them but once, earlier that same day, and still a good many miles behind them, and though their horses were weary after four long days on the trail, he and his companions had pushed their mounts to the limit in the last few hours, so that when they dismounted among the skin lodges of Black Kettle's people, the animals just stood there, lathered and blowing hard, legs splayed and heads hung low.

As a cavalryman Gunnison's first concern was always his mount, a deeply ingrained habit that, this once, he forgot as he came face to face with Gordon Hawkes.

The mountain man appeared unchanged in the years since they had last met, still tall and lean and wide in the shoulder, the eyes in his bearded face as piercingly keen as ever, the gaze direct and unafraid of anything. Though Gunnison was not in uniform, Hawkes recognized him immediately, and the lieutenant detected both curiosity and caution in the man's expression. But for the moment the mountain man was occupied with other matters. Both Eliza and Grace ran to embrace him enthusiastically. Not given to public displays of affection, Hawkes nonetheless kissed them both, indifferent to the fact that more than a hundred Cheyenne were witnessing the joyful reunion.

Hawkes could tell that something was wrong. His wife and daughter were trail-worn; their weariness was evident in the way they leaned against him for support. And the horses they had come in on were on their last legs, too. He looked to William Bent for answers. The trader was in the middle of a reunion of his own; his wife and sons had gathered to welcome him home. But he cut that short in order to respond to the silent question in the mountain man's eyes.

"There's a bunch of Colorado Volunteers on our trail," he announced. "They never got close enough for me to make sure, but I'm betting they're being led by your friend Captain Talbot. They've been after us ever since Denver, but we managed to stay out in front of them. Don't know that we could have for much longer, though." He glanced at the horses.

The majority of the Indians present did not speak or understand English, so they could not decipher Bent's words. But a handful knew enough to pick up the gist of what he was saying, and the word that Colorado Volunteers were on the way spread quickly.

"How many?" asked Hawkes, as calm as the eye of a hurricane.

"Maybe thirty," guessed Gunnison.

Hawkes turned his attention back to the lieutenant.

"I guess I need to know if you're here to try to arrest me—again."

Gunnison shook his head. "No, I'm not. Though I probably should be. The governor has revoked your amnesty."

"I'd have been mighty surprised if he hadn't. So if you're not here for that reason, then why are you here?"

"He lent me a hand in getting your wife and daughter away from Denver," said Bent.

"Governor Evans placed us under house arrest," explained Eliza. "He wanted to lure you into a trap, Gordon."

"You asked me to go to Denver to fetch them," said Bent. "With the lieutenant's help, that's what I did."

"I owe you," said Hawkes, the gaze he leveled at Bent filled with gratitude. Expressing his deepest feelings had never been easy for him and he didn't know what else to say, even though he knew that what he *had* said was woefully inadequate. He glanced at Gunnison. "You, too, I reckon."

"You don't owe me a thing," replied the cavalryman.

Hawkes still didn't have his answer—why the lieutenant had stuck his neck out to free Eliza and Grace. But it would have to wait. An argument had broken out between some of the Cheyenne. He wasn't surprised to find that Wolf Chief was involved. What did surprise him was that Black Kettle was right in the middle of it, too.

Wolf Chief and Horse Catcher had asked Black Kettle for permission to ride out and meet the Colorado Volunteers. For the sake of the women and children, the soldiers could not be allowed too near the village, they argued. But Black Kettle would not give the Wolf Soldiers his blessing.

"The bluecoats did not come to attack us," he said, and turned to William Bent. "Little White Man, you must leave and you must take these people with you." His angry gesture included Gunnison, Hawkes, Eliza and Grace. "When the soldiers see that you are not here they will go on their way."

"You are angry at me," said Bent, "because you think I have brought more trouble upon your people. And I guess maybe you have a right to be. But I don't honestly think it makes much difference in the long run. The governor wants all the Indians out of Colorado. Those that aren't driven out will be killed. It's as simple as that, I'm afraid. Those Volunteers out there won't pass up a chance to fight the Cheyenne. They have orders to do just that at every opportunity. And if I'm right, they're being led by a real Indian hater."

Black Kettle grimly digested all that Bent had told him, then looked at Horse Catcher and nodded reluctantly. "The Wolf Soldiers will ride out to meet the soldiers," he said.

"Every warrior to his horse," said Bent. "If we go against them in great numbers they will pull back and we may avoid bloodshed."

Black Kettle nodded. Bent had given him a glimmer of hope. "If they do pull back you must not go after them," he told Horse Catcher, the pipeholder of the Wolf Soldiers.

"We should kill them all when we have the chance," argued Wolf Chief, shaking a clenched fist.

"We will do as you say," Horse Catcher told Black Kettle.

With a sound of pure frustration escaping his lips, Wolf Chief whirled and stalked away. *That one and Captain Talbot are two of a kind,* mused Hawkes. *They want a bloodletting and they don't really care who gets hurt by it. They long for an excuse to kill that which they hate. Each other.* He knew what both Talbot and Wolf Chief were about. Once upon a time he had been just like them.

Bent turned to his son Charlie. "Get me a fresh pony. I'm going with them."

"So am I," said Hawkes. He looked at Eliza, saw the worry in her eyes, and knew she would refrain from giving voice to the concern she felt. "In a way I'm the one who is responsible for all this," he explained.

"No, I think I am," she said softly. "If I had never gone to Denver in the first place . . ."

"What about you, Lieutenant?" Charlie Bent asked Gunnison.

Gunnison shook his head. "Colorado Volunteers or not, those are still soldiers out there. They ride under Old Glory. I'm a soldier, too, and I will not fight them."

Cheyenne warriors going off to war—Gordon Hawkes had to admit that it was a stirring spectacle.

It didn't seem to take them any time at all to get ready and ride out to meet the Colorado Volunteers.

It occurred to the mountain man that maybe they had been ready for a very long time. For himself, he scarcely had time to fetch the dun mustang, check his Plains rifle to make sure it was in perfect working order and give his wife and daughter a hug before two hundred mounted braves were on their way out of the village. He knew that the warrior societies of the Plains tribes were well drilled. Many white men made the mistake of thinking there was no discipline among Indians because they did not march or attack in the kinds of formations they were accustomed to. But a boy was trained from early childhood to be a warrior, and to do his fighting in coordination with other braves.

Each warrior clan, like the Wolf Soldiers, had its leader, or pipeholder. In the case of the Wolf Soldiers it was Horse Catcher. He and the other war chiefs signaled their men, and each other, in a variety of ways, depending on the circumstances at hand. Smoke and mirror signals were used when the distance between clans or units was great. Today there was no need for these, and the war chiefs resorted to communicating with the lance, or horse movements, or blanket waving. The pipeholders had spent a lot of time working with each other so that they were skilled in coordinating the movements of the different elements of the Cheyenne force.

The Cheyenne men had not had time to paint their faces or their horses for war, but they wore their war shirts and carried their shields and lances, both aflutter with eagle and hawk feathers, as well as their bows and quivers full of arrows. Hawkes noticed that some of the braves had gashed their lower legs. This was a sign that they were out for revenge. The mountain man looked for Wolf Chief among the Indians but could not spot him; still, he was confident that Wolf Chief had cut himself as well. It was the mark of a zealot. The mood among the warriors was one of grim determination. They were resolved not only to protect the village but also to pay the bluecoats back for the unprovoked attack at the Platte River. Hawkes wondered if Horse Catcher and the other war chiefs would actually be able to keep their men from launching an assault on the column of soldiers, as they had promised Black Kettle they would do.

It wasn't long before he found out. They rode but a few miles before spotting the Colorado Volunteers. Instantly the Cheyenne warriors split into three groups. One rushed forward to within a half mile of the soldiers while the other two galloped off to the flanks. This stopped the bluecoats in their tracks. Expecting an attack, they dismounted and formed a ragged square with their mounts in the center. But the pipeholders signaled one another, and in unison the three warrior groups pulled up. Their positions left the soldiers with but one avenue of escape—back the way they had come.

Riding with Bent and the trader's sons in the center group, Hawkes watched the soldiers and thought how easy it would be to kill them all. They were outnumbered at least seven to one, and while they were armed with rifles, and could probably inflict heavy losses on the Cheyenne, the outcome would never be in doubt. But the mountain man thought that Black Kettle was right to try to avoid spilling blood. To attack these Volunteers would be to play right into the hands of Governor Evans and Colonel Chivington. Those two would gladly sacrifice the lives of thirty men, mused Hawkes, for their deaths would trigger a full-scale conflict. And Black Kettle probably knew that while his warriors would be victorious on this day, they would most certainly lose the war. The enemy could afford to lose thirty men. The Cheyenne could ill afford to lose a like number.

In the end, it all depended on the man who was leading the column of soldiers. Was it Talbot? At this distance Hawkes couldn't tell. He hoped not. Because Talbot's hatred for Indians made him unpredictable. A rational commander would survey the situation and understand immediately that he had only one viable option. Retreat. By their maneuvering the Cheyenne were dictating precisely that outcome. But a man like Talbot would not cotton to being dictated to, especially not by redskins. Such men might prefer a glorious death to the ignominy of backing down before a people he considered his inferiors. If the soldiers didn't turn back, the Cheyenne would have no choice but to kill them. It was as simple as that.

For a few tense moments there was very little movement on the field. The Cheyenne sat their prancing ponies and stared at the distant bluecoats, who stared right back over their rifle sights. The omnipresent wind that scourged these arid plains moved a pall of dust across the scene, leaving grit in Hawkes's eyes and on his tongue as he licked dry lips. He had ridden out with the Cheyenne because it seemed to be that siding with them—sharing the danger with them—was the least he could do since he was in large measure the reason the soldiers had come here in the first place. But if this standoff turned into a scrape, then what would he do? His dilemma was this: He was done with killing, no longer had much stomach for it, and this was no place for a man so squeamish. *If the Cheyenne ride against those men,* he told himself, *I will have to ride with them. But I will not take another life. No matter what.*

Then he asked himself: *Not even to save your own hide?*

Bent was right. He had no business being in the middle of this trouble. He needed to take Eliza and Grace home and keep himself up in the high country, too, since a war was not a very good place for a man who wouldn't fight.

There was movement in the square of bluecoats.

"Well, that's that," said Bent, astride a Cheyenne war pony that was chafing at the bit and fiddle-footing excitedly, annoying the mountain man's high-strung mustang. "They're leaving. They're turning tail."

With relief Hawkes could see that this was apparently so. The soldiers were mounting up. In a loose formation they were going back whence they had come, keeping their mounts to a walk and their eyes on the Cheyenne horde. Hawkes figured that to a man they were expecting the warriors to jump them now that they'd shown the white feather. That was, after all, what they would do if the situations were reversed.

"Call it turning tail if you like," replied Hawkes.

"But saying it that way makes them sound like cowards. And it's not cowardice to walk away from a fight you know you can't win."

He surveyed the Cheyenne positions. There was some movement among the warriors—aggressive forward movement—and he heard taunts hurled at the departing soldiers from various points. Here and there a warrior kicked his pony and rushed forward a few dozen yards, only to draw up sharply. Horse Catcher and the other pipeholders were doing what they had told Black Kettle they would do. There was no attack on the bluecoats. Hawkes could only imagine how disappointed Wolf Chief and the other hotspurs had to be at this moment. And he wondered if they were as sure as he was that they would get another chance to kill the soldiers.

The pipeholders met and briefly conferred. By the time they were done, the Colorado Volunteers were a couple of miles away, and all that could be seen of them was telltale dust marking their progress across the sagebrush plain. Scouts were sent out, several pairs of them, to shadow the soldiers. They would be told to remain unseen. Of that Hawkes was certain. The Cheyenne just wanted to be certain that the Volunteers didn't double back.

That done, pipeholders led the rest of the warriors back to the village. They displayed no exuberance at having faced down the bluecoats. Scarcely a word passed between them. They knew, mused Hawkes, that what had happened here today hadn't really resolved anything, and that the Cheyenne nation still faced the gravest crisis in its history.

*   *   *

"One thing is certain," said Bent, sitting around an evening fire with Hawkes and Gunnison and his sons. "After today's little standoff, the governor will consider every Cheyenne to be a hostile. Just a couple of weeks ago I was advising Black Kettle to go to Fort Lyon and by so doing prove to Evans that he was sincere about wanting peace. But he would be foolish to go now. It's too late for that."

"Just as well," said George Bent.

"It must be hard on you," said Gunnison. "Being part white and part Indian."

"Not really," replied George. "Not about white and red, anyway, but right and wrong. If the whites in this territory were minding their own business and the Cheyenne were the ones making war on them I wouldn't be here."

Gunnison nodded. He couldn't argue with that perspective.

William Bent glanced across the fire at Hawkes. "I reckon you'll be going home now that you and your family's together again."

"We'll leave first thing in the morning."

That left a bitter taste in Gunnison's mouth. The thought that in a matter of hours he and Grace would go their separate ways, with no guarantee that they would ever see each other again, made him feel empty inside.

"What about you, Lieutenant?" asked the elder Bent.

"I've got to get back to Fort Lyon," said Gunnison, hoping he didn't look or sound too disconsolate. "Major Merritt needs to know what's been going on. Hopefully he'll see fit to make a report to Washington."

"What for?" asked George. "You think anybody in Washington is going to do something about all this? You think they'll actually try to stop Evans and Chivington?" His tone suggested that he didn't think there was any chance at all of that happening.

"I don't know," confessed Gunnison. "But I do know the major won't like what he hears."

The elder Bent just shook his head. "The folks back in Washington have their hands full with the Southern insurrection. They'll have neither the time nor the inclination to worry about an Indian war out here."

"I hope you're wrong."

"What I'm wondering," said George, "is what will your major do when the governor asks for help in his little war. It occurs to me, Lieutenant, that the next time we meet it might be on opposite sides of a battlefield."

Gunnison got to his feet. "I think I'll take a walk before I turn in," he said, and left the fire.

Bent watched him go. "I'm sure glad I'm not in his shoes."

"Why do you say that?" asked Hawkes.

"Couple of reasons. One is he can't decide between an obligation to do the right thing and his duty as an officer in the Army."

"He made the right decision once, when he helped you free my wife and daughter."

"Well, that's true enough."

"You said a couple of reasons. What's the other one?"

Bent smiled faintly. Apparently Hawkes had been too preoccupied with other matters to notice the way his daughter and the lieutenant looked at each other. And he wasn't about to be the one to enlighten him.

"It's not important," he said.

Walking through the Cheyenne village, Gunnison made for Sand Creek. Reaching it, he followed its course until he was clear of the skin lodges. Only then did he stop to sit on the rim of a low-cut bank. He wanted to be alone with his misery. The moon was just rising, bathing the plains in its pale silver-blue light. There were at least a million stars in the sky. It was a beautiful night, a cool dry breeze whispering through the sage, and coyotes on a distant butte yapping enough to start some of the Cheyenne camp dogs howling. Ordinarily Gunnison would have appreciated the tranquillity of the scene. But he doubted now that he would ever enjoy anything again—not if Grace Hawkes wasn't around to share it with him.

"Lieutenant?"

It was her voice, and for a brief moment he thought he was dreaming, but there she was, in the flesh, standing only a few feet away, her pale hair gleaming in the soft moonlight. She had traded in her travel-worn clothes for a deerskin dress that Bent's wife had given her. It fit her slender form loosely. Gunnison scrambled to his feet.

"Miss Hawkes—I didn't hear you."

She smiled. "You must have been very deep in thought. And please, after all that we've been through together don't you think it's time we were on a first-name basis?"

"Yes, of course."

Stepping closer, she glanced away, across the dark plains, as she asked, "What were you thinking about just now?"

"You."

"That was what I hoped you'd say."

"Tomorrow you're going home. And I have to go back to Fort Lyon. And I . . ." He shook his head.

"Was wondering if we would ever see each other again."

He had to smile, in spite of his anguish. "You're easy to talk to. You seem to know what I'm thinking."

"Possibly because I'm thinking the very same thing that you are. But I have a feeling we will see each other again."

"You sound awfully certain," said Gunnison, well aware that he didn't sound sure at all and wondering if she really believed that they would. Or was she simply putting on a brave front? Telling him that just to make him feel better?

"We will. It was meant to be. Once this is all over. I would go with you now, Brand, if I could."

He was stunned. "You would? Honestly?"

"Yes I would," she said, quite earnest. "But If I did, my father would come after us and probably kill you."

She looked serious, only it was a facade, and one she could not maintain for long. She laughed at the expression on his face, and he had to laugh right along with her.

"No, he wouldn't," she said. "I wouldn't let him."

He took a chance and reached out to touch her

cheek, and Grace leaned her head into the palm of his hand.

"Does he know you're out here now? With me?"

"My mother knows. I told her I wanted to tell you good-bye."

"And she didn't mind?"

"Well, I wouldn't say that. But she's getting used to the idea that I'm fond of you." Grace smiled. "I told her she had better get used to it since you were all I was going to talk about from now on."

"Fond of me," said Gunnison, repeating the words just so he could hear them again. They were music to his ears.

"Yes, that's right. Here. Let me show you."

She stepped right up to him, so that their bodies were nearly touching, and wrapped her arms around his neck. Standing on tiptoe, she brushed her lips across his.

Gunnison thought his heart was going to explode. Her kiss sent a fire racing through his body, igniting his passion, so that he wrapped his arms around her and pulled her tightly against him and kissed her back, a long hungry kiss that stole her breath away. She surrendered to him, but only for an instant, and then panic set in, and she laid her hands on his chest and pushed away suddenly, gasping. Mortified, he let her go.

"I'm sorry," he breathed. "I—I don't know what came over me. Please forgive me, Grace."

She turned away from him and jumped off the bank to the sandy creek bottom, wading into the shallows. Standing there a moment, her back to him, she stared off across the moonlit plains. Gunnison was petrified with fear that he had gone too far, and that because he had she would leave him, and he could not bear to think that they might part on such terms. Yet he could think of nothing to do or say to make amends.

Then, wordlessly, she lifted the deerskin dress up over her head and let it drop.

Spellbound, all Gunnison could do was stare at her firm slender body, pale in the moonlight, the most beautiful sight he had ever beheld.

Chin tucked, she looked over her shoulder at him through a veil of yellow hair, and her eyes burned with a secret fire.

"Come say good-bye to me, Brand," she said in a husky whisper.

He jumped down off the bank, forgetting everything in that magical moment—the nearby Cheyenne village, her father, the stars, the past and the future. She began to walk along the creek through the shallows, away from the village, and he followed, gazing at her, at her long lithe legs and her narrow waist flaring into rounded hips that swayed with such a natural and unpretentious rhythm when she moved. Gunnison shed his shirt, hopping on one foot to get rid of the boot on the other foot, then hopping on the other to be rid of the boot on the first. She glanced back again, smiling at him, a smile full of promise, and he hastily unbuckled his belt and stepped out of his trousers—and only then did she stop and turn as he moved to her, and their bodies seemed to melt into one. This time she returned the passion of his kiss, her arms locked remorselessly around his neck, just as her legs were locked tightly around his waist. Dropping to his knees, he laid her gently down in the shallows. The cool water was like a salve on their burning flesh. She gasped, her warm sweet breath on his face, as they became one. The slow and gentle rhythm of their lovemaking soon quickened into a thrashing shudder, and he smothered her sharp, querulous cry of release with his mouth. For a long while they lay there, still joined, her trembling body entwined with his.

Much later, when he had found his voice, Gunnison said, "Grace—I want you to marry me."

"I will," she whispered, and then giggled. "I guess we had better get married, after this!"

He grinned down at her.

"Have you ever been happier, more content, than you are at this moment?" she asked.

"No. Never."

"Me, either."

"I'll speak to your father in the morning."

"No you will not. Tomorrow I am going home and you will go do your duty, and when these troubles are all behind us, then we will be together forever."

"What if he doesn't approve? I mean, well, I don't think he cares much for me."

"Well, you did try to arrest him once, remember." She laughed softly. "But I care about you. And when my father sees how happy you make me, and how I simply could not live without you, he will give his blessing. You'll see. I want you, Brand Gunnison, and no other. Forever and ever."

He kissed her again, then began to lift his weight off her. "Guess we had better be getting back," he said reluctantly. "Someone might come looking for us. If we get caught like this I doubt they'll ever let us see each other again."

"Oh no you don't," she said, and threw a leg over him, rolling him over. Straddling him, she leaned forward to put her hands on his shoulder to pin him down. "You're not getting away from me that easily."

He could have gotten free, but he didn't want to. He never wanted to be free of her. Reaching up with both hands, he brushed wet tendrils of golden hair from her cheeks. Then his hands moved light as feathers down over her shoulders, over her breasts that seemed to have been molded for his hands alone, and Grace closed her eyes and moaned with the pleasure his touch gave her. Aroused, he found her ready for him again, and they made love there beneath the moon and a million stars, with the coyotes on the nearby butte yip-yipping a serenade.

Chapter Nine

When Governor Evans and Colonel Chivington arrived at Denver's city jail, the man they had come to see was sprawled on a narrow wooden bunk in a small, stinking cell, snoring loudly.

"My God," said Evans, gazing through the strap iron of the jail cell at the man. "I can smell him from here."

Chivington nodded. So could he. The prisoner positively reeked of whiskey. He turned to the jailer. "This is James Beckwourth? The legendary Beckwourth?"

The jailer grunted. "No, sir. This is the *real* James Beckwourth. A drunken old man. He spends more time under this roof than I do."

Evans scowled, reviewing in his mind what he had heard of the man in the cell. Jim Beckwourth had come west in 1824 with a party of fur trappers led by William Ashley—what turned out to be the initial expedition of the now-famous Rocky Mountain Fur Company. Born in Virginia, Beckwourth was a mulatto, but among the mountain men the color of one's skin mattered less than whether one had the requisite grit and skill with weapons to be the kind of man others could depend on. Beckwourth had plenty of courage, and he was about as talented with rifle or knife as any other in that band of men who blazed the westward trails. Certainly, William Ashley had come to rely on him; it was Ashley who made Beckwourth the fur company's representative among the Crow Indians.

Beckwourth's job in that capacity had been to persuade the Crows that their time was better spent trapping beaver—the pelts of which they would turn over to the company for the usual trade goods. But the Crows had not been very obliging in that regard, much preferring such activities as stealing the horses and raiding the villages of their perennial foes, the Blackfeet. Since he couldn't change them, Beckwourth decided to join them. He was the one who changed, living among the Crows and becoming one of them, so much so that when a fellow trapper named Zenas Leonard happened upon a Crow encampment on the Shoshone River sometime in the early 1830s he found Beckwourth virtually indistinguishable from the Indians. The mulatto had taken several wives and become a highly regarded warrior. He spoke the Crow language better than he did his own, and had willingly assimilated into the Crow way of life.

Later, Beckwourth became something of a hero among the Crows, being instrumental in the defeat of the Blackfeet and their Piegan cousins in a major battle between the Crows and their northern enemies. For a reason unknown to anyone except Beckwourth himself, however, he abruptly left Crow country for good around 1837. Subsequently, he spent a few years on the Santa Fe Trail, and then opened up a mercantile in Denver. Governor Evans had heard rumors that Beckwourth was drinking up all of his profits from the enterprise. Now he realized that those rumors were probably true, and he began to have second thoughts about the proposition he had intended on making to the mountain man.

"Yep, this is the famous Jim Beckwourth," drawled the jailer sardonically. "He's a big talker, that one. Why, just the other day he was telling me how he wrestled three grizzlies in one afternoon, and still had the strength to go home and make love to all four of his wives." The jailer shook his head. "All the Blackfoot Injuns he's said he killed, I'd be surprised if that whole tribe hasn't been wiped off the face of the earth."

"Wake him up," snapped Evans. "I haven't got all day."

"Sure thing, Governor." The jailer went back into the front room, returning with a bucket and hurled its contents through the strap-iron cell door. Evans hoped the bucket contained water, because a few drops splattered on him. Drenched, Beckwourth groaned and rolled over, the rickety bunk groaning even more loudly as he moved. The jailer seemed to take it as a personal affront that his efforts to rouse the prisoner had failed—and he blamed Beckwourth for it. Scowling, he drew what looked to Evans like the handle of a sledgehammer from under his belt. A leather strap had been secured to one end, and the jailer slid his hand through this, got a good grip on the club and began hammering the strap iron with it, swinging for all he was worth and striking the iron close by the prisoner's head.

"Get up, you stinking nigger! There's somebody here to see you, you drunken black Injun. I said get the hell on your feet, you goddamn son of a bitch!"

Beckwourth rolled off the bunk and lunged at the strap-iron door, snarling like a wild animal, his actions so sudden, so furious, that the startled jailer jumped back. Apparently this was the reaction Beckwourth had hoped to elicit; he threw back his head and laughed uproariously. Turning an ugly dark shade of red, the jailer glanced at Evans, wondering if he could get away with going into the cell and beating the mulatto mountain man into a bloody pulp with his "head buster." Evans was watching him with hooded eyes that reflected disapproval and disgust.

"I think that will suffice," Evans told him dryly. "Now leave us alone."

"Yes, sir," muttered the jailer, crestfallen. He left the cell block, closing the door behind him.

Watching him go, Beckwourth drawled, "That pasty-faced little bastard. I think I might scalp him when I get out of here this time."

"No you won't," said Evans. "Because when you get out of here you're going to be working for me."

"And why would I do that?"

"Because otherwise you might not ever get out."

Beckwourth took a closer look at Evans. He seemed to be having a little trouble with his vision. "I've seen you before," he said. "Just can't seem to recall the name."

"Good God," said Chivington distastefully. "This man is a hopeless drunkard, Governor."

"Governor?" Beckwourth blinked. "Oh yeah. The governor, that's who you are. Tell me something. Who made you governor, anyway? I know for damn sure we never got to vote on it."

"The president."

"Is that right. Governor, will you do me a small favor?"

"What do you want?"

"Tell this dandy here that I might be a drunkard, but I ain't hopeless. And I ain't no swish, either, which he is, looks like to me."

"Swish?" asked Chivington suspiciously. "What is a . . . ?"

"A homosexual," said Evans.

Chivington glared at Beckwourth. "Why you . . ."

"That'll do, Colonel," snapped Evans. "So, Mr. Beckwourth, I am told you are one of the best scouts in these parts. When you're sober, that is. Is this true?"

"I could track a field mouse in a hurricane," replied Beckwourth confidently.

Evans smiled faintly. "I also heard you are prone to exaggerate your skills."

Beckwourth shrugged. "Maybe just a little." He cocked his head to one side and looked quizzically at the governor with narrowed eyes. "Now what's this about me working for you?"

"We need your help, Mr. Beckwourth. The Colorado Volunteers are all that stand between the good decent folk of this territory and the savage Indians who have made war against us. But for a token force at a few scattered outposts, the United States Army has no presence here, occupied as it is with the prosecution of the war in the East. That is why it falls to Colonel Chivington here and his brave and hardy men to make the Colorado Territory safe for settlement."

Evans paused in his oration to draw a breath, and Beckwourth seized the opportunity to interrupt. "You sure talk handsome," said the mountain man, shaking his head in admiration. "But I still don't see where I fit in."

"The colonel's Volunteers can do the job, I am confident of that. But against the Indians they need scouts. I want you, Mr. Beckwourth, to form and lead a corps of scouts to serve with the Colorado Volunteers."

"A corps? How many men in a corps?"

Evans glanced at Chivington—then he realized that the colonel would have not the slightest clue how many scouts his regiment would require. "Let's say twenty," replied the governor.

"What Indians are we talking about, anyroad?" asked Beckwourth.

"The Cheyenne and the Arapaho, of course," said Chivington.

Beckwourth squinted suspiciously. "The Cheyenne ain't at war with us," he said. "And most of the Arapahos don't want no trouble, either. It's just a handful of troublemakers that have been hitting the wagon trains and such."

"Oh, so you know all about it, then," said Chivington dryly. He was still smarting over the remark about his sexual preferences. "Pretty amazing, I must say, for a man who hasn't stayed sober more than two days out of a week."

Beckwourth walked to the rear of his cell and put his back against the wall, folding his arms. "I ain't going to work with this pompous ass, Governor. Sorry."

"I will make it worth your while," said Evans. "I think the chief of scouts should make one hundred dollars a month."

"You can buy a lot of rotgut with that kind of money," remarked Chivington. "Of course if you're caught drinking while on duty I'll have you clapped in irons."

"Colonel, do you mind?" asked Evans, thoroughly exasperated. He was tired of standing here, smelling the stench of the cell block, and he wanted to be done with this business. Chivington wasn't making things any easier.

"That is a lot of money," conceded Beckwourth.

"A few days ago a contingent of the Volunteers was ambushed by a far superior force of Cheyenne warriors near Sand Creek," said Evans. "It is a miracle that they escaped with their lives. You can't depend on miracles, Mr. Beckwourth, but I believe I can depend on you. With scouts the Volunteers would not ride into ambush again. So now you see why I have come here today and made you this offer. Your country will not forget your services to the cause of peace and progress."

"I don't care about all that. But a hundred dollars *is* a lot of money."

Chivington snorted his contempt.

"Then we can rely on you?" Evans asked the mulatto.

Beckwourth nodded. "Sure. I guess I'll give it a try."

"Good!" said Evans. "I will see to it that you are released today. Come to my office first thing in the morning."

"And come sober," added Chivington.

"You sure you won't reconsider, Governor—and let me scalp that jailer?" asked Beckwourth.

Evans left the cell block, herding the colonel out before him, pausing only long enough to tell the jailer that he wanted Beckwourth turned loose at once. A moment later he was on the street, filling his lungs with hot dusty air.

"I have to say, Governor, that Beckwourth is most assuredly not a man you can depend on," protested Chivington.

"Your regiment needs scouts," reminded Evans. "Beckwourth knows the Indians and their ways as well as anyone. He has lived among them for years, after all. Who else are you going to recruit who has the necessary skills? Most of his peers—men like William Bent and Gordon Hawkes—their sympathies lie with the hostiles. All Beckwourth seems to care about is money."

"And whiskey."

"I can handle that."

"But what if you're wrong, sir? What if it turns out Beckwourth cares about more than just money and whiskey? He's gone native once before. What if he does that again? Turns his back on his own kind. Sides with the Indians?"

"Then he'll be a traitor, won't he? And you can have him shot."

When Gunnison arrived at Fort Lyon he had his uniform back on and had discarded the civilian clothes he'd acquired in Denver in order to disguise his identity while helping William Bent secure the freedom of Grace and her mother.

No sooner had he dismounted than a burly sergeant by the name of Crocker came up to take charge of his horse.

"Good to see you again, Lieutenant," said Crocker through a wad of chewing tobacco. "I'll tend to your mount for you, sir."

"Thanks, Sergeant. Where is the major?"

"In his quarters, I reckon. Packing up all his personal belongings."

"What? Packing up? What for? Where is he going?"

"He ain't seen fit to tell me that, Lieutenant. But he's been replaced. We got us a new commanding officer."

Gunnison stared at Crocker. He couldn't believe his ears.

"That's the gospel truth, Lieutenant," promised Crocker. "This new major—Blalock's his name—brought the orders with him. Just showed up right out of the blue. He's a West Pointer, I hear. Just like yourself. Made a name for himself at Chancellorsville, or Fredericksburg, one of them places. If you don't believe me, go see for yourself."

Gunnison felt compelled to do just that. He went straight to Major Merritt's quarters, knocked on the door and went in when the major told him to do so. The first thing he noticed was the trunk on the floor, filled with Merritt's personal effects, the lid still open as the major placed the last of his books within it. Gunnison read the titles of the top volumes—Boswell's *Life of Johnson* and the *Histories of Herodotus*. That was one of the things he had always admired about Merritt—the man was a thinker. He was well read. Something of a philosopher himself, in fact. He was a gray, rail-thin man of medium height, unprepossessing physically, but intelligent and fair, with an orderly mind and a common-sense approach to life. He had not attended the military academy; instead, he'd worked his way up through the ranks, having served, like Gunnison's father, in the Mexican War. Merritt had been a lieutenant in a regiment of Kentucky Volunteers. After the war he had managed to get into the regular Army. It said something about the man, in Gunnison's opinion, that he had achieved the rank he now held, given that West Pointers dominated the Army's officer corps. It had taken Merritt his entire career, and it was as far as he would go, but it was further than many others had come.

"Ah, Lieutenant," said Merritt. "Very glad to see you made it back before my departure."

"What's happening here, Major? Sergeant Crocker tells me you've been removed from command."

"Reassigned. A post in Michigan, up near the Canadian border, I believe." Merritt smiled wanly. "Well away from the war. Any war."

"But why are they doing this?"

Merritt gave him a long, somber look. "You'd better close the door, Lieutenant."

Gunnison realized then that he had left the door open, and turned to shut it.

"I don't know this for a fact," said Merritt, "but I have a strong suspicion that Governor Evans has stolen a march on us."

"You mean you think the governor is behind this?"

"As I said, I have no solid evidence to substantiate that. Not yet, anyway. But I won't be surprised should I discover that the governor wrote a letter to Washington, a letter that prompted the war department to send Major Nathan Blalock out here to take over."

Gunnison carefully considered Merritt's words. There was no question but that the major had somehow fallen into disfavor in Washington. To be replaced in this manner—so summarily, without warning—was a discourtesy to an officer, and his new assignment to some backwater posting on the Canadian border was further proof. That wasn't the way the Army normally treated an officer of twenty years' service.

"And why would the governor complain about you, Major? You haven't done anything to him."

"No, I haven't done anything—and he wasn't going to give me a chance to do anything, either. Don't underestimate Evans, Lieutenant. He's a clever one, that man is."

"This has everything to do with the Indian situation, doesn't it, sir?"

Merritt headed for a table where a bottle of sherry

stood, clapping a hand on Gunnison's shoulder in passing.

"You're a smart fellow, Gunnison. Have a drink with me."

Gunnison was not fond of sherry, but he didn't even consider refusing the major's request. Merritt poured, gave one glass to Gunnison and raised the other in a toast.

"To your health, Lieutenant."

"And to yours, Major."

They drank, and Gunnison tried not to betray his dislike for the sherry.

"I'm proud of the fact that I have established good relations with many of the Indian leaders in these parts," said Merritt. "Black Kettle, Roman Nose, Little Raven— I consider then all to be friends. And, more to the point, I believe them to be honorable men. My opinion about the Cheyenne and the Arapaho is no secret. And it is not an opinion shared by the likes of Governor Evans."

"So you think he made a preemptive move to get you out of the way before he starts his war against the tribes in earnest."

Merritt nodded. "I believe he and Colonel Chivington are planning to do something that they know I would strongly oppose. Now they won't have to worry about me or what I would do in response."

"What about this Major Blalock? What do you know about him, sir?"

Merritt finished off his sherry, put the glass down, picked up the bottle and crossed back to the trunk. He put the bottle in the trunk and shut the lid, securing the latch.

"I hear he drives his men hard, and often takes

big chances in his search for glory. His commands suffer heavy losses in action. But he doesn't answer for that because he generally carries the day thanks to courage and audacity. What his opinion of Indians is, I have no idea."

"I suppose we will find that out soon enough," said Gunnison.

"Well, I think that's everything." Merritt looked around the room.

"I'm very sorry to see you go, sir. It was an honor serving under you."

Merritt stepped forward and extended a hand. "It was my privilege to serve with you, Lieutenant. You are a first-rate officer. I predict you will go far."

Gunnison shook his hand and thanked him for the compliment.

"Tell me," said Merritt. "What happened in Denver?"

"I helped William Bent get Eliza Hawkes and her daughter away from the Volunteers."

Merritt raised an eyebrow. "You don't say."

"Yes, sir. We reunited them with Gordon Hawkes, the man accused of killing several of the Volunteers at Burn's trading post a couple of weeks ago. The Volunteers pursued us all the way to Black Kettle's village on Sand Creek, but were turned away by the Cheyenne warriors."

"I see. I have to ask—why did you take such a risk?"

"Because I happen to be in love with Gordon Hawkes's daughter."

"Well I'll be damned." A slow grin creased Merritt's face. "Congratulations, Lieutenant."

"For being in love, sir?"

"That, and for giving the governor's mustache a good tweaking."

Gunnison smiled. "Thank you, sir. But I don't think I'll get a commendation for it."

"No, I doubt it. A court-martial, perhaps."

"I wasn't recognized. I took off my uniform."

"Then I recommend we keep this strictly between ourselves. I wish you the best of luck. You're going to need it in the weeks to come."

"Yes, sir," said Gunnison grimly. "I think you're right about that."

When the warriors from the Northern Cheyenne band led by Roman Nose arrived at the Sand Creek village, Wolf Creek was making war arrows. Every brave learned from an early age how to make arrows, but he excelled at it. He made the shafts from the wood of birch saplings which he had cut the previous winter, when the sap was down. Each shaft had been cut the length of his arm from the elbow to the tip of his middle finger. They were straight and about as big around as his little finger. After harvesting and cutting them he tied them in bundles of twenty, wrapped the bundles in hide and hung them from the top of his skin lodge. The smoke from his lodge fire served to season the wood in the weeks that followed.

After the shafts had been sufficiently seasoned, Wolf Chief had peeled the bark from them and scraped them with his knife until they were very smooth. Inevitably a few had to be straightened further; this he accomplished by rubbing buffalo fat on the shaft, then heating it over the fire and bending it with his hands until it cooled. On one end he then cut a deep U-shaped notch to fit a bowstring. At the other end he cut a slit not more than an inch deep. Into this he fit the arrowhead. The latter was made from sheet iron which he had acquired from the Arapaho. They had gotten it from the barrel bands and wagon wheels of the white man's prairie schooner. Wolf Chief was able to cut twenty arrowheads from a barrel band.

It was the arrowhead that distinguished a hunting arrow from one made for war. The former was a long, tapered blade securely fastened to the shaft, while the latter was shorter and sharper, with the shoulders angled to form barbs. The arrowhead was loosely attached to the shaft, as it was intended to become detached within the body of the enemy.

After securing the arrowheads with sinew, Wolf Chief cut three shallow grooves the length of the shaft. These represented lightning, and like all Cheyenne braves Wolf Chief believed these symbols would make his arrows fly true and swiftly, and strike with great force, just as lightning did. After the grooves had been cut, he used a bone brush to paint his identifying marks on each shaft: a broad yellow band flanked by two red ones. The last step was fletching the arrow with the feathers of the hawk and the eagle, three on each shaft, glued and then secured with buffalo sinew. The glue was made by boiling buffalo horns in water.

Wolf Chief lived with his mother and sister, and provided for them, as he was unmarried, and because his father had died several years earlier of the white man's plague they called cholera, which he had contracted during a visit to a trading post. His mother and sister had been busy of late preparing a new war shirt for him. It was long, extending nearly to his knees, and had quilled yellow shoulder bands, and more bands, also yellow, on the sleeves. Zigzagging red lines extended the length of the shirt, and he was wearing it on that day to signify his readiness for war against the whites, as well as a silent protest against Black Kettle's intransigence in holding firm to his misguided ideas about living peacefully with the white man.

It was Horse Catcher who came by the skin lodge to tell him that the Northern Cheyenne braves had come.

"They come to speak for Roman Nose," said the pipeholder. "We should go and find out what they have to say."

Wolf Chief couldn't have agreed more. He left his war arrows and went with Horse Catcher to the center of the village where Black Kettle's skin lodge was located. Other braves were making their way through the teepees in the same direction. A crowd had already gathered there, and when he arrived Wolf Chief learned that the men sent by Roman Nose were in Black Kettle's lodge with the chief. There was a lot of speculation concerning the reason for this unexpected visit. Some believed that it was a harbinger of good news—that Roman Nose had decided to go to war against the whites. Others thought it was probably bad news—that the bluecoats had launched an unprovoked attack against the Northern Cheyenne. Wolf Chief did not even bother speculating. He had a premonition that no matter why the Northern

Cheyenne had come to Sand Creek, their coming would bring about momentous changes.

The assembled Cheyenne fell silent as Black Kettle emerged with the two envoys from Roman Nose. It escaped no one's notice that Black Kettle looked very unhappy.

"Roman Nose has decided to fight the white man," he announced grimly.

Wolf Chief let out a jubilant shout of approval—as did dozens of other warriors, a totally spontaneous release of pent-up frustration that made Black Kettle look even less happy than he had been before.

"He has asked that I allow Two Birds to speak to you," continued Black Kettle, with a gesture at one of the envoys. "This I have agreed to do."

He nodded at Two Birds and stepped back as the Northern Cheyenne warrior took a step forward to gravely survey the circle of intent faces.

"All know that Roman Nose, like all Cheyenne, has tried for many winters to live in peace with the white man. But he knows now that this was a mistake. The white men do not want peace. If they did they would not be attacking our villages and our hunting parties. It is time to show the whites that they have made a mistake killing our young men, our women, our children. I do not need to remind you of what happened to Lean Bear. Many of you saw it with your own eyes. He signed the treaty paper. He gave his word to live in peace. He kept his word. Yet the bluecoats shot him down. That is what will happen to all the Cheyenne, sooner or later, unless we show the white man the error of his ways. Roman Nose himself will lead us against the bluecoats. When we have defeated them, the White Father will realize his mistake and ask for peace. Then perhaps he will make a treaty that he intends to keep."

Two Birds paused and glanced at Black Kettle. "Roman Nose has told me to say that he has great respect for Black Kettle and the others who are opposed to war. They are doing what they think is best for the Cheyenne. But Roman Nose is taking a different path. And he asks all his brothers who want to follow that path to ride with him against the bluecoats."

Black Kettle stepped forward. "I will not ride with Roman Nose. I will not raise a hand in anger against the white man even though there is good reason to do so. I will not because there are too many of them, and too few of us. But I will not stand in the way of those of you who do want to fight. I know that many of you do, and you are free to go back with Two Birds to join Roman Nose. I will not stop you."

Sadly, Black Kettle turned and went back into his skin lodge.

There was no elation in the gathering of Cheyenne warriors, even though the hearts of many of them were gladdened by this welcome news. For himself, Wolf Chief did not hesitate.

"I will ride with Roman Nose," he declared loudly.

Most of the other warriors spoke up to say the same thing. Wolf Chief noticed that Horse Catcher was not one of them.

"You will not go with us?" Wolf Chief asked him. "Roman Nose has given us our one chance to save our people."

Horse Catcher shrugged. "Maybe that is true. But it concerns me that we would leave our own families unprotected when we all ride away to fight."

"When they know that all the Cheyenne are gathered to do battle they will not even think about attacking our villages. They will be too worried about protecting their own towns and wagon trains."

"I hope you are right," said Horse Catcher dubiously.

"Stay here, then, if you want to." Wolf Chief tried to sound indifferent, though he wanted the pipeholder to ride with them. He and the other Wolf Soldiers depended on Horse Catcher for leadership.

"No, I will go with you."

In the end, nearly all the warriors in Black Kettle's band decided to go, leaving only a handful behind.

Gordon Hawkes was glad to be back in the high country, relieved when he and Eliza and Grace left the open sagebrush plains and struck the trail that led up through the wooded foothills toward Dead Horse Pass. He felt too exposed in the low country. There were too few places to hide if trouble came your way. And there was entirely too much trouble on the plains these days to suit him.

It was his intention to wait until they had gotten home to ask Eliza about Grace. He could tell something was wrong. His little girl had changed, virtually overnight, or so it seemed to him. She was too dreamy and distracted, and that wasn't at all like her. She was constantly lost in her thoughts, paying no attention to her surroundings. And she hardly ate a bite. Hawkes began to wonder if perhaps she was ill, and his concern for her welfare prompted him to broach the subject with Eliza ahead of schedule.

They had stopped for the night on a wooded slope, still a long day's ride from the crest of Dead Horse Pass. Hawkes tended first to the horses, as was his habit, but when Eliza sent Grace off to fetch some wood for a fire, he set that task aside and walked over to his wife.

"Something's wrong with her," he said, watching Grace through the trees. "Haven't you noticed?"

"Wrong? Whatever do you mean?"

Hawkes peered at his wife. "You mean you don't see it?"

Eliza hesitated. Of course she knew exactly what he was talking about, but her first instinct had been to pretend that she did not, in the hopes that her husband would drop the matter. She quickly realized that she had misjudged; he wasn't about to let it go. The expression of concern on his face testified to that.

"See what?" she asked.

"I think she might be coming down with something," he fretted.

Eliza had to laugh. She couldn't help it. Her hand flew to her lips and she tried very hard to stifle the laugh, but he looked at her with suspicious eyes and she laughed even harder then.

"What's gotten into you?" he asked, annoyed by her laughter.

"Nothing, dear. Nothing at all," she said, getting a grip on herself. "You're quite right. Our little girl *has* come down with something. But trust me, it isn't fatal."

"What is it, then?"

"She's in love."

Hawkes stared at his wife.

"I can't believe you didn't notice the way she and that lieutenant were looking at each other, Gordon."

"Gunnison?"

Eliza nodded. "Yes. Lieutenant Brand Gunnison is all our daughter can think about."

"My God," breathed Hawkes, horrified.

"Well, now, it was bound to happen someday, dear."

"Yes. Sure. But not him!"

"And why not? He is a good, decent young man. When he arrested you at Gilder Gulch he was only doing his duty. Surely you don't hold that against him. I mean, I seem to recall you said some nice things about him."

"I said he was a good soldier. But Christ, Eliza— she's only sixteen!"

Eliza made a face. "Oh really now, Gordon. Girls, Indian and white alike, often marry at that age out here."

"*Marry?* Don't tell me marriage has been mentioned."

"The morning we left the Cheyenne she informed me that the lieutenant had posed the question. And she said yes."

Hawkes ran a hand over his face, struggling to come to terms with this news. "You gave your blessing?"

"Not exactly. I told her this was neither the time nor the place to talk of marriage. And she agreed that it wasn't. She said they would not be married until these Indian troubles were resolved. But she also told me, in no uncertain terms, that Brand Gunnison was the only man for her."

Hawkes shook his head. "Well," he muttered, struggling to find the words to express himself, "I guess this was bound to happen sooner or later. I just—just didn't expect it to happen so soon!"

"I know, Gordon." Eliza put a hand on his arm. "It's always difficult for a father to understand why his daughter would need to have anything to do with another man. But look at her, dear."

Hawkes looked, though it was almost painful to do so.

"Our little girl has grown up into a young woman," said Eliza pensively. "She has her dreams, and her desires. Much as we may want to, we can't keep her to ourselves forever."

Hawkes nodded. Unable to speak further on the subject, he went back to the horses, feeling a hollowness not unlike what he had experienced upon hearing of the death of his son.

Once through Dead Horse Pass, they had five more days of rough travel ahead of them. But they knew the way quite well and it held no surprises for them. Now it was Hawkes's turn to seem distracted, so much so that at one point Grace asked her mother if something was the matter with him.

"Oh, he just has a lot on his mind," replied Eliza, with a faint smile, and left it at that.

They reached home without incident. The cabin was as they had left it over a month ago. Located in a remote valley, its exact location was unknown to anyone but themselves, as far as Hawkes knew. When they had moved here some years back he had carefully scouted the valley, and had been unable to find any sign that humans had passed through it recently, much less lingered there. Since then he had seen no one in the cabin's vicinity, though the previous winter he had found the tracks of several unshod ponies in the snow marking the passage of Indians.

Eliza was glad to be home. They didn't have much in the way of possessions, but that had never bothered her. Material things were of little consequence in her opinion. They had all that they required to live comfortably. Every now and then, when they ventured out to a trading post for supplies, she would pick up a bolt of cloth or a book. So she had curtains on the windows and Grace had several dresses, and the cabin could boast of a library consisting of nine books. Eliza figured that was more books then anyone else in the mountains could claim to own. She had read them all, cover to cover, several times, and with them she had taught both Cameron and Grace how to read.

The day after their arrival Hawkes went hunting, and Grace used the opportunity to speak to her mother about his recent behavior.

"My father," she said gravely, "knows how I feel about Brand, doesn't he?"

"Yes. He could see that something was the matter with you, dear. He thought you were ill. So I told him the truth. I won't lie, not even for you, Grace."

"How did he take the news?" asked Grace, though she had a hunch she already knew the answer.

"Well, it will take him a little while to get accustomed to the idea."

"Because of Brand."

"No, no. Because you're his little girl."

"But I'm not a little girl anymore, Mother."

"I realize that. And so will your father, eventually. He just doesn't want to lose his daughter, that's all. It's perfectly understandable."

"I see." Grace thought it over, brows knit as she concentrated on the problem.

"Are you sure he is the only one for you, dear?" asked Eliza.

"Oh yes." Grace smiled dreamily, remembering. "I simply can't imagine spending my life with anyone else. He is so strong and brave, and yet so gentle. He treats me like a—like a princess."

"Of course. That's exactly what you are," said Eliza wryly.

Grace giggled. "Really? I don't recollect you ever called me a princess, Mother. You did call me a little devil on several occasions, though."

"More than several," said Eliza, and laughed.

Grace laughed with her, but then her laugh died, and her smile faded quickly.

"Mother, I'm so worried. I can't bear the thought of anything happening to Brand."

"Nothing will happen to him. Don't worry."

"But you can't know that. Life can be so cruel sometimes, you know?"

Eliza's thoughts turned to Cameron. She swallowed the lump in her throat and nodded. "Yes, I do know. Still, it does one nary a bit of good to worry about things one has no control over."

"If Brand were killed I—I just don't know if I could go on."

"Yes, you most certainly could," said Eliza sternly.

"You can survive anything. Believe me, you can. And by the way, what would your lieutenant say if he heard you utter such nonsense?"

"He would be upset with me, I suppose."

"Yes. Because he would want you to live, and more than that, to be happy."

"I could never be happy," said Grace earnestly.

"As long as you lived he would live, too—in your heart. Don't you see?"

"He would live in more than my heart, if I was carrying his child."

Eliza gave her daughter a sharp, penetrating look. "Is that your way of telling me that . . . ?" She didn't finish.

"Yes, Mother." Grace did not avert her eyes. "We did. And it was the most—the most sublime and wonderful moment. I—I wish I could describe it."

"You don't need to. I don't want to hear it."

"Are you angry with me?"

"Not angry. A bit disappointed."

"Was it like that for you, too? When you met Father?"

"If you are referring to when we first made love, I will not discuss it. That is a personal matter."

"But when you first met him. Did you know, at that moment, that he was the one?"

"No, not really. I liked him well enough, I suppose, when we first met. But no, it wasn't until later. After your grandparents were killed by the Flatheads, and your father saved me, and took me up into the mountains and looked after me and kept me safe. One morning I woke up and it seemed so natural, so right, being with him, that I decided I would not be with anyone else ever, and I knew I would never want to be."

"That's how I feel where Brand is concerned."

"Then I expect that the two of you will be together forever. Though I do wish you had waited until after the marriage, Grace."

"I know I should have. But I just couldn't. Just in case—in case we never did see each other again, I would at least have that one night . . ."

Tears suddenly welled up in her eyes and she quickly left the cabin. Eliza didn't try to stop her.

That evening Grace went to bed early without supper.

"Is she okay?" asked Hawkes.

"Oh for heaven's sake," said Eliza, exasperated. "I do wish the two of you would start talking to each other! No, she's not okay. She's worried sick. She's deeply, genuinely in love with her lieutenant and she seems convinced that something will happen to him."

"I guess it's possible," allowed Hawkes.

"Gordon!"

He sighed. "She really feels that strongly about him?"

"It is not a passing fancy, so just get used to the idea."

"You don't have to snap my head off."

"Well, it's just that I know what's going to happen."

"Want to tell me, so I'll know?"

She looked him squarely in the eye and said, "You're going to go back down there when everything breaks loose and people start killing each other, just to make sure he comes through it alive."

Hawkes shook his head. "No, I don't think that will happen, Eliza. I've got no business being in the middle of a shooting war."

"Nonsense. You've never minded your own business before, and you won't start now."

He grinned at her. "Never?"

"Well, almost never. But tonight you're going to mind your business. You're going to make love to me, Mr. Hawkes."

"I am?"

"Yes, you are. Just in case you decide to leave tomorrow."

"Eliza, I'm telling you . . ."

She kissed him, deeply, passionately. "Don't tell me anything," she whispered. "Just show me."

Chapter Ten

Camp Weld didn't amount to much—two rows of small adobe buildings facing a dusty parade ground with a flagpole right in the center. Aside from some corrals and outbuildings, that was it, with the whole surrounded by a low rock wall. Denver was a half day's ride away, and the mountains were a low, ragged, blue suggestion along the western horizon. In the other three directions stretched endless sagebrush plain. It was, thought Governor Evans as he approached the outpost, a pretty bleak vista. He couldn't imagine of what value this land would ever be to his own kind. You sure couldn't farm it and expect to make a living. You might be able to raise livestock on it, but that would be no easy task considering the sparse graze and lack of water in the hot season.

Personally, the governor could have cared less if the Indians kept this land, since it was practically worthless anyway. He harbored no animosity toward the redskins, though he could work up plenty of genuine-sounding indignation against them when he spoke to his constituents. Thing was, he needed to

drive the Cheyenne and the Arapaho off this land
because to do so would be politically advantageous
to him. Using the Indians in this way did not give
him pause. He never had second thoughts about it.
They were here and they could be of some use to
him and they were, after all, only Indians. It never
occurred to him that this callous indifference to the
suffering of the Indians might be deemed by some
to be worse than the hatred men like Captain Talbot
harbored in their hearts for the red man.

What Evans was doing and the reasons he had for
doing it were cold-blooded, thought Major Edward
Wynkoop as he watched the governor's party approach. Accompanying Evans was Colonel John
Chivington and Jim Beckwourth, along with a small
detail of Colorado Volunteers. A tall, ungainly young
man with bristling sideburns flaring from gaunt
cheeks, Wynkoop watched the horsemen approach
from Camp Weld's gate—a square-cut timber laid
across a pair of stout uprights. Surveying the camp
with a jaundiced eye, Wynkoop wasn't sure why a
gate had been erected in the first place, when one
could simply climb over the low perimeter wall at
any point. But, for better or worse, this post, and its
nineteen-man garrison, was his command, and he
was trying to make the best of it.

As the governor and his companions drew closer,
Wynkoop reminded himself that while Evans himself
might not deserve his respect, the position that the
man held did, and the major resolved to exercise unflagging courtesy. After all, Evans was here at his
behest. Wynkoop had arranged for the governor to

meet Black Kettle of the Cheyenne and One Eye of the Arapaho, in what might well amount to a final bid for peace on the frontier.

Wynkoop stepped forward to offer up his hand when Evans arrived at the gate and checked his horse.

"It's good to see you, Governor. Thank you for coming."

"I'm happy to do it, sir," replied Evans, without conviction. "I will do anything in my power in order to resolve our present difficulties with the tribes."

"That's good to hear, sir." Wynkoop knew full well it was an outright lie, too. The "present difficulties" were largely of the governor's own making. And the only reason he was here was because he had to leave the impression that he had gone the extra mile, had exhausted all the options, before he went to war against the Cheyenne and the Arapaho. Wynkoop's invitation had been one he could not refuse, however much he might have wanted to. Wynkoop had relied on that fact. Evans was here not of his own accord but under duress, of sorts. And Wynkoop couldn't help but derive some small measure of satisfaction— carefully masked, of course—from that.

Evans glanced beyond Wynkoop, scanning the parade ground. "Are the chiefs here, then?"

"Yes, sir. They arrived yesterday morning."

"Well then, let's get on with it, shall we?" Evans sounded about as enthused as a man on the verge of visiting a dentist.

"Yes, sir," said Wynkoop. "Right this way, Governor."

They proceeded across the parade ground and into

one of the adobe buildings. Black Kettle and One Eye, accompanied by William Bent, all sat on blankets spread out on the warped plank floor. Bent was surprised to see Jim Beckwourth walk in with the governor and Colonel Chivington.

"Hello, Jim. Didn't expect to see you here today."

Beckwourth grinned. "Howdy, Bill. You know me. Always turning up in the strangest places."

"Mr. Beckwourth," announced Chivington, "is chief of scouts for the Colorado Volunteers."

"Is that right," said Bent coolly. "And how did they talk you into something like that, Jim?"

Beckwourth shrugged. He could tell that Bent disapproved of the company he was keeping, and the mulatto mountain man really couldn't blame him. "They paid my bail," he said. He meant it as a joke, but it fell flat, and it was obvious that Bent didn't find it at all amusing.

"Can we get on with this, Major?" asked Evans. He looked around for a place to sit. There was a battered kneehole desk in the room, and a single chair behind it. "Where am I to sit?"

Wynkoop gestured at Army-issue blankets spread on the dusty floor.

"You must be joking," said Evans. "Colonel, bring me that chair."

Chivington didn't think that was any way to speak to a man of his rank—then he remembered that he held that rank only because the governor had seen fit to give it to him. Before commanding the Colorado Volunteers he had been but an itinerant Methodist preacher. So if Evans spoke to him as though he were a house slave, without so much as a "please" or "thank you," there wasn't really a whole lot he could do about it. He went to the desk, lifted the chair, and carried it back. Evans pointed to the spot where he wanted the chair to be placed and Chivington placed it there. The governor sat down, facing the Indians and, ever conscious of his dignity, brushed trail dust from his trouser leg.

"Shall we begin?" he said. It was a rhetorical question. He was ready, and he wanted to make this meeting as brief as possible, since his plans included a prompt return to Denver. He had no intentions of spending the night at Camp Weld.

Bent spoke to Black Kettle in the Cheyenne tongue, and the chief nodded his assent, so Bent turned to Evans and said, "I am permitted to speak for Black Kettle when I tell you, Governor, that we have a problem with your recent proclamation."

"Which proclamation might that be?" asked Evans, though he knew perfectly well which one.

"I believe Mr. Bent is referring to this one, Governor," said Wynkoop, drawing a paper from under his tunic and unfolding it to read: " 'I hereby authorize all citizens of the Colorado Territory, either individually or in such parties as they may organize, to go in pursuit of all hostile Indians on the plains, scrupulously avoiding those who have responded to my call to rendezvous at the points indicated; also to kill and destroy as enemies of the country wherever they may be found all such hostile Indians."

Evans raised an eyebrow. "And where do you find fault with that, Mr. Bent?"

"No Indian has responded to your call to rendezvous. None of them trust your Indian agent, Colley, to provide them with enough food to get through the winter."

"No Indian has responded—exactly," said Evans, as though he felt this alone was complete vindication.

"So what you've done is declare open season on all Indians, sir," said Wynkoop.

"All hostile Indians. I make that clear."

"But in your mind all Indians are hostile since none responded to your call," said Bent. "Governor, can you honestly sit there and call Black Kettle a hostile? This man who has always been committed to living in peace with the whites, and who has put his personal reputation—and, I might add, even his safety at times—on the line in an attempt to be true to that commitment?"

Evans stared blankly. His mind had wandered as he tried to decide what he would have for supper tonight when he got back to Denver. "What was the question?"

"Can you sit there and call Black Kettle a hostile?"

"No, of course not." It seemed to Evans a small enough point to concede.

"Then could you explain how the citizens of Colorado are supposed to distinguish between Black Kettle and a real hostile?" asked Bent.

Evans frowned. He didn't like being put on the spot. "I don't see why I have to explain anything."

Bent was not famous for his patience. He glanced at Wynkoop, perturbed. The major realized that now was the time to intervene before Bent got angry and said something ill advised.

"The Indians have a serious problem with Sam Colley, Governor," he said. "The Indian agent is, it appears, selling for his own profit some of the allotments due the Cheyenne and the Arapaho according to the terms of more than one treaty. And furthermore, he was recently overheard to say that in his opinion the best food for the Indians right now was a dish of powder and lead."

"He said that?"

"That's what I've heard."

"I can only say that every man is entitled to his opinion in this country," said Evans.

"Ochinee," said Bent, motioning to the Arapaho sitting on the other side of Black Kettle from him, "the man you know as One Eye, has also risked everything for peace."

One Eye spoke slowly and solemnly, and Bent translated when he was done.

"Ochinee says he spoke with Bull Bear of the Cheyenne and Little Raven of the Arapaho not long ago. Bull Bear's brother, Lean Bear, was killed without provocation by the Colorado Volunteers."

"The report I have read indicates he was leading a charge against the troops," said Chivington.

"That's bullshit," snapped Bent. "Ochinee says Bull Bear told him that the white men are foxes and the Indians cannot trust them to keep a peace. The only thing the Indians can do is fight. Little Raven agreed with Bull Bear. This is the same Little Raven who signed the peace treaty at Fort Wise a few summers ago. Little Raven said he would like to shake hands with the white man, but the white man does not want his hand in friendship, so war is the only alternative."

"Which proves that to question the sincerity of the

Indians who signed the peace treaty is completely justified," said Evans.

"You're missing the point entirely," said Bent. "Ochinee goes on to say that he was ashamed to hear Bull Bear and Little Raven say such things. And he has given his word to Tall Chief—Major Wynkoop— that if the Arapaho did not act in good faith he would fight on the side of the white man."

"Tall Chief?" asked Evans, smirking.

Wynkoop's cheeks reddened. "Well, sir, that's what some of them have taken to calling me. At any rate, in exchange for that pledge I gave one of my own. That I would arrange this meeting and try to help make a peace in order to avoid further bloodshed."

"You're very free in speaking for the United States Army," said Evans critically.

"It was more along the lines of a personal pledge, sir. I gave it as a gentleman rather than as an officer."

Black Kettle had been intently watching the governor's face throughout the meeting, and only now did he speak. When he was done, Bent translated his words.

"Black Kettle says there are bad Indians and bad white men. The bad men on both sides are to blame for this trouble."

"What is he implying?" asked Chivington defensively.

"He's just making an observation, Colonel," replied Bent dryly. He refrained from adding, *But if the boot fits, Chivington, by all means go ahead and wear it.*

"Black Kettle also says that all they ask is that they may live in peace. He wants to shake your hand on

it, Governor. He wants to bring good news back to
his people so that they can sleep peacefully. We have
been traveling through a cloud, he says, and all he
wishes is for his people to be able to come out into
the open and be safe. So he asks that you tell all the
white people in Colorado that the Cheyenne are not
their enemy, so that the Cheyenne will not be mistaken for same. He has come to talk plainly with you.
His people must live near the buffalo or they will
starve. Beyond that there are no demands. When he
came here he did so without apprehension, and with
hope in his heart. And when he goes back to his
people he prays that he can tell them that he has
taken your hand and all will be well from this day
forward."

"It is a shame you did not respond to my summons to come to Fort Lyon and thereby demonstrate
your desire for peace, then," said Evans coldly.
"Now I fear it is too late. Because now your young
men have gone into an alliance with the Sioux, who
are at war with us."

When Bent translated this, Black Kettle looked
shocked and responded rapidly, with great feeling.

Bent said, "He does not know who could have told
you such a thing, but—"

"It doesn't matter who told me. I'm satisfied that
it is in fact the case."

"The Cheyenne have not made an alliance with the
Sioux. It's true that some of the braves from Black
Kettle's band rode to join Roman Nose, who has decided he has no choice but to fight. But Black Kettle
did not condone it."

"So really, Governor," interceded Wynkoop, "at

this point they are only asking that you make a distinction between the hostiles and the ones who desire peace."

"You're far too gullible, Major," said Evans. "The Indians know we are at war among ourselves back East. They see this as their best, perhaps their only, opportunity to drive us out of this country. They try to deceive us by extending the olive branch in one hand while raising the tomahawk against us with the other. And when they are called to task on this, they shrug and protest that they have no control over their warriors. If they have no control over their own people then they should not be chiefs in the first place." The governor turned to Bent. "You tell them this. That it is utterly out of the question that they can be for peace while being on friendly terms with our enemies. I am referring to the Sioux."

"But that's just not true," said Bent, outraged. "The Cheyenne have had nothing whatsoever to do with the Sioux nation."

"I have reliable information to the contrary."

"Where did you get this information?"

"As I have said before, that is of no consequence. I know it is true. I will not be deceived by your protestations of innocence. It is dishonorable, in my opinion, to sit there and say you want to shake my hand in friendship while probably at this very moment your warriors are attacking a wagon train or a stage station and slaughtering innocent people."

"Black Kettle is the most honorable man I know," said Bent.

Evans stood up. "I don't think anything else needs to be said." He nodded curtly at Bent, Black Kettle and One Eye. "Good day to you. Major Wynkoop, I would have a word with you, outside."

Wynkoop followed Evans and Chivington and Beckwourth out into the hammering heat.

"Major," said Evans thinly, "the president and the war department gave me authorization to raise the Third Colorado Regiment because I convinced them that it was necessary to do so, since the Indians in the territory posed a very real threat."

"That's not the only reason you raised it, sir," said Wynkoop. He was angered by the way Evans had comported himself earlier, and he caved in to a youthful indiscretion even though he knew he might regret it later. "There were a lot of men in this territory who came here for the express purpose of getting out of fighting in the war back East. They thought they had succeeded, until President Lincoln started conscription. To avoid being drafted, those men pressured you to raise a regiment that they could volunteer for. They figured fighting Indians would be a lot easier than taking on Confederates. I think they are beginning to find out differently now, by all accounts."

Evans glowered at the major. "I raised the Third Colorado for a war. What would I do with them if I made peace instead?"

"I can hardly believe you are telling me this, Governor. If you're being straightforward with me why can't you be the same with Black Kettle?"

Evans smiled thinly. "I'm telling you because you are young and rash. And so you will know why I am going to remove you from command of this post.

Captain Anthony of the Volunteers will relieve you. You will take your soldiers to Fort Lyon and report to Major Blalock."

"Governor, you don't have the authority to—"

"Oh but I do. I have declared a state of martial law in the Territory of Colorado, effective until further notice. That temporarily places all United States regular troops at my disposal. Until, at least, such time as I hear to the contrary from Washington. And that may very well take a good long while, Major, since it appears that the hostiles have destroyed the telegraph line."

Wynkoop shook his head. "I have to hand it to you, sir. When you make up your mind that you want something you don't leave anything to chance."

Evans was pleased. "I try my best not to. Since you are at present directly under my command, Major, I order you to arrest William Bent."

Wynkoop was flabbergasted. "What?"

"Are you hard of hearing, Major? I said arrest William Bent."

"You must be joking."

"I assure you I am very serious."

"But why? What crime has he committed?"

"I suspect him of conspiring to free a couple of prisoners who by my order had been placed in the custody of the Volunteers."

"You have proof to substantiate this charge?"

"A good soldier does not question orders," said Chivington. "He simply obeys them."

Wynkoop glared at the colonel. "How would you know what a good soldier is supposed to do?"

"I'm not going to debate this matter with you, Major," said Evans. "Either you carry out my orders or I will have you arrested."

Wynkoop decided that the governor was mad. He would never get away with what he was trying to do. Yet it could not be denied that he had the authority that he was so recklessly, so boldly, exercising. And there could be no doubt that his threat needed to be taken seriously.

"Very well," said Wynkoop, the bitter taste of bile in his mouth. "I'll take Bent into custody." *Better me*, he reasoned, *than some of the Colorado Volunteers. If they did it, Bent might wind up dead.*

"Good. You will have him taken to Denver under close guard. There he will be placed in the city jail until it can be determined whether he was in fact involved in the crime which I earlier described."

"Yes, sir."

Evans nodded, quite pleased with himself, and with the way things were going.

As they rode through the gate of Camp Weld, beginning the journey back to Denver, Evans turned to Beckwourth.

"Your scouts, are they reliable? I refer to the men who told you that most of the braves from Black Kettle's band have joined up with Roman Nose."

"I rely on 'em," said Beckwourth, "so I reckon you can, too."

"And how many warriors would that give Roman Nose?"

"Can't say for sure. Maybe as many as six or seven hundred."

"That's nearly as many men as we have in arms,"

said Chivington, unable to mask his anxiety. The thought of an Indian horde of that size caused a chill to run down his spine.

"Don't worry, Colonel. We'll make it easy for you. As soon as we arrive back in Denver you will make arrangements to lead a large force against Black Kettle's village on Sand Creek."

"With what orders, sir?"

"The regiment was raised to kill Indians, Colonel. And that is what they should do."

"Excuse me," drawled Beckwourth, "but you mean you're going to attack a village filled mostly with women and children and old men?"

"Precisely," said Evans. "It will serve several purposes. First, it will expunge the stain of dishonor brought upon the regiment by the retreat of Captain Talbot's command a few weeks ago, when faced by braves from that very village. Secondly, it will give the Volunteers some much-needed experience in battle."

"That wouldn't be much of a battle, I'm thinking," remarked Beckwourth. *More like a massacre*, he thought to himself.

"Thirdly, it will force the Southern Cheyenne to desert Roman Nose. They will go back to their villages in order to protect them. That is when the Volunteers will march against Roman Nose and win a great victory that will make this territory safe, once and for all."

"Brilliant strategy, Governor," said Chivington. "I was thinking along the same lines myself."

"Of course you were," said Evans dryly. "Colonel, be sure to take Captain Talbot along with you to

Sand Creek. He has the right idea when it comes to dealing with hostiles. And you'll be going, too, Beckwourth. Your job will be to make certain the Volunteers are not discovered by the Indians—until it's too late."

James Beckwourth didn't say a word.

Lying on his belly just behind the rim of a low grassy swell, Beckwourth eyed the speck of light in the night-dark plain before him. That was a campfire, located about a thousand yards away, to the northeast, and he knew who that fire belonged to—a pair of Cheyenne scouts.

About four miles to the northwest was Chivington's column, also in night camp. So far as Beckwourth knew, the Cheyenne scouts were unaware that several hundred Colorado Volunteers were so close. By tomorrow, though, they would find out. That was why they had to die.

Every night since the column had left Denver, Beckwourth would ride on ahead, always accompanied by one of the three other scouts assigned to Chivington's force. Tonight it happened to be a man named Harker, a Canadian who had once been a trapper with the Hudson's Bay Company, before coming here to hunt for gold. He had been a patron of Beckwourth's store, which had become a kind of gathering place for all the old mountain men in these parts. They would come and sit around and swap tall tales, and Beckwourth hadn't minded at all. He was an ardent teller of tall tales himself and could hold his own with the best of them. It had been largely from this group of men that he had recruited the scouts for the Third Colorado Regiment. Harker had been only too happy to sign up. He disliked Indians in general and ached for action. That, mused Beckwourth, was a common complaint among men of his ilk. In this wild country they had lived on the edge every single day. Pretty soon the fear and excitement had become an addiction. Such men did not know how to adjust to civilized living. They didn't really feel alive unless they were taking chances.

"This is just like old times," murmured Harker, who was lying bellydown on Beckwourth's right. He sounded very content. "Why don't we just go on in and finish them off now, Jim?"

Beckwourth shook his head. "Too risky. One of 'em might get away. No, we wait until the fire dies. Then we can go, when they're asleep." He glanced at Harker. "No guns, though. We have to use our knives, not bullets. Might be more Cheyenne near enough to hear gun talk."

"That suits me," said Harker. Killing didn't bother him too much, be it with rifle or knife or bare hands. He had always lived by one cardinal rule—kill or be killed. That didn't make him bloodthirsty. He didn't especially like killing. He just didn't mind it. It was just one of those things a man had to do if he wanted to survive out here. He had to eat and sleep and kill to stay alive, it was as simple as that.

Beckwourth, though, *was* bothered. He had been bothered ever since riding to Camp Weld with Governor Evans a couple of weeks ago. Unlike Harker and many other mountain men, he had lived among the Indians and had come to realize that they were human beings, just like any other race, and no better or worse. He didn't like what Evans was doing to start a war. There was no call for that. The Indians were no real threat. The governor had manufactured this crisis for his own personal gain. And that wasn't right. He was going to sacrifice a lot of people on the altar of his own ambition.

As a mulatto whose mother had been a slave back in Virginia, Beckwourth knew all about the prejudice that many white people had when it came to persons of a different color. Perhaps that was why he had been able to see Indians in a different light from many of his peers. And why he could empathize with them in this particular case. It made him mad that Evans had assumed he would have no conscience in this matter. He figured that was because he was a "nigger," and as any white man "knew," black and red people were inferior creatures unacquainted with such attributes as a conscience, and with no comprehension of morality or integrity. People without honor. But Evans had misjudged him.

Still, mused Beckwourth, *here I am, in a real box.* Evans and Chivington were playing for very high stakes, and if he did not go along with them he would pay a steep price. He might even pay with his life. Walking away was just not an option. They would not let him walk away. He glanced at Harker, who was eagerly focused on the faraway fire. *I could kill ol' Harker here and go over to the Cheyenne.* But that was crazy. And it was as suicidal as trying to walk away. The Cheyenne were doomed. They were going to die. It was a grim awakening for Jim Beckwourth to realize that he did not have the courage that might enable him to give up his own life for what was right. But he was getting old, and while often his life seemed to be hardly worth the grief it brought him, on the other hand it had become all the more precious to him because he had so little of it left. Beckwourth didn't think much of Evans or Chivington, or of this whole business, but he thought even less of himself.

"The fire's died down," said Harker.

"Yeah. Let's get it over with."

They walked their horses in closer, five hundred yards, before ground-hitching them and proceeding the rest of the way on foot. They approached downwind of the camp, so that the Cheyenne ponies could not pick up their scent and give the alarm. Beckwourth wasn't sure whether both of the scouts would be asleep or not. It might be that they were taking turns staying awake and keeping a lookout. Not that it really mattered. There was not the slightest doubt in his mind how this would turn out. Those Cheyenne braves were on their way to the happy hunting grounds and that was all there was to it.

As they drew closer Beckwourth saw that one of the braves was stretched out on the ground, wrapped in a blanket. The other was standing. He had heard something, but it hadn't been them; the Indian had his back to them and was gazing into the darkness in the opposite direction. *He's going to a better life*, thought Beckwourth, *and I'm signing my own ticket to hell.*

"I'll take the one standing," whispered Harker, barely loud enough for Beckwourth to hear, and then the Canadian moved on, the blade of the knife in his hand catching a glimmer of starlight. One of the Cheyenne ponies whickered, and the Indian began to turn, but it was too late. Harker drove the blade into his left side, just below the ribcage, angling it so that it penetrated the brave's heart and killed him instantly.

Beckwourth moved in, pouncing on the sleeping Indian, bringing his knife to the man's throat even as he awoke. But the mulatto hesitated, and the Cheyenne threw him off and reached for his war lance. That was when Harker hurled the knife he had just pulled from the corpse of the other brave. The second Indian cried out, and fell dead.

Harker retrieved his knife, wiping blood from the blade onto his trouser leg and looking at Beckwourth with a grin on his face.

"Damn, Jim, you must be gettin' old to let that buck get the better of you like that."

Beckwourth just nodded. He did feel very old at that moment.

Harker walked over and cut the throats of the Cheyenne ponies. They could not take the chance that one of the horses would get free and return on its own to the village that lay, by Beckwourth's calculations, no more than ten miles to the east.

"You going to lift their hair?" asked Beckwourth.

Harker looked at the dead Indians. "Nah. Their scalps ain't worth nothing. Best we be getting back to the column."

Beckwourth nodded again. He could not bring himself to look at the Cheyenne corpses, and promptly left the camp, making his way back to the place where they had left their horses. He was eager to be away from the scene of what he knew would turn out to be the worst act he had ever committed.

And he couldn't help but wonder if he was going to commit even worse ones tomorrow.

Chapter Eleven

There were nearly seven hundred of them, just about every Colorado Volunteer that had been fit to ride and fight, and they were accompanied by a battery of four mountain howitzers. Colonel Chivington was in command and the orders he gave to his subordinates were concise. "We have come to kill Indians," he told them. "I believe it is right and honorable to use any means at hand to kill them. And please remember that nits make lice." He was not deterred by news brought to him by Beckwourth's scouts—that a band of Arapaho had camped across Sand Creek from Black Kettle's Cheyenne. He had come to believe of late that he was on a mission from God, and that he was destined to be a hero in the campaign that rid the West of the redskin scourge.

They attacked at dawn, a cold, bleak, gray dawn, for summer was well and truly over now, with the first snow not far in the future. The Cheyenne and Arapaho encampments contained no more than six hundred people, and more than two-thirds of them were women and children. Many of the Cheyenne braves had gone north to join Roman Nose, and a large portion of those that had remained behind were out hunting for buffalo, as it was time to begin laying in winter stores of meat and buffalo robes.

George Bent awoke to the sound of many horses, an incessant thunder rolling across the sagebrush flats. He sat up in his blankets and looked across the still-dark skin lodge at his mother, Yellow Woman, who had also risen.

"Are those buffalo?" she asked.

"No," said Charlie Bent as he leaped to his feet. "Buffalo sound like life. That sound is the sound that death makes."

A shout came from outside, a cry of alarm quickly echoing from a dozen more voices throughout the village. George and his brother grabbed their weapons, in George's case a war lance and a percussion pistol his father had recently given him and for which he had only a handful of cartridges. Charlie laid hands on a bow and quiver of war arrows. Both young men were clad in buckskin leggings and hunting shirts. Emerging from the skin lodge with their mother, they paused to look about them. A column of soldiers was coming straight down along the creek toward the village. Another, smaller column raced across the flats to the west, heading for the Indian horse herd being held south of the encampment. All about them men, women and children were pouring out of skin lodges. For a moment the Bents were at a loss as to their best course of action. Then the first gunshots rang out, a sharp crackling sound that shattered the morning. George glanced east—saw the blood-red smear of light along the horizon that presaged the sunrise—saw, too, dark shapes scurrying among the teepees of the Arapaho band led by Left Hand.

"Come on, Charlie," he said. "We have to get our mother to safety."

Most of the Cheyenne were on the move, fleeing to the center of the village where Black Kettle's skin lodge was located—and, more important at that moment, where he flew the United States garrison flag on a tall pole. The Cheyenne hoped that the flag would protect them. George Bent knew better. His only hope was that all the other men in the village would collect at the center and, once united, turn to fight the bluecoats. But even if they did, the outcome did not appear to be in doubt, at least to George. This time there were just too many soldiers. The full military might of the Territory of Colorado had descended upon them this day. The words of the Cheyenne death song formed in George Bent's mind. *Nothing lives long, only the earth and the mountains.*

Reaching the vicinity of Black Kettle's skin lodge, George saw the old chief standing with the flag pole in hand, and calling for his people to congregate around him, assuring them that the flag would protect them. Some of the Arapahos had crossed Sand Creek, likewise seeking the protection of the flag. Among them was Left Hand. About sixty Cheyenne and Arapaho warriors took their place along the outer edge of the milling crowd.

The bluecoats appeared, galloping through the teepees, their rifles and pistols spitting flame—and the shooting did not cease when they saw the flag. Women and children screamed in terror, knowing that all was lost. George saw Cheyenne falling on all sides. He whirled, shouting above the din to Charlie, ordering his younger brother to take their mother and flee. Then he turned back to face the bluecoat onslaught, as did a few dozen other warriors, while the women and children scattered. He saw Left Hand striding toward the soldiers, holding up his hands and calling for them to stop in English. Several bullets struck him at the same time, and he crumpled to the ground. George calmly raised the percussion pistol and fired into the oncoming mass of horsemen. As the powdersmoke cleared, he saw with satisfaction that he had emptied one saddle.

The thin line of Cheyenne and Arapaho warriors disintegrated in seconds, with most of them cut down in a hail of bullets. George Bent made a break for the creek. As he neared the creekbank, a bullet caught him in the hip and he toppled. He managed to crawl to the edge and look down into the creekbed, only to watch in helpless horror as a wave of mounted Volunteers swept down onto a mass of women and children, cutting them down with pistol, rifle and saber. George knew then that his worst fears had come to pass. The soldiers were making no distinctions: All Indians were to be killed, from the oldest man to the youngest infant. His cry of rage brought unwanted attention: another bullet struck him and he slid down the sandy bank, and as a blackness swept over him his last thought was of his father, and how fortunate it was that he was not here to witness the slaughter, to feel the heartbreak.

Within twenty minutes it was over.

Jim Beckwourth surveyed the carnage with bleak eyes. The ground was littered with dead and dying Indians. And as if that were not enough, the Volunteers were looting the village, in search of souvenirs. In some cases the souvenirs turned out to be quite gruesome. Beckwourth saw a soldier cut out the private parts of a young Cheyenne girl and stretch them over the pommel of his saddle. The private parts of a brave were cut off by another Volunteer, who cheerfully announced that he was going to make a tobacco pouch out of them. Many scalps were taken, even from the very young. Beckwourth saw quite a few children among the dead, even some infants, and in one case an unborn baby which had been cut from its dead mother's womb and left to die in the dirt.

Sickened, and almost delirious with rage and self-loathing, Beckwourth began to look for Chivington, having in mind to kill the colonel, and by so doing atone at least in part for the crimes that had been done here. But before he could locate Chivington he found George Bent—and a soldier just seconds away from taking the half-breed's hair. Beckwourth leaped from his horse and gave the man a good hard kick in the ribs, sending him sprawling into the shallows of Sand Creek.

"What the hell do you think you're doing?" shouted the Volunteer, leaping to his feet.

"This is George Bent, William Bent's son," said Beckwourth, his voice deceptively calm, but with the fires of hell blazing in the caverns of his eyes. "He's half white. And furthermore, he ain't even dead yet."

"Hell, I can see that. But he's good as dead, and I ain't about to waste a bullet. As for him being half white, then I say all the more reason to kill him."

"I'm half white," said Beckwourth. "Maybe you want to kill me, too."

The soldier just glared at him.

"Now go away," said the mountain man.

The soldier looked into the old mulatto's eyes . . . and went on his way.

Beckwourth knelt to determine the extent of the wounds that George Bent had sustained. One in the leg, and a deep bullet graze in the side. George had lost a great deal of blood. He was breathing shallow and was very pale, his skin cold and clammy to Beckwourth's touch. The mountain man calculated that George's chances of surviving were downright slim. Still, he bound up the wounds as best he could to slow the bleeding and keep the flies out of them. Then he sat down next to the young half-breed and fired up a pipe, to wait and see whether George kept breathing.

Gazing at the Indian dead strewn along the creek bed, Beckwourth wondered what had become of Charlie Bent and the mother, Yellow Woman. This had been a slaughter, but it could have been worse. Many of the Cheyenne and the Arapaho had gotten away, most of them on foot. This was because Chivington's men were amateurs and poorly trained. And as a rule they weren't the best shots. There seemed to be no desire among them to pursue the escaped Indians, either. The Volunteers were too busy collecting mementos. Besides, they had lost the element of surprise now. None of them wanted to risk riding into an Indian ambush. They had done plenty of killing today, so they were satisfied.

Beckwourth watched them, bluecoated vultures scavenging the village, with a loathing that reached into every fiber of his being. He had seen a lot of gory work in his forty-plus years in the wild country, but some of the atrocities he witnessed this day were more brutal than anything he had seen before. It made him want to throw up. His own role in what had transpired made him sick to his stomach, too. He had not lifted a hand against the Indians, but that certainly was no mitigating circumstance. He was as guilty as Chivington and any of the Volunteers who had participated in this massacre. The gravity of his sin was such that he knew a kind of hopelessness; nothing he could ever do would serve to make amends for this heinous association.

Movement on the other side of the creek interrupted this grim reverie, and Beckwourth looked up to see two Indians being escorted by a trio of Volunteers. Only the prisoners weren't Indians. Not entirely. One was Charlie Bent. The other was even more obviously a half-breed. His hair was a light brown color, his complexion lighter even than Charlie's. Upon reflection, Beckwourth figured that this was the reason they were both still alive, though he had doubts that they would stay alive for very much longer. They were both bruised and bloodied.

They moved on, paying Beckwourth no mind, or anything else, for that matter. Charlie Bent kept his eyes downcast, perhaps not wishing to view the carnage all around him, and Beckwourth was glad of that, because Charlie was in a bad enough way without seeing his brother George's bloody body.

Getting to his feet, Beckwourth lifted George up in his arms and carried him downstream, continuing until he was well beyond the last corpse. A quarter mile from the village he arrived at a tangle of dead-wood piled up against a bank where the creek turned sharply, washed there by a flash flood no telling how long ago. Behind a shattered log he placed George Bent, out of the sight of anyone who might come this way.

"I'll try to get back here to check on you, boy," muttered the mountain man, though he knew George could not hear him. "You just hang on, now. Me, I'm going to see if I can't at least save your brother."

Rising, he retraced his steps, and continued on past the spot where he had found George, until he reached the place where the Volunteers were re-grouping, at the northern end of the village. He saw Chivington then. The colonel was conferring with his lieutenants, and again Beckwourth had that errant thought about going right up to the colonel and cutting his heart out. But he didn't do it. He had something more important to attend to now. Searching for Charlie, he finally spotted him, sitting on the ground among some wagons into which the soldiers were loading their dead and wounded for transport back to Denver or Camp Weld, which Chivington had recently appropriated from the regular United States Army. A pair of rifle-toting Volunteers were standing guard over Charlie. Beckwourth didn't hesitate. He walked right up to them.

"What are you doing, Charlie?" he asked Bent.

Charlie looked up at him, his eyes blank.

"You know him?" asked one of the Volunteers.

"I guess I'd better know him. He's one of my scouts."

"What? He ain't no scout. He's a fucking breed."

"You calling me a liar?" asked Beckwourth, his cold eyes hooded like a snake's.

The Volunteer hesitated. "I ain't never seen him before today," he muttered.

"There are a lot of things you don't see. That's why you need scouts like Charlie and me, I reckon."

The other Volunteer laughed. "He got you there, Ben."

"He put up a fight," said Ben. "Was he one of yours why would he do that?"

"Probably thought you were aiming to kill him," said Beckwourth. "And that is what you aim to do, isn't it?"

"Ben did," said the second Volunteer. "I was the one thought we might ought to bring him in alive, seeing as how he's at least half white."

"Being half white don't count for much," said Ben resentfully.

"I could have told you that," said the mountain man.

"I didn't mean that," said Ben.

"Come on, Charlie," said Beckwourth, praying that Bent would just keep his mouth shut and do what he was told.

Charlie stood up. It looked like doing that took a great deal of effort on his part. He swayed uncertainly for a moment. Beckwourth figured he'd had a rough go of it today. Putting an arm around the young Bent's shoulder, Beckwourth walked away from the two befuddled Volunteers.

When they were out of earshot of anyone else,

Beckwourth said, "I'm going to put you on one of those wagons with the dead and wounded, Charlie. Come night, when they make camp, you slip away nice and quiet-like. You understand what I'm telling you, boy? They won't even know you're gone." The mulatto frowned, wondering if he was getting through. "You getting any of this, Charlie?"

Charlie looked at him with bleak, bloodshot eyes. "My brother George. What's become of my brother?"

"He's alive," replied Beckwourth, even though he wasn't absolutely sure that that was still the case. "I've seen him. Don't worry about that now. Just keep your sights set on staying alive yourself."

Charlie kept staring at him. "Why are you doing this?"

Beckwourth grimaced. "That doesn't matter. You clear on what to do? It's the only way you'll get clean away, I reckon. If I leave you to wander around out here you'll run crossways of another one of these bluecoat butchers for sure. And next time they'll probably just kill you and be done with it."

Charlie nodded. "I'm clear."

Beckwourth took him back to the wagons and selected one that was fast filling up with wounded. He told the officer in charge of the detail that Charlie was one of his scouts. The officer took one quick look at Charlie's bruised and bloodied face and nodded. Beckwourth helped him up into the wagon. And he waited until all the wagons had been filled and the caravan was on the move. He was glad to see that only a small detail rode along, and he didn't figure Charlie would have much trouble getting away under cover of night. The soldiers would be keeping an eye out for hostiles coming into camp, not anyone sneaking out.

His thoughts returning to George Bent, Beckwourth went back to the creek and the deadfall where he had concealed William Bent's eldest son. But George was gone. The mountain man saw footprints in the sand that hadn't been there earlier. They had been made by someone wearing moccasins. Beckwourth took a long look around but saw no one. The Cheyenne had come back for their own. The question remained: Would George Bent live?

Gordon Hawkes saw the smoke from miles away. Someone was in his valley and they weren't trying to hide the fact. He figured it had to be white men. Indians weren't so careless in savage country.

He was out hunting when he saw the smoke. The trees were turning and the nights had grown cool and now was the time to be laying in a supply of meat for a winter that might come early and with a vengeance. The cabin was several miles away, and he considered going back to warn Eliza and Grace, just in case the smoke meant trouble and something happened to him when he investigated it. But night was only hours away, and he chose to do his investigating while there was light enough to see exactly what he was getting into.

Riding to within a quarter mile of his destination, he tethered the mountain mustang and went the rest of the way on foot. There was only one man tending the fire that made all that smoke. He was cooking a rabbit on a stick. His horse stood nearby. The man wore buckskins and a coonskin cap. He looked every inch a mountain man, but Hawkes had never seen him before.

Wary of a trap, Hawkes circled the camp, looking for sign, and when he found the tracks he was looking for he saw only one set of them. So the man was traveling alone, it seemed. But where had he come from, and where was he going? Hawkes considered his options. He could wait and see if on the morrow the stranger moved on out of the valley. Or he could confront the man now. Since he wanted to sleep that night, Hawkes opted for the latter course of action

He moved in on the man from behind, making about as much noise as a butterfly landing on a leaf, but when he was still a good hundred feet away the man at the fire spoke up without turning his head.

"Hope you ain't aiming to bushwhack me. That would make me feel downright foolish, seeing as how I came here against my better judgment in the first place."

"Get up and walk away from that rifle," said Hawkes.

Sitting on his heels near the fire, the man looked at the long gun that was lying on the ground within reach. Then he put the cooking rabbit down, got up and took ten paces before turning to face Hawkes, arms held out away from his body.

"The name's Claymore Jones. Well, that ain't my real name, but it's the handle I've used ever since I left Texas back in '43."

"What are you doing out here?" asked Hawkes.

"I carry a message for a Gordon Hawkes, also known as Henry Gordon. Might that be you?"

"A message from who?"

"Alonzo Burn. He's an old friend of mine. We go back a ways. He would have delivered the message himself, except he's stove up. Some bastard shot his kneecap off."

Hawkes moved in closer. He didn't lower the Plains rifle. "I'm the one you're looking for."

Claymore Jones nodded. "Figured as much. Alonzo told me what you looked like. And he told me you was meaner than hell with the hide off. Said you'd like as not just clean my plow before I got the chance to tell you why I come. When he told me your name I knew that was so. I've heard some tales about you, Hawkes. They say fifty tough hombres have come after you on account of you got a price on your head, and not a one of 'em has ever been heard from again. They say you was captured by the Sioux and managed to get away from five hundred bucks out to take your hair. They also say you cleaned out a whole gold camp in revenge for the killing of your son."

"They say a lot of things that aren't true."

Claymore Jones grinned. "Well, that's gospel. But I figured enough of it had to be true to make coming here a fool's errand. Still, Alonzo and I go back a ways, and I owed him, so here I am."

"What's the message?"

"He wanted me to tell you this. William Bent was arrested by order of the governor. He's being held at the jail in Denver. He also said to tell you that the Colorado Volunteers attacked Black Kettle's village. Had to have been three weeks ago, by now. Killed hundreds of Cheyenne women and children. A real massacre."

"Jesus," muttered Hawkes. It wasn't as though the news came as a surprise to him. He had been expecting something like this to happen. His first thought was of Bent's family, the man's two sons and Yellow Woman. Had they been in Black Kettle's camp the day the attack had come? They probably had been. Had they survived? He wondered if Bent himself knew what had become of them. Even if they were dead it would be better to know the truth than to wonder.

"The talk is that Cheyenne and Arapaho warriors have joined up with the Sioux and are going to ride straight into Denver and kill every last white person they find," said Claymore Jones. He laughed a short, bitter laugh. "Can't rightly say I'd blame them if they do."

Hawkes simply shook his head. He felt disgust, anger—anger directed at Evans and Chivington for orchestrating this bloody little war. Anger, too, at Black Kettle, for having put his faith in the garrison flag that the government had given him at Fort Wise. And anger at himself as well, for hiding out up here in the high country.

"How about some rabbit?" asked Claymore Jones. "There's enough to go around."

"No thanks. Tell me, why did Burn ask you to give me this message?"

Claymore Jones shrugged. "He just said he thought you would want to know, seeing as how you were a friend to the Cheyenne."

"I'm not, really."

"Well, me, neither. But I'd be lying if I said it would bother me if the Injuns did turn Denver into a graveyard."

Hawkes gave him a hard look of disapproval. "There are innocent women and children in Denver, too. Just as innocent as the women and children who were at Sand Creek. What's the difference?"

"I guess that's right," said Claymore Jones, grudgingly. But it was obvious that he still didn't really care what happened to Denver or its inhabitants. "So what are you going to do?"

"About what?"

"Just figured Alonzo wanted you to know because he figured you would do something about it, that's all."

His laugh sounding hollow, Hawkes said, "I'm just one man. Not a whole lot I can do."

He knew, though, exactly what he had to do. He had known from the moment Claymore Jones had given him the news.

The other mountain man shrugged. "Well, it's none of my business and I aim to keep it that way. I'll just have my dinner and be on my way. Alonzo told me that after I gave you the message I should just keep moving. Not to take it personal if I didn't get an invite from you to stick around."

"No offense, but I think he's right. I think you should move on."

"Hey, that's fine by me. And you don't have to fret none, Hawkes. I ain't going to tell nobody where they could find you. Way I got it figured, you and me, we have some things in common. One being that we're both on the run from something. I've been on the run since '43. Can't ever go back to Texas, that's for sure. I've learned a thing or two since then. Mostly I've learned to mind my own business. To live and let live. So me, I'm just going to head a little deeper into the mountains and find me a nice quiet place and make myself comfortable and wait out the winter, and come green-up I'll probably mosey on down to the plains and see who's left standing."

Hawkes nodded. "Then I guess that's it." He didn't thank Claymore Jones for bringing him Alonzo Burn's message. He wasn't thankful. He turned away and left the camp.

But he didn't go far, finding a good spot from which he could watch, concealed, while Claymore Jones ate his dinner. He figured Jones knew he was doing just that, too.

When he had finished off the rabbit, Jones killed the fire and mounted up and rode west. Hawkes went back to his mustang and followed the man's trail, keeping an eye peeled for ambush. Alonzo Burn might have thought Jones was a man who could be trusted, but Hawkes didn't trust him at all. It hadn't escaped his notice that Burn had learned his true identity. That didn't surprise him. He figured by now that nearly everyone in the territory knew who "Henry Gordon" really was, now that he stood accused of killing several Colorado Volunteers. Claymore Jones might or might not be a man who understood the value of minding his own business— but certainly he was a man who understood that there was value in turning in another wanted man.

But, in the end, Claymore Jones did exactly what he had said he would do. He rode west and by the end of the day was well removed from the valley. Only as nightfall approached did Hawkes, fairly well satisfied, go home.

Eliza was waiting for him at the cabin door, worried that he had been gone for so long; he seldom stayed away past sundown. If the fact that he had returned empty-handed from a hunting trip wasn't enough to indicate that something was amiss, the troubled expression on his face surely was.

"What has happened?" she whispered.

"It's started," he said flatly.

She knew precisely what he meant by that, and what the consequences of it were for them.

Looking her straight in the eye, aware that he wasn't telling her anything she didn't already know, Hawkes said, "I'll have to go. Leave first thing in the morning."

Eliza nodded, experiencing that old familiar fear, a fear no less acute for its familiarity. Her husband, the man she loved more than she loved life itself, was going to go away from her again, going into harm's way, going where the odds were high that he would never return. And if that happened, what would she do? How would she survive the loss? She had told her daughter that a person could survive anything, and she'd sounded very certain when she had said it, and Grace believed her because she'd proven it, proven it by surviving the deaths of her parents and of her only son. But in her heart of hearts Eliza wasn't sure she could actually survive the loss of this man, who was the very breath of life for her. This was an agony that she could never express to him, but then she didn't have to, because Hawkes could see it, right there, in those blue eyes.

"What are you going to do?" she asked.

"William Bent is in jail in Denver. I've got to get him out. And I've got to find out if his family is still alive. The Volunteers attacked Black Kettle's village. Many women and children were slaughtered."

"Dear God." Eliza's hand flew to her throat.

Hawkes reached out and took that hand in his and brought it to his lips. "I have to do this," he said, an apology of sorts, and a woefully inadequate one as well.

"Yes, you do," she said firmly, supportively. She knew it was a matter of conscience with him, and more than that, a matter of honor, because William Bent had been a good friend, had rescued her and Grace and reunited them with Hawkes. Her husband could not sit by and do nothing. And he would not have been the man she loved, had he been able to.

"I better see to my horse," he said, reluctantly letting go of her hand.

"One more thing you can do while you're down there," said Eliza.

"Yes, I know," he said. She didn't have to spell it out for him. In fact, he had already thought about it—about making sure somehow that Lieutenant Brand Gunnison wasn't lost in the bloody insanity that had erupted in the plains below. It was a commitment he had made silently and without question, quite aware that by so doing he accepted the fact that Grace was no longer a little girl, that she had grown up and fallen in love and would one day go away from him, and that this did not in any form or fashion abnegate his responsibility to see to her happiness.

Chapter Twelve

When he got to Denver Hawkes stole the first horse he could find.

It was late at night. He had waited on the outskirts of town for darkness to come, and then he had waited some more, until the streets had quieted down. He didn't bother trying to devise some elaborate scheme to free William Bent. Nor did he worry about scouting out the lay of the town. He had never been to Denver, but going in just to familiarize himself with it, and to discover the exact whereabouts of the jail where Bent was being held was not an option open to him. Captain Talbot and some of the Colorado Volunteers had gotten a good look at him back at Burn's trading post, and for all he knew they had broadcast his description. He couldn't take the chance. He wouldn't do Bent much good if he ended up in the next cell.

So he had just walked in, keeping to the night shadows as much as possible, and taking the horse, which was tethered with some others in front of a saloon, and then he walked on, leading the stolen pony along with his own mountain mustang, and a block farther along the street he passed yet another watering hole, just as a man emerged, a bit uncertain on his feet. Hawkes stopped, keeping the stolen horse between himself and the man, with his own mustang on the other side of him, and asked where the jail might be.

The man squinted into the darkness, trying to get a better look at Hawkes, but unable to see much of anything, not only because it was a dark night but also because the horse was in the way, and because he was more than halfway to being good and drunk. He shrugged and pointed along the street. "It's down about two blocks, on your left. How come you want to go to jail, mister?"

Hawkes didn't respond, just continued on his way. When he reached the jail he tied the two horses up out front and pulled the Plains rifle free of his saddle's tie and, looking up and down the street, went to the door and rapped on it with the butt of his rifle. There was no light in the front windows, so he tried the latch, but the door was bolted from the inside, and he rapped on it again, louder this time.

"Okay, okay!" came a slurred and exasperated voice from inside. "Hold your damn horses. I'm coming, damn it."

Hawkes heard the bolt being thrown. The door's hinges creaked as the man opened it. The mountain man didn't hesitate. He drove the butt of the Plains rifle into the man's face. The jailer fell backward, blood spewing from his nose and mouth. When he hit the floor he was out cold. Hawkes stepped inside, kicking the unconscious man's legs to one side so that he could close and bolt the door.

The room was dark. Hawkes located an oil lamp

and lighted it. He stood in an office, furnished with a battered desk, a gun case, a blackened stove and a narrow cot where it appeared the man he had just hit had been sleeping. A ring of keys dangled from a peg beside a door fashioned from thick, iron-reinforced timbers. The door was locked, and it took Hawkes a moment to find the key that would unlock it. That done, he stepped into a darkened cell block.

"Who is that?" asked someone in the cell immediately to his right.

"I'm looking for William Bent."

"Hawkes?" Bent's voice issued from the darkness of the cell to the left. His eyes gradually adjusting, the mountain man stepped to the strap-iron door and began to test the keys in the lock.

"What are you doing here?" asked Bent.

"Getting you out."

"You shouldn't have come. There's nothing but death down here. Go back to your mountains and stay alive."

"I will. But first there are a few things I have to see to."

A key turned, the lock scraped, the door opened.

"Hey," said the prisoner in the cell opposite Bent's. "Let me out. Let me out . . . or I'll sound an alarm."

"No you won't," said Hawkes. "Because if you did I'd have to come back and shut you up."

He followed Bent out into the office. "Did you kill him?" Bent asked, nodding at the jailer sprawled on the floor, his face covered with blood.

"No." Hawkes opened the gun case, took a rifle and pistol from it and handed the weapons to Bent.

He found a cartridge pouch that seemed to be pretty full and gave this to Bent as well.

"Evans has finally done it," said Bent bitterly. "He's got his war now. He started it by sending the Volunteers against Black Kettle's village. The bloody bastard."

"I know. I heard about it."

Bent clutched his arm. "My family. My boys. Do you know if . . . ?"

Hawkes shook his head.

"Beckwourth came to see me two days ago," said Bent. "Said he had seen both George and Charlie alive after the massacre. He did what he could to help them. But he doesn't know where they are now, or even if they're still alive. Seems that George was pretty badly shot up . . ." Bent's voice began to tremble and stopped.

Hawkes could sympathize. He knew exactly the kind of torment Bent was suffering at this moment. He had experienced it himself, during the long ride to Gilder Gulch not too many years ago, when he had not known for certain whether his son Cameron was alive or dead, fearing the worst while hoping against hope for the best.

"Where would they go?" he asked.

Bent shook his head. "No way to be sure. They might have gone with the rest of the survivors. Or they might have gone to my ranch. It's about two days from Sand Creek."

"I didn't know you had a ranch."

"Not much of one. But that's just it—not many folks know about it."

"Then that's where we'll go."

Bent looked at him. "I'm grateful to you, Gordon. Bad enough to be locked up in that iron cage. But it was pure hell being stuck in there, not able to look for my people, to get to them, to help them when they needed me."

"There's a horse for you right out front. Go get on it. We'll just ride out of here nice and easy."

"The town's full of Volunteers," said Bent. "They're sticking close because there's a rumor that Roman Nose plans to attack Denver."

"Let's go." Hawkes blew out the lamp.

They stepped out onto the street. All was quiet. Hawkes shut the door and tossed the keys aside. Mounting up, they turned their horses south, down the street up which Hawkes had come. They were halfway home when, as they passed the saloon, Hawkes spotted Captain Talbot and another officer of the Colorado Volunteers emerging from the watering hole.

Talbot glanced with idle curiosity at the two passing horsemen and immediately recognized Hawkes and Bent.

Cursing, he groped for the pistol at his side.

"Go!" Hawkes roared at Bent, and as the latter kicked his horse into a gallop, he spun his mountain mustang toward the saloon and rammed his heels into the animal's side. The mustang was not one to tolerate rough handling. It lunged forward, snorting, chomping at the bit as Hawkes tightened up on the reins and rearing up. Talbot flung himself sideways to escape the flailing hooves. Jerking the horse's head sharply, Hawkes turned his mount and lashed out with a kick that propelled the other officer through the saloon doors. Then he kicked the mustang into a leaping gallop, riding low in the saddle. Talbot scrambled to his feet and got off one shot at him, but the bullet passed over the mountain man's head.

Within moments they were well clear of Denver. The long strides of the mountain mustang brought Hawkes abreast of Bent, and he called for the other man to stop. They both checked their horses and turned in the saddle to scan their back trail.

"Think they'll come after us?" asked Bent.

"That was Talbot. What do you think? But he won't find us in the dark." Hawkes looked at Bent. "Now, let's find this ranch of yours."

William Bent's ranch didn't amount to much—an adobe hut standing forlornly in the middle of the vast sagebrush plain. Hawkes had no idea why Bent had even built it in the first place, but he didn't ask for details and Bent never offered him an explanation. In fact, they scarcely spoke during the four-day journey. Hawkes didn't fault him for that. He was worried sick about his family and could think of nothing else. The hope that he would find them safe at the ranch was, at best, a slender one, but he clung to it fiercely. And, as luck would have it, they *were* there.

As they rode up it was Charlie they saw first—he emerged from the hut with a rifle in hand. Bent leaped from his horse and embraced his son. Hawkes was moved. But it seemed to him that Charlie wasn't. In fact, the younger Bent seemed very reserved.

Hawkes wondered if it was his imagination, or had Charlie actually stiffened as Bent threw his arms around him?

"George," said Bent. "And Yellow Woman. Are they . . . ?"

"They're inside," replied Charlie.

Bent rushed into the adobe. Hawkes dismounted, aware that Charlie was watching his every move in a less-than-friendly fashion.

"Did they let him go?" asked Charlie.

"Not exactly."

Charlie's gaze shifted to the plains beyond. "Were you followed?"

"Not for long. We shook loose of them a few days ago."

"I guess you know what happened at Sand Creek."

Hawkes nodded. He could see the cuts on Charlie's face that had not quite healed. "I was truly sorry to hear about it."

"Yeah," said Charlie bitterly. "We're all sorry."

He turned and went inside. Since he hadn't been invited to do so, Hawkes didn't cross the threshold. He took the horses to the nearby well, loosened the cinches, and gave them water. Then he fetched pipe and tobacco and had a smoke, contemplating his next move. He had done a good bit of what he'd wanted to accomplish already. William Bent was out of jail and now he was reunited with his family. So far so good. It had been a lot easier than he had expected it to be. The next task would prove far more difficult, he was sure. Just how was he supposed to make certain that Lieutenant Brand Gunnison didn't get himself killed in this Indian war?

William Bent appeared in the doorway, looking pale and shaken.

"Gordon, you had better come in here."

Hawkes followed him inside. George Bent was sitting up on a narrow wooden bunk over in one corner of the room. His leg was bandaged, as was his midsection. He looked gaunt, weak. Yellow Woman stood near him, her back to a wall and her face a stoic mask betraying nothing. Charlie moved to the door, standing just inside it so that he could keep one eye on the countryside. They were fugitives now, and acting like it. Hawkes knew how they felt.

"They say Black Kettle and many of the survivors of the attack went east, into the Smoky Hill country," Bent told him. "Yellow Woman brought George here in the hopes that Charlie would show up, which he did some days later. Now they're planning to rejoin what's left of the band."

Hawkes nodded. "When are you all leaving?"

"We aren't," said Bent flatly. "They are."

"Why aren't you going with them, Bill?"

"That's not what they have in mind."

Hawkes shook his head. "Afraid I don't follow."

"We have decided," said George Bent.

"Decided what?"

"We have forsaken the blood of our father. We will never again have anything to do with the white man. From this time forward we are only Cheyenne. Nothing more, and nothing less."

"I still don't see—" began Hawkes.

"They don't want me to come along," said Bent.

Hawkes stared at Bent, then at Charlie and finally at George. "You're kidding. This is your father, boy."

George just shook his head and looked away. Hawkes glanced at Yellow Woman. "Don't you have something to say about this?"

"She already has," said Bent wearily. "She has sworn that she will never again live with a white man."

Hawkes looked into Yellow Woman's eyes—and saw nothing there but a smoldering resentment. He had a hard time accepting the situation, and while he knew that it was really none of his affair, he felt compelled to speak his mind just the same.

"I reckon what you all have seen and been through was about as bad as it gets. What was done to you and your people is a terrible thing, done by bad men. But that's no reason to forsake your own father. Your husband, Yellow Woman."

"Just let it go, Gordon," said Bent.

"But it just isn't right," protested Hawkes.

Taking a last look around the room at his family, William Bent said, "What is?" and walked outside with his head down.

Hawkes lingered, biting down hard on the anger that welled up inside him. "One day," he rasped, "you'll see how big a mistake you just made."

"Our mistake," replied Charlie bitterly, "was ever being born. Our father is living a lie. Red and white won't mix. Can't live together. It just won't ever happen. I would cut my wrists open if I thought I could get rid of all the white blood in my veins. We want nothing to do with a people who could do what was done at Sand Creek."

"It's not the blood in your veins that makes any difference," said Hawkes. "It's what in the heart. And your father has a good heart."

Charlie didn't respond to that, and neither did the others. Hawkes searched their faces, hoping for some sign that they were reconsidering their decision, but he saw nothing of the sort. He couldn't fathom why or how they could do what they were doing, but apparently it made perfect sense to them, and they felt justified in doing it. Shaking his head, Hawkes gave up and walked outside.

William Bent was standing at the well, looking off into the distance. Hawkes figured he wanted to be alone. He had isolated himself for many months following the death of his son, trying to deal with his grief, and for a time he hadn't even allowed Eliza to get close. Bent had just lost his entire family. It seemed to Hawkes that in many ways this was a more profound loss than had they all been slain by the Colorado Volunteers. So he kept a respectful distance, busying himself with tightening the cinch of the saddle on the mountain mustang and trying to think of something to say to Bent, even though he knew there was really nothing he could possibly say that would make this any easier on his friend.

Eventually Bent turned to him. His face was like stone, as expressionless as Yellow Woman's had been, and it betrayed none of the pain he was experiencing.

"I want to thank you, Gordon," he said, extending a hand. "Now if you will take my advice you'll go home to your family."

"I have a few more things to attend to first."

"What would happen to Eliza and Grace if you got killed down here? Go home and wait until these troubles are over to see to your business."

"I wish I could, Bill. I really wish I could. But I just can't. Not yet. There's something you don't know. My daughter has fallen in love with that Army officer, Gunnison. I need to make sure he comes out of this alive."

"And just how do you propose to do that?"

Hawkes smiled ruefully. "I wish I knew," was his fervent reply. "What about you? What are you going to do now?"

Bent glanced at the adobe, and for an instant the pain glimmered in his eyes. "I have to make sure they get safely to where they're going."

"I reckon they'll come to their senses, Bill. Just give them time. They've been through hell and they're not thinking straight. But right now it doesn't look like they're going to invite you to come along with them."

"They won't know I'm around."

Hawkes nodded. He understood now. Bent was going to shadow Yellow Woman and his sons during their trek to the Smoky Hill country to join what was left of Black Kettle's band.

"Good luck to you, then," he said.

"Same to you, my friend. And, Gordon, don't go getting yourself captured by the Volunteers. I expect Governor Evans would have you hanged before you could say a prayer."

Hawkes nodded. There wasn't a doubt in his mind that William Bent was absolutely right.

When Major Nathan Blalock told Brand Gunnison to enter his office when the lieutenant knocked on the door, he didn't turn away from the territorial map on the wall behind his desk. He already knew, or thought he knew, why Gunnison was here, and he wasn't interested. He was far more intrigued by the map, particularly by the distance between the Powder River at the top of the map and the Smoky Hill country located at the bottom right corner.

"Good morning, Lieutenant," said Blalock.

"Morning, sir."

Blalock counted to thirty before turning, wanting to make Gunnison wait, for no other reason than that he thought it was important, especially when taking over a new command, to establish that he had total mastery over even the smallest matters at Fort Lyon. This was especially important with men like Gunnison, who were inclined to independent thought and action. Blalock harbored no personal animosity toward the lieutenant. In fact, he thought that in some respects they were a lot alike. He liked to think that he was inclined to independence and audacity and he was well aware that he had a reputation for challenging authority himself at times. Gunnison struck him as an officer made from the same mold. But in this case Blalock was the authority—and he knew he had to make it absolutely clear to Gunnison that he would brook no insubordination.

Settling into a chair behind the desk, Blalock said, "So tell me what it is that you wanted to see me about, Lieutenant."

"I expect you already know, Major."

"The incident at Sand Creek would be my guess."

"Incident?" Gunnison shook his head in disbelief. "I'd call it a massacre, sir. Cold-blooded murder."

"Would you now." Blalock reached for the humidor on the desk and extracted a cigar from it. The humidor had been a gift, as he recalled, from General Hooker—just one in a long line of incompetent commanders of the Army of the Potomac who had been outplanned, outmarched and outfought by the rebels under the Gray Fox, Robert E. Lee. Hooker had led the Union Army to defeat at Chancellorsville, but it could have been much worse. Blalock was convinced—as were most of the newspaper editors and armchair generals—that his audacious rearguard action had kept Stonewall Jackson's hard-fighting Confederates at bay while the Federal Army made an orderly withdrawal from the swamps and thickets of the battlefield. General Hooker had been aware of this, too. It had been bad enough that he'd been whipped; his career would have been destroyed had the defeat turned into a rout. Major Nathan Blalock had prevented that from happening—and the fact that he'd lost more than a third of his horse soldiers in the process only served to render the deed more heroic. So Hooker had presented him with the humidor. More than just a token, it was an acknowledgment of his debt.

"What would you call killing women and children, sir?" asked Gunnison.

Blalock scratched a sulfur match to life on the edge of the desk and meticulously fired up the cigar, puffing a screen of pungent blue smoke between himself and the lieutenant. He had no intention of answering Gunnison's question. It was irrelevant, not to mention that it verged on insubordination.

"I've read some of the reports you wrote regarding your activities against the Arapaho Dog Soldiers. You are a very capable field officer, Lieutenant. But in my opinion you have a bit too much admiration for your adversaries. Respecting your enemy's prowess is one thing, but you go beyond that. To effectively wage war you have to at least feel that you are on the right side, fighting for the right cause—and that your enemy is not. I'm not sure you believe that, where the Indians are concerned. In fact, there are some in this very fort who think you are an Indian lover."

"I don't admire the Dog Soldiers who have been attacking the wagon trains, sir. They are in the wrong and should be hunted down and punished, and that's what I've tried to do. But I don't hold what they do against all of the Arapaho people. I know that it's not just Arapaho Dog Soldiers that do wrong. In fact, some of my own kind have done worse—at Sand Creek, for instance."

"Ah yes, Sand Creek. Colonel Chivington has said that there were a great many warriors there. In fact, a band of Arapaho had joined up with Black Kettle's Cheyenne. The colonel has said that many of the Cheyenne women were fighting, too, and killing Volunteers who had no choice but to defend themselves."

Gunnison scoffed at that. "I seriously doubt it, Major. And I'd be amazed if you actually believed that poppycock."

"Why do you doubt it?"

"They can't have it both ways, sir. The governor is saying Black Kettle's warriors went north and joined Roman Nose, and even the Sioux. And now Chivington says the warriors were at Sand Creek? As for the women fighting, maybe they were just fighting for their lives. Indian men are trained from childhood in the ways of the warrior. Women are not. It's very rare, in fact, to find a woman warrior among the Plains tribes."

"Well," said Blalock, with a faint smile, "I suppose what I'm getting at is that you are a first-rate officer, Gunnison, and you have the ability to go far in this Army. But you are going to have to abandon this quixotic notion that the Indian is worthy of consideration. There can be no doubt that we will prevail against them. And the wars we fight against them will provide men like you and me with great opportunities for advancement."

"I see," said Gunnison coldly. "I believe you and Governor Evans have the same outlook in that regard. That's convenient."

Blalock stood up and turned to the map. "The governor has employed a man by the name of James Beckwourth to form a corps of scouts for the Colorado Volunteers. It seems that Beckwourth, though, has vanished. He had a business in Denver, but apparently he has simply walked away from it. A good many of his scouts have also made themselves scarce following Colonel Chivington's campaign against the Cheyenne."

Their consciences must have been bothering them, thought Gunnison, but he kept his mouth shut. He was in no mood for any more lectures from Blalock.

"For that reason we aren't sure where the enemy is." Blalock reached up to run a finger along the line of the Powder River at the top of the map. "It is generally accepted that Roman Nose has amassed a considerable force somewhere up in this country. It is believed that he has been joined by Arapaho Dog Soldiers and Sioux warriors. He may have as many as three thousand warriors. And it is feared that he will strike at Denver itself."

"I doubt that he has that many men, sir," said Gunnison. "And while I believe he does have to strike somewhere soon, it won't be at Denver."

"How can you be certain?" Though he would never admit such a thing, Blalock realized that Gunnison had more experience than he with Indians and the tactics they employed.

"That's just not in keeping with the way the Indian wages war, Major," replied Gunnison. "They don't go looking for the decisive battle. They employ hit-and-run tactics. They avoid the strength of their enemy and strike at his weakest points. That's why they attack wagon trains and isolated stage stations, not major towns or our forts. This isn't cowardice on their part. Just common sense. They realize that they can't afford heavy losses in battle. That's why if you are attacked by them and badly outnumbered you may still survive, if you can hold them off and make wiping out your command too costly for them to accept."

I see," said Blalock. "It is also believed that there is a large group of Cheyenne and Arapaho somewhere down here." He pointed at the Smoky Hill country. "The same Indians that Chivington engaged at Sand Creek."

Engaged. Gunnison had a bad taste in his mouth. *That was a nice way of putting it.*

"We suspect that those Indians will attempt to reach the Powder River and join Roman Nose," continued Blalock. "I want you, Lieutenant, to go find out where they are, and how many of them there are. Our task is to prevent them from joining up with Roman Nose."

"Our task, sir? We have received orders from the war department to get involved in the governor's war?"

"It is not the governor's war, Lieutenant. It is a conflict between the Sioux, the Cheyenne and the Arapaho nations against the United States. And no, I have had no direct orders from Washington. But I have been in communication with Governor Evans. He has declared martial law in the Territory of Colorado. And since that is the case, we are under his command."

"The Indians in the Smoky Hill are no threat, sir."

"Not so long as they are prevented from joining forces with Roman Nose. That is precisely what we are going to prevent."

Blalock walked away from the map, going to a window that overlooked the fort's parade ground. It was an overcast and blustery day. A stiff wind that carried the promise of rain came out of the northwest to punish the flag that flew over the post. The first storm of winter was on its way, or so said the men who were more familiar than he with the weather in these parts. Troops were conducting a mounted drill on the parade ground, and Blalock watched them for a moment. By and large the men in his command were capable horsemen and good shots. They matched up well with the troops he had led to glory on the battlefields back East. But his predecessor,

Major Merritt, had been lax when it came to drills and discipline. So Blalock had worked the men, pushed them hard. They grumbled now, but they would appreciate him later, when they saw action and survived because of the training he was subjecting them to.

And they *would* see action. Blalock had no intentions of sitting here in this dreary frontier outpost twiddling his thumbs while others waged a war and earned the laurels that would accrue from its successful prosecution. He hadn't been particularly pleased with his new assignment at first. A man who thrived on war, he had been sorry to leave behind so many as-yet-untapped opportunities for glory. And, too, he had suspected that some of his superiors had been eager to send him away, as his exploits had captured the imagination of a Northern public that had far too few reasons to cheer the Union Army in the early years of the conflict. Envy, Blalock surmised, had colored the judgment of his superiors. He made them look incompetent or, worse, spineless. But they would not be rid of him that easily. Thanks to Governor Evans he had a new war, and he would find a way to become the hero of it. That wouldn't be easy, with a command that numbered less than one hundred men, and with the competition of fellow glory seekers like Evans and Colonel Chivington. But long odds had never bothered Nathan Blalock.

"The Indians at Smoky Hill should be considered noncombatants, Major," said Gunnison. "With that in mind, what am I to do, exactly, once I do locate them?"

"You will send a message back to me," replied Blalock. "Keep an eye on them, and wait for me to get there."

Gunnison knew he was about to step across the line with his next question, but he didn't care. He had to know the answer.

"And then what will happen, sir?"

Blalock turned from the window and smiled coldly. "Then I will take command and do as I see fit."

"That wouldn't include another massacre like Sand Creek, would it, sir?"

"As I said, Lieutenant, you are a splendid field officer. You show great promise. So I am inclined to overlook this insubordination. But I will act upon the next—if you are foolish enough to do it again."

"Yes, sir."

"You leave tomorrow. That is all, Lieutenant."

Gunnison gave Blalock a brisk salute—something that, unlike his predecessor, the major insisted upon even at the conclusion of a private conference. Then the lieutenant left the headquarters building. He paused just outside, feeling slightly sick to his stomach, because he knew that his hunch—the one that told him Major Nathan Blalock fully intended to finish the job Chivington had started at Sand Creek—was correct. And he was going to be right in the thick of things. William Bent's words came back to him then. *One of these days you're going to have to stick your neck out and make a stand for what's right.*

But if he did that his career would be over. He would be cashiered at the very least, if not court-martialed. He might be thrown in prison. And then what would he do about Grace Hawkes? Even more than was usually the case, she was very much on his mind now. Because he knew what she would expect him to do, regardless of the consequences. Yet the price would be so high. He felt trapped, and there was no way out of the dilemma that he now faced.

Spotting Sergeant Crocker ambling across the parade ground, Gunnison called him over.

"We're going out tomorrow, Sergeant, with the entire troop. Inform the men."

"Yes, sir!" This was good news to Crocker, who chafed at long periods of inactivity confined to the post. "What are we going to do, Lieutenant, if you don't mind me asking?"

"Our orders are to locate Black Kettle's Cheyenne."

Crocker grinned. Like Gunnison, he knew what that meant. But unlike the lieutenant, he wasn't at all averse to the prospect. As far as the sergeant was concerned, the Army existed to fight. Not guard wagon trains or put up telegraph lines or sit around in dusty outposts behind crumbling adobe walls. And he didn't much care who the Army was fighting at any given time, either.

"Well, sir," he said, his creased, jowly face splitting into a big yellow-toothed grin, "I'd say it's about time we got an invite to the dance."

"That will be all, Sergeant," said Gunnison, feeling very much alone . . . and less than proud, for the first time in his career, of his uniform.

Chapter Thirteen

When Wolf Chief heard that Horse Catcher wished to have words with the other Wolf Soldiers from Black Kettle's band, he was pretty sure what the pipeholder was going to say. A few days ago news had reached them of the massacre at Sand Creek—news that had made Wolf Chief sick with fear and anxiety, for he had no way of knowing what had become of his mother and sister.

As he had thought, Horse Catcher told the warriors who answered his summons—over a hundred—that they needed to ride south, locate the survivors of the massacre and see to it that they reached the Powder River safely. It was their duty to do this.

Wolf Chief was torn. They had only just begun to conduct raids against stage stations and trading posts and wagon trains all along the Republican River. It bothered him that they had not made one, big concerted attack on the whites—Denver was a perfect target, in his opinion. They were certainly strong enough. Roman Nose had formed an alliance with Spotted Tail's Brulé Sioux and Pawnee Killer's Oglala Sioux. With bands of northern Arapaho Dog Soldiers and Cheyenne Wolf Soldiers, there were thousands of warriors congregated in several large encampments along the Powder River. Never had so many Indians from so many different bands joined together in common cause. And yet while there was a unity of purpose—to make the white men pay for all the broken treaty promises and all the indignities heaped upon the tribes over the years—the leaders could not seem to agree on a strategy.

Roman Nose wanted to strike with all their might at Denver, but others balked at that suggestion, preferring instead to carry out a series of raids to keep the whites guessing. Winter was coming, and now was not the time to launch a major campaign, they said. Better to wait until spring. For now they were safe; the whites did not dare march into the Powder River country, and the raids would keep the blue coats spread thin. The buffalo were plentiful along the Powder River, and as there were so many mouths to feed, about eight thousand Cheyenne, Sioux and Arapaho combined, hunting had to be a priority. And far more hunting parties than war parties were going out.

None of this, of course, was to Wolf Chief's liking. But he could not argue against the need to provide a winter store of meat for the encampments. He had come here to fight, to kill as many whites as possible before he fell in battle. He knew the Indian cause was doomed, regardless of whether they attacked in force now or waited until the spring. He knew he was going to die, as would all his fellow Wolf Soldiers. His one desire was that they be given the opportunity to die with honor in battle, and not starving to death on some wretched reservation. The leaders were thinking about the future—as if there was one! Wolf Chief knew better. But he could hardly speak out to say there was not much point in worrying about whether the people had enough to eat this winter, since they were as good as dead, anyway.

Still, he could not deny that he wanted to find out whether his family lived, so he could not bring himself to reject Horse Catcher's plan. Unfortunately it was becoming more and more apparent that Roman Nose would not prevail this winter. They were not going to attack Denver. This way, said Horse Catcher, they could bring their families back here to the Powder River where they would be safe from the bluecoats, and the Wolf Soldiers would not miss anything but an occasional raid during their absence. Nearly all the warriors present agreed. So did Wolf Chief. Horse Catcher went to Roman Nose and informed him of their decision. This was mere courtesy, as Roman Nose did not have the authority to tell them not to go. On the following day they rode out, ninety warriors in all, heading south in the direction of Sand Creek. Normally there would have been high spirits and a good deal of bravado associated with the departure of braves. But this time the Wolf Soldiers were a grim and silent lot, as solemn as a funeral procession.

Gordon Hawkes reached Fort Lyon without meeting any difficulty along the way. The difficulties arose when he got there. He could not just walk in and ask to see Lieutenant Gunnison; after what had happened at Alonzo Burn's trading post he could no longer rely on the Henry Gordon alias. It was possible that no one in the fort would know his true identity. But if someone did . . . well, he just couldn't take the chance. If he fell into the hands of the Colorado Volunteers he was as good as dead, and since the governor had declared martial law in the territory the regular Army was now under his direct command. The men in Fort Lyon weren't Volunteers, but they might as well have been.

Nonetheless, he was determined to find out where Gunnison was. That would be the first step. Beyond that he wasn't sure just what he could do to guarantee the lieutenant's safety. To what extent was the Fort Lyon garrison involved in Governor Evans's little war? Hawkes needed answers. But how was he going to get them? He spent most of one day on the rim of high ground about a half mile from the outpost, trying to figure that out. One thing was certain—he wouldn't find out a whole lot like this.

At dawn the following day he saw dust off to the east. Saddling the mountain mustang, he rode out to investigate. The dust was made by the passage of several wagons heavily laden with buffalo hides. There were eight buffalo runners in the crew, five riding in the wagons, and three on horseback. Seeing them, Hawkes had an idea how he could get into Fort Lyon without, hopefully, drawing much attention to himself. As far as what he would do then— well, he would worry abut that when the time came.

The horseman in the lead of the caravan called a halt when he saw Hawkes riding in, and every man in the crew reached for a weapon. The lives these men led were hazardous, so they weren't the type to take chances or let down their guard. Hawkes checked his horse about thirty yards shy of the wagons.

"Howdy, boys," he said affably. "Looks like you had some luck."

"Luck has nothing much to do with anything," said the rider in front. "It's all about a good rifle, a keen eye and a steady hand. Most of us are crack shots—as you may yet discover unless you're right quick about telling us who you are and what you want."

"I do a little scouting for the Army," said Hawkes, improvising as he went along. "Wondering if you've had any trouble with Indians, or even seen any sign of them."

"We seen sign," said the buffalo runner. "Plenty of sign. But no Injuns. That surprised me, too. We were expecting trouble, what with everything that's happened. Way the redskins see it, the shaggies all belong to them, and we're just poachers."

Hawkes nodded. "Well, I'm going on to Fort Lyon. Thanks for the information."

"That's where we're headed."

"Reckon I might as well ride along with you, then."

"Suit yourself. Get 'em rolling, boys!"

The caravan moved on, and when they neared the Army outpost, the leader told the others to pitch camp outside the walls of the fort. Then he and the other two on horseback rode into the fort. Hawkes went in with them. They weren't challenged by the sentry at the gate. It was abundantly clear what they were, and equally clear why they were there. And as far as anyone could see, Hawkes was one of them. The buffalo runners tethered their horses in front of the sutler's store and went inside. Hawkes lingered outside, scanning the parade ground, noting everything that was going on inside the fort and keeping an eye peeled for Gunnison. Nobody paid him much attention. The garrison as a whole assumed he was just another buffalo hunter and that made him a man whose presence was, at best, tolerated—certainly not one that they cared to associate with to any extent.

He stood out front of the sutler's for a while, and when a soldier passed within earshot he called out to the bluecoat, motioned him to come closer and asked him casually if Lieutenant Gunnison was around.

"Why do you want to know?" asked the soldier, annoyed at the interruption.

"He's sort of a friend of mine," said Hawkes. "Last I heard he had been posted here."

"You heard right. But he's gone. Rode out two days ago with his troop."

"You have any idea where he went? Or when he'll be back?"

"The major sent him south to find the Cheyenne they say are down in the Smoky Hill country."

Hawkes nodded. "Obliged," he said.

The soldier went on his way. Hawkes mounted up and rode out of the fort. Going to the buffalo runners' camp, he loitered there until night had fallen, drinking strong coffee and eating hump meat and listening to the hunters tell their stories. The leader returned from the fort's sutler with tobacco and whiskey, and before long the buffalo runners were well on their way to being inebriated. Later that night

Hawkes rode away and no one even noticed. He headed south, on the trail of Gunnison's detail.

The first day out of Fort Lyon, Hawkes cut sign that he was confident had been made by Gunnison and his men: the tracks of over twenty iron-shod and grain-fed horses along with several pack mules. But he doubted that the weather would hold long enough for him to take full advantage of the find. And he was right. On the very next day a storm rolled in quickly from the north, dumping rain and sleet, and this was backed up on the following day by the season's first snow. All Hawkes could do was keep heading south and hope for the best as the weather obliterated the sign. He knew, roughly, where the Smoky Hill country was. Finding Gunnison would be more a matter of luck than anything else, though.

This time, at least, luck was with him. A week out of Fort Lyon he cut sign again, the tracks of shod horses and mules. It had remained bitterly cold since the blue norther had roared through, and though the sun had been out for several days it had no heat, and the snow remained on the ground. This made following the soldiers' trail that much easier. Hawkes could tell that he had gained at least one day on them; they were only about twenty-four hours ahead of him now. Hawkes pushed the mountain mustang, and the horse responded readily, so that three days later, when Hawkes figured they were getting close to the Smoky Hill country, he finally spotted the men he was after.

They spotted him, too, and the column of bluecoats halted to let him catch up. Again Hawkes realized that he was taking a big chance. What if someone in the detail besides Gunnison knew his true identity? But it was a chance he felt he had to take.

Recognizing Hawkes as he drew closer, Gunnison told Sergeant Crocker that he knew the buckskin-clad rider and went out to meet the mountain man, stopping Hawkes beyond earshot of the other soldiers.

"What the hell are you doing here, sir?" asked the lieutenant. "Grace—is she all right?"

"She's well," replied Hawkes. "And she's the reason I'm here."

Gunnison grimaced. "I take full responsibility for what happened, Mr. Hawkes. But I don't regret it. And if you are here to take issue with me for what I've done, I'm afraid it's just going to have to wait. I have a mission to accomplish, and I will not get into a brawl with you in front of my men."

"Take responsibility for what?" asked Hawkes, eyes narrowing into slits.

Gunnison blinked. He had just assumed that the mountain man had learned about the night he'd spent with Grace at Sand Creek, making love under the stars, and that Hawkes had tracked him down in order to have an old-fashioned reckoning.

"Exactly what are you here for, Mr. Hawkes?"

"I'm here because my daughter seems to think she can't live without you, Lieutenant. I've come to make sure you don't get yourself killed."

"You're taking a risk, sir, and for no good reason. The one thing I don't need is a nanny."

"You'll just have to tolerate my presence, I reckon."

"I don't have to do anything of the sort."

"And just what is it that you're taking full responsibility for, Lieutenant?"

Gunnison drew a long breath. "I made love with your daughter, sir."

Hawkes sat quite still in his saddle for a moment, digesting this news. Finally, he said, softly, "And you say you don't regret it."

"No, sir, I do not."

Hawkes nodded. Then he hit Gunnison, his fist connecting solidly with the lieutenant's chin, so quick that Gunnison didn't even see the punch coming. It was a powerful blow, very nearly knocking him cold, and the next thing he knew he was on the ground, dazed, and scrambling to avoid being trampled by his own horse, which was shying away from the mountain mustang as the latter pivoted, snorting and biting.

"Now do you regret it?" asked Hawkes.

Checking the column of bluecoats, the mountain man saw what he had fully expected to see: a dozen rifles aimed right at him. One man, a sergeant, was riding straight for him with pistol drawn. Hawkes raised his hands, clinging to the mountain mustang with his knees, but he wasn't sure if the gesture would save him. Then Gunnison was on his feet, shouting at his men to hold their fire. The sergeant arrived, pulling his horse alongside the mountain man's, and Hawkes didn't flinch as Crocker placed the barrel of his pistol about an inch from his temple.

"Put it away, Sergeant," snapped Gunnison crossly, and when Crocker hesitated, added, "Put it away, god damn you."

Crocker reluctantly obeyed. "Who the hell is this man, Lieutenant?"

Gunnison glowered at Hawkes, holding his jaw. "A friend," he mumbled.

"Oh," said Crocker. "I never would have known."

Gunnison touched his mouth. Between Hawkes's knuckles and his own teeth—which he also checked to make sure they were all still in their proper place—he had a cut and badly swollen lip. He glanced, annoyed, at the blood on his fingertips.

"Sergeant, go get my horse."

"Yes, sir. But, well, shouldn't I disarm this pilgrim first, sir?"

"You should do what I tell you to do," snapped Gunnison.

As Crocker went off after Gunnison's straying mount, the lieutenant looked up at Hawkes and said, "I guess I owed you that much. But with all due respect, if you hit me again you're going to have one hell of a fight on your hands. Sir."

"Well, I would sure as hell hope so."

"And I do not regret what happened because I am in love with your daughter and intend to marry her at the first opportunity."

"I see," said Hawkes. "I guess you'd better, now."

"That's exactly what she said." Gunnison couldn't help but smile at the thought of her, and how she had looked in the moonlight as she had uttered those words. "But you don't need to worry about me. I can take care of myself."

"Maybe so, but I'm going to stick close just the same."

"That might be a little hard to explain."

Hawkes surveyed the column of troops. "Looks to me like you could use a scout."

"It isn't a job that would be to your liking. I'm to find Black Kettle's Cheyenne and inform Major Blalock of their whereabouts."

"Why does he want to know? Black Kettle's people aren't a threat to anyone. They never were, and they sure aren't now."

"That's not the point."

Hawkes grimaced. "Does your major intend to finish the job that Chivington started at Sand Creek? Is that it?"

"I don't know, for certain," admitted Gunnison.

Crocker returned with the wayward horse.

"Sergeant, Mister . . . Smith here is going to be riding scout with us for a while."

Crocker gave Hawkes a long look. It wasn't necessarily a hostile look, but it wasn't very friendly, either, and it was obvious that the sergeant didn't think it was all that great an idea to have him along. "Whatever you say, Lieutenant." He handed Gunnison the reins to his horse and returned to the column.

"You sure you want to do this?" Gunnison asked Hawkes.

"Are you sure you do?"

"No, I'm not. But I don't have any choice. I've been given my orders."

"When you get your orders to kill Cheyenne women and children, are you going to obey them, too?"

Without a reply, Gunnison put boot to stirrup and mounted up to follow Sergeant Crocker back to the column.

*   *   *

Since he was passing himself off as a scout, Hawkes had to act like one, so he spent his time well in advance of the column. That suited him just fine. He didn't much care for the prospect of riding with the soldiers, anyway. He kept his distance even in night camp, making his own fire some distance from the cavalrymen. That was just his way. He preferred his own company, and it didn't really have much of anything to do with the fact that he was a fugitive from the law. He had always been a loner, even as a youth back in Ireland, so being on his own had seldom been much of a burden on him. Eliza had once told him that it was because he was afraid to get close to anyone, afraid of being hurt, because people always seemed to let him down. They died on him, or deserted him, or turned on him. Hawkes figured she was pretty close to right. His father had died during the crossing to America. Bewildered by grief and laudanum, his own mother had abandoned him. He had been befriended by William Drummond Stewart, a Scots adventurer, and he supposed that Stewart had been a good friend, but he'd also been a slave to his own wanderlust and had soon moved on. Hawkes's first love, the Absaroke girl named Mokamea, had deserted him. Hawkes had never had many friends. These days he considered Jim Bridger one, and William Bent another. But, at least among his own kind, that was about it.

As for Indians, many of the Absaroka Crow had befriended him. And then there was Pretty Shield, the young Sioux woman who had kept him alive with her love during his long captivity among the

Dakotas. He had not seen her since the business at Gilder Gulch following the death of his son, and he supposed that was for the best, because he had feelings for her, feelings that were inappropriate for a man who was married to another woman. Still, he often wondered what had become of her.

These thoughts brought him around to Grace—more specifically, Grace and Gunnison and what the future held in store. He had lost his son and soon, if he did his job and managed to keep the lieutenant alive, he would lose his daughter, too. At times he wondered if he wouldn't have been better off remaining isolated from everyone. The price to pay for getting close, for loving someone, was high indeed. When Grace left it would just be him and Eliza, and one day one of them would be alone, as well. Was that the way it was supposed to be? That hardly seemed right. He could only conclude that life was a painful journey, interrupted briefly by interludes of joy that were soon gone, leaving only a wake of bittersweet memories.

He knew that Gunnison was a decent young man, in spite of the fact that he put duty before conscience—and in spite of his having slept with Grace. But Hawkes had no desire to befriend the lieutenant, even though the man was destined to become his son-in-law. Besides, but for the fact that they both loved Grace, they had very little in common.

So the mountain man kept to himself, and always before daybreak he would be gone from the camp, ranging well ahead of the column. The land changed, from flat and arid sagebrush plains to rolling prairie. He knew they were entering the Smoky Hill country.

But where were the Cheyenne? He could find no sign of them. He did see plenty of buffalo sign, however, and one day came upon a small herd. He shot a bull and took the meat back to the soldiers. They were grateful for fresh meat, having gone two weeks now on hardtack and smoked beef. On that occasion, anyway, even Sergeant Crocker seemed glad to have Hawkes along. The mountain man took a few cuts of hump meat for himself, cooked it over his own fire and ate alone.

Riding out the next day, Hawkes took extra care. He figured that where the buffalo were, the Indians were probably near at hand, especially this time of year. Sure enough, he found not only more buffalo, but spotted a small Cheyenne hunting party as well. They didn't see him, though. They were too busy with the job at hand, and he was too adept at remaining unseen. From afar he watched them hunt, admiring the skill and daring they displayed as they rode straight into the herd, firing arrows into the great shaggy beasts at almost point-blank range, so close that the slightest miscalculation would mean almost certain death. They brought down several buffalo and butchered them on the spot. Unlike white hunters, though, they took nearly everything, not just the choice cuts of meat and the hide, but also the sinew, the hooves, the horns, certain of the internal organs. All of this they loaded onto previously assembled travois, and when they left the killing ground, heading east, Hawkes followed them at a good distance, hoping that they would lead him to Black Kettle's band. This was exactly what they did.

The Cheyenne were on the move. Men, women

and children on the march, strung out for over a mile, with their pack animals and camp dogs and travois laden with their meager possessions. There were several hundred Indians in all. Hawkes got close enough to notice three things. There was no sign of the garrison flag that Black Kettle had once put so much store by. There were relatively few warriors among the refugees. And the Cheyenne seemed to have far fewer horses than should have been the case. Hawkes figured that was because they had lost many when the Volunteers attacked the Sand Creek village. He wondered if Yellow Woman and her sons, George and Charlie, were with this group. And if so, where was William Bent these days?

Having seen what he needed to, Hawkes rode away, returning the way he had come. By nightfall he had rejoined Gunnison's column—as darkness descended on the prairie their campfires guided him in. All the way back he'd debated whether to tell the lieutenant about his discovery. The Cheyenne were off to the east, and Gunnison had been traveling south, so it would be possible to deceive him, to say he had found no sign of the Indians they sought and get away with the deception. As he made his night camp a short distance from that of the soldiers, Hawkes mulled it over. And then Gunnison walked over and forced a decision.

"Any luck?" asked the cavalryman.

Hawkes grimaced. "I found them. Black Kettle's Cheyenne. They're about seven, eight miles east of here and traveling north."

"You're sure it's Black Kettle?"

"I'm sure. They're in a pretty bad way. Don't have much left after what happened at Sand Creek."

Gunnison gave him a long, speculative look. "I'm a little surprised, frankly, that you're telling me this."

Hawkes shrugged. "Maybe I shouldn't have. That remains to be seen."

"What do you mean by that?"

"I mean it kind of depends on what you're aiming to do now."

Gunnison stiffened. "You're talking like you think I have a choice. Well, you're wrong about that. I don't. What I do have are orders. I may not like them, but then that doesn't really matter. I don't have the luxury of only obeying the orders that I approve of."

"You could decide to just keep heading south—and we would miss them altogether."

"Damn it," rasped Gunnison. "What are you trying to do? Test me? If that's what you wanted to happen you could have just not told me."

"I reckon that's so," said Hawkes. "I guess I figured that in the long run it wouldn't make any difference. Black Kettle's people are trying to join the rest of the Cheyenne up along the Powder River. That's plain. They're not doing this because they want any part of the war. They're doing it because that's the only place they'll be safe. You know that as well as I do. But I also know they're not going to make it. Not without a lot of help."

"Oh, and I suppose you are suggesting that I help them accomplish what my commanding officer is determined to prevent."

"No," said the mountain man quietly. "That would be expecting too much."

Gunnison was thoroughly annoyed. "Tomorrow we will ride east and locate those Indians."

"And then what?"

"And then I send a man back to Fort Lyon to report to Major Blalock and tell him what we've seen."

"And *then* what?"

"That isn't up to me."

"Like I said," muttered Hawkes, "they're never going to make it to the Powder River."

They spotted the Indians around midday, and Hawkes took note of the fact that the Cheyenne had not made very good time. Many of the women and children were on foot. Gunnison surveyed the band with a pair of field glasses, which he offered to Hawkes with the comment that the Cheyenne looked to be in poor condition. The mountain man declined the offer. He didn't need the field glasses to confirm what he already knew. And then, from several points along the column, mounted warriors split off and rode toward them.

"It seems they have spotted us," remarked Gunnison.

Sergeant Crocker barked an order, and the troopers brandished their Sharps carbines. Still watching through the binoculars, Gunnison was torn between observing the warriors—he made it out to be about thirty of them—as they gathered to form a ragged line on prancing ponies between the soldiers and the rest of the Cheyenne. He could see signs of panic among the women and children and old men. Some were making haste to the north while groups broke off to flee eastward. Still others huddled together in stationary clusters, uncertain what to do.

"Lieutenant," said Crocker, "looks to me like they aim to charge right into us."

"Don't shoot," said Hawkes.

"I give the orders here," snapped Gunnison.

"Don't you understand? They're just defending themselves. Every time they've seen a blue uniform lately their people end up dying."

"Here they come, sir," said Crocker. "Get ready, men. They'll soon be in range."

Sure enough, the Cheyenne warriors were advancing, holding their horses to a trot.

Hawkes swung the mountain mustang around to put himself between Gunnison and the oncoming Indians. "Lieutenant, tell your men not to shoot, damn it."

"What would you have me do?"

"Pull back."

"You must be joking," said Sergeant Crocker.

"They won't come after us," said Hawkes.

"I am under attack, sir!" shouted Gunnison.

"They will not follow!"

"And if they do?"

"Then you can start shooting. But they won't."

Gunnison looked from Hawkes to the Indians to his men.

"They're in range now, sir," said Crocker, wanting the order to open fire.

"Let's get out of here, Sergeant," said Gunnison.

"Lieutenant!" Crocker injected into that single word all the protest he could muster as he stared at Gunnison in disbelief.

"I said pull back, Sergeant."

Red in the face, Crocker snapped orders at the soldiers. They whipped their horses around and kicked them into a gallop. Gunnison and Hawkes brought up the rear. Looking back, they saw that the Cheyenne warriors were not pursuing them.

Two miles form the Indian column Gunnison called a halt. He dismounted and in a fit of frustrated rage hurled his hat to the ground.

"I am not in the habit of running from a fight!" he shouted at Hawkes.

The mountain man just sat his horse and didn't say anything.

"If you want my opinion," growled Crocker, "we should go back there and kick the hell out of them redskins."

"Shut the hell up, Sergeant," snapped Gunnison. "My orders were to find the Cheyenne, not engage them in battle. Pick a man to ride back to Fort Lyon."

"Yes, sir."

With one last angry look thrown at Hawkes, Gunnison took a dispatch book from his saddlebags, sat on his heels and began to compose a report to Major Blalock.

Watching him, Hawkes wondered if the lieutenant understood that he was writing out a death warrant for Black Kettle's Cheyenne.

Chapter Fourteen

They camped that night several miles away from the scene of the confrontation with the Cheyenne. Gunnison posted extra sentries, and Hawkes thought that was a good idea. There was no way of anticipating what the Indians might do. Black Kettle's people had been pushed into a corner. They were desperate and that made them unpredictable. And the warriors were ready to die. That was obvious by their willingness to ride straight at Gunnison's command. With their carbines, the bluecoats could have mowed them down. The Cheyenne weren't stupid. They knew this was the case. Normally that was a situation an Indian brave would avoid at all costs. They were not suicidal, but Black Kettle's band had nothing to lose anymore. So Hawkes couldn't be sure that the warriors would not launch an attack on the soldiers' camp that night, and he, too, stood guard, just in case, forsaking any sleep whatsoever.

Dawn came without any sign of the Cheyenne, and Hawkes rode out to have a look around. He found sign indicating that the Cheyenne had continued northward. He wasn't surprised. What choice did they have? Turning back would not save them. He doubted that very many of them actually believed they could reach the Powder River and safety, especially now that their whereabouts had been discovered by the enemy. Hawkes went back to Gunnison and gave him the news.

"Then we will follow them," said the lieutenant. "We'll keep our distance, try to stay out of sight, but I won't let them get too far ahead."

"You don't have to worry about that," said the mountain man. "You want to find them again, that won't be a problem."

"My orders were not just to find them—but rather to find them and then keep track of them until Major Blalock arrives."

"But they'll know we're here. They won't have to see us to know that. And they may turn and put up a fight."

"I will not run away a second time," said Gunnison firmly, and Hawkes knew he meant every word of it.

"I'll keep track of them," he said. "You just stay well back. At least a half day, even more."

"Don't try anything. Don't even think about trying to lead me astray."

"You have my word on that."

Gunnison nodded. He thought he knew Hawkes well enough to rely on the man's word. But he couldn't resist adding, "I just don't know where you stand in all this. You're going to have to pick a side soon enough."

"We'll all have to do that," replied Hawkes.

He rode on well ahead of the column. Picking up the Cheyenne sign again, he followed it.

And rode right into an ambush.

The man literally came right up out of the ground. He had excavated a shallow hole and laid down in it and covered himself with dirt, and then waited until Hawkes was passing by, only a few feet away. Startled, Hawkes's horse snorted and jumped sideways so violently that it nearly unseated its rider, and by the time Hawkes had recovered the ambusher was on him, leaping through the air to hit him hard and knock him out of the saddle. Impact with the ground knocked the wind out of him, and in the next instant Hawkes found a knife pressed to his throat. He remained very still, because he recognized the man who straddled him, and who held the blade to his throat.

It was William Bent.

"You better have a damned good reason for being here, Gordon," rasped Bent.

"Let me up and I'll tell you."

Bent thought it over. He hesitated, and Hawkes realized that the Cheyenne weren't the only ones who were in a desperate situation. So was Bent, or he would never have contemplated, even for a moment, cutting a friend's throat—which was precisely what he was contemplating now.

"Okay," he said at last, and got up to back off a few steps, knife in one hand and a pistol in the other, a look of grim determination on his face.

Laboring to suck air into his tortured lungs, Hawkes got to his feet. He saw that the mountain mustang stood a dozen strides away. Most horses would have strayed farther or run off altogether, but not the mustang. His sheathed Plains rifle was tied to the saddle, and it might as well have been on the moon. The only weapon he had on his person was a knife. But then, he had no intentions of killing anyone, least of all William Bent.

"I kept telling you to go home," said Bent. "To stay out of this."

"I wish I could. But I can't, not any more than you can."

"My family is in danger. Yours isn't."

"There's a lieutenant out there who might be family soon."

"So Gunnison is leading those bluecoats. That's why you're here."

Hawkes nodded. "And your family—they're with Black Kettle?"

It was Bent's turn to nod. "Followed them all the way from the ranch. And I reckon I'll keep following until . . . until they get where they're going."

"They won't get that far." Hawkes could sense that he wasn't telling Bent anything he didn't already know. "Gunnison sent a messenger back to Fort Lyon. Before long there'll be a lot more soldiers here, led by a man who won't back off the way Gunnison did yesterday."

"Yeah, I saw that. But I was too far away to recognize you or the lieutenant. Now it makes sense to me. I couldn't figure it out at the time. George and Charlie were probably with that bunch who rode out to fight you. They didn't stand a chance, and I reckon they knew that. I was just about to ride in and join them, whether they liked it or not, and then Gunnison fell back. I guess he still hasn't decided to follow his conscience, seeing as how he's still following the Cheyenne instead."

"He has his orders."

"There's going to be some killing soon. I hope you realize that, Gordon. You managed to avoid it yesterday. But you won't be able next time."

"I can only try."

"It's just too late. You're on the wrong side, too."

"I guess it might look that way to you," conceded Hawkes.

"It sure as hell does. I know why you're doing this. But if you start killing Cheyenne to protect your lieutenant, then you and I become enemies at that moment."

"I don't intend to let that happen."

Bent's laugh was bitter. "Of all people you should know by now that it doesn't matter what we intend to have happen."

With that he sheathed his knife, stuck the pistol under his belt and walked away over a low grassy rise and out of sight without once looking back. Hawkes mounted up and waited until he heard the sound of a horse at a gallop, a sound that quickly faded away. Bent was riding off to the north, following the Cheyenne. Considering the position of the sun in the western sky, Hawkes turned back south, expecting to rejoin Gunnison's command a little before sundown.

Hawkes didn't tell Gunnison about his run-in with William Bent. He didn't see any good reason to do so. For the next five days they continued to follow

Black Kettle's band, keeping their distance. Gunnison calculated that Major Blalock would catch up with them no sooner than a fortnight after he had dispatched the messenger to Fort Lyon. Until then he would keep tabs on the Cheyenne, as ordered. Beyond that he didn't even want to speculate what would happen. But he had a bad feeling in the pit of his stomach. In fact, it had been there ever since he had left Blalock's office with his orders.

Hawkes had a bad feeling, too—and not only because he worried about what would happen once Blalock showed up. Another winter storm blew through two days after Bent's ambush, dumping more snow and sending temperatures plummeting. He could tell by reading the sign that the Cheyenne were suffering badly. Black Kettle did not dare send out warriors on hunting forays, for fear they would clash with soldiers. And now game was scarce. His people were short of provisions. And since they had lost most of their horse herd during the massacre of Sand Creek, the majority of them had to walk through the deep snow, which slowed them down even more. They were tired, cold, hungry and afraid. Hawkes couldn't be sure, but he had a hunch the Indians knew by now that the bluecoats were following them. He hadn't seen a single Cheyenne for a week, but that didn't mean they hadn't seen him, or Gunnison's column. And if they knew, they might decide at any moment to turn and fight.

Then—a new and unexpected development. Hawkes saw where eighty or ninety riders on unshod horses had joined Black Kettle's band. They had come from the northwest, and it wasn't hard to figure out who they were. Hawkes made haste back to the column and told Gunnison about what he'd found.

"What do you make of it?" asked the lieutenant.

"It could only mean one thing. The Wolf Soldiers have come back. They must have learned what happened at Sand Creek."

"Eighty of them, you say."

"At least. Probably more."

"How many fighting men does that give Black Kettle now?"

"Who knows. We saw about thirty the other day. So you have to figure they outnumber us at least six to one now. Like as not the odds are worse than that."

Gunnison nodded. "I suspect they haven't tried to drive us off before because there were so few of them. Now that's no longer the case. Now I guess it depends on Black Kettle's frame of mind."

"Don't be too sure. Those Wolf Soldiers may not pay Black Kettle much heed anymore. He didn't want them to go off and join Roman Nose, but they did it anyway. No, if they decide to tangle with you, Lieutenant, they'll do just that whether Black Kettle approves or not."

"And you're thinking that's exactly what they'll decide to do."

"They want revenge," said Hawkes.

"Well, you know all about revenge."

"That I do. I know what they're feeling right now, and how they're thinking. And we both know what they're capable of doing."

"I will withdraw," said Gunnison, "if that's what you're getting around to."

"You don't want to fight them."

"I'll do what I have to. If they attack, we'll fight. There will be no running away this time."

Hawkes nodded. Gunnison's pride had been injured by turning tail. He could hardly blame the young lieutenant on that score, or for a decision to defend himself if attacked. Gunnison had his orders—and he was going to obey them, come what may, and it didn't seem to Hawkes that there was much point in discussing the matter further.

At dawn the next morning Hawkes rode out as the soldiers broke camp. He kept his eyes peeled for Cheyenne Wolf Soldiers and also for game. Deer tracks in the snow led him to a clump of trees near a frozen stream, and before long he had flushed the deer and brought two of them down with a couple of well-placed shots. He realized that the gunfire might attract the wrong kind of attention, but that didn't really matter, since he intended to ride right up to the Cheyenne today.

Tying one deer down behind the cantle of his saddle and draping the other one across the pommel, he pushed the mountain mustang into a canter and by midmorning had nearly caught up with the Indians. He wasn't too surprised when William Bent made an appearance, coming up over a rise and galloping down a long slope to catch up with him. Hawkes slowed the mountain mustang but didn't stop, and Bent fell in alongside and looked at him like he was a lunatic.

"You're getting way too close, Gordon. Back off."

"I'm going in. I want to talk to them."

"Time for talking is past. We tried that." Bent glanced at the deer. "Who's that for?"

"The Cheyenne. They haven't been doing much hunting."

"Hard to do when you're on the run." Bent nodded. "It's a nice gesture. But it won't feed too many."

"It's a start. And I figure there's a chance they might not kill me, at least not right off, if I'm bringing them something."

"A peace offering? They might just figure it's another trick. Don't do it, my friend. Besides, I think the Wolf Soldiers have come home."

"I know. That's why I'm doing this."

"The Wolf Soldiers are not going to want to talk."

"I hope you're wrong. But if you're not, I'd be obliged if you would get word to Eliza that I won't be coming back. It would be better if she knew I was dead than to not know anything. That happened once, when the Dakota Sioux took me prisoner, and it was plenty hard on her, not knowing from one day to the next if I was dead or alive."

Bent shook his head. "I don't rightly know what you're trying to prove, Gordon. It's little wonder that you've gotten into so much trouble in your life. You just can't seem to mind your own business."

Hawkes had to smile. "You know, I've heard that said."

Bent had to smile back. "I sure hope I don't have to kill you myself, because I like you."

"Feeling's mutual. And I hope you don't have to, either."

"Well, if you insist on going in, reckon I'll go with

you. Because I sure don't want to have to give Eliza that kind of news."

"You may not be any more welcome than I am, Bill."

"I realize that. But we might as well go ahead and find out."

So they rode in together. Before long they spotted the tail end of the ragged Cheyenne column, and almost immediately a dozen mounted warriors galloped out to intercept them. They were all Wolf Soldiers, and they looked none too friendly. Hawkes noticed that Wolf Chief was not among them, and he wondered if the brave he had saved at Burn's trading post—it seemed like years ago instead of only a few months back—had gotten his wish and died in battle with the blood of slain white men on his hands.

Hawkes let Bent do the talking—and Bent talked for a while. Then the warriors conferred among themselves very briefly before one spoke curtly to Bent and motioned toward the Indian column.

Bent's sigh of relief was audible. "So far so good," he told Hawkes. "They'll let you go in. But whether you get out alive or not, that's something else again."

"Never cross a bridge until you come to it," said Hawkes.

"They know you're the one who's been scouting for the bluecoats. They know I've been following them, too, but then they know why I'm doing that, and I don't think they hold it against me."

The Wolf Soldiers escorted them the rest of the way. As they moved to the head of the column, Hawkes got his first close look at the Cheyenne, and what he saw only confirmed his suspicions: These people were suffering. And they were scared, too, almost without hope. He could see that in their eyes as they watched him like hunted animals watch an approaching predator, knowing the end is near and helpless to prevent it.

As they drew near the head of the caravan a group of mounted Indians broke free from the rest and came out to meet them. As the riders stopped their horses, the rest of the Cheyenne kept trudging northward through the snow. How many steps, mused Hawkes, from here to the Powder River? Not that it really mattered. However many there were it was too many for these people in the condition they were in.

Among the horsemen who had come out to meet them was Black Kettle. Horse Catcher, the pipeholder of the band's Wolf Soldiers, was also present. And so was Wolf Chief. Hawkes sensed that William Bent was disappointed because neither of his sons had come out, and every now and then he would glance to his right, at the human stream of misery plodding past, in hopes, Hawkes supposed, of catching a glimpse of the family that had forsaken him.

"Why have you come here?" Black Kettle asked Hawkes. He was much changed since Hawkes had last laid eyes on him. He looked gaunt. He was, thought Hawkes, a broken man, a man, perhaps, who would have preferred to lie down and die, but who did not have that luxury because his people still depended on him for leadership.

Hawkes said, "I've come to warn you. But first, here is some fresh meat for your people."

Black Kettle gazed inscrutably at the deer. Then he

nodded, and two of the Wolf Soldiers relieved Hawkes of the kills and rode away. The others remained, watching the mountain man like vultures observing the final struggles of a dying animal, hoping, he figured, for one word from Black Kettle so that they could kill him on the spot. Hawkes silently, vehemently, cursed Governor Evans and Colonel Chivington then—not because their actions had placed his life in jeopardy but rather because of what they had done to these peace-loving people.

"Warn us?" asked Black Kettle. "We know the bluecoats are following us. What we don't know is why they are doing this. We rode out to fight them because we thought that was why they had come. This has always been the case before. Instead, they ran away. But they do not go home."

"They had orders to find you, and then keep track of you, until reinforcements come."

"And when the other bluecoats come?"

Hawkes could tell that Black Kettle already knew the answer to that question. "Then I reckon they'll attack," he replied.

Some of the Wolf Soldiers muttered angrily among themselves, until Black Kettle silenced them with a curt gesture.

"You ride with the bluecoats. Why are you telling us this? Did they send you? Do they know you are here?"

"No, they don't know." Hawkes drew a long breath, shaking his head. "Look, I know I can't stop this fight. But my daughter is in love with the man who leads the soldiers that are following you. He doesn't want a fight, either. But he's a soldier, and he has orders, and he won't run away a second time. I'm just trying to keep him alive. I figure your Wolf Soldiers are going to attack him. But that would be a mistake."

Why would it be a mistake?" asked Black Kettle. "You are right. The Wolf Soldiers want to fight. And why shouldn't they? You say the bluecoats will attack us when more of them come. If we kill the ones who are here now there will be fewer to attack us later."

"It would be a mistake because many of your warriors would die."

"They are not afraid to die. They know they will anyway, when the soldiers attack."

Hawkes grimaced. He didn't particularly like what he was about to do. But he was boxed in, and saw no other alternative.

"I'll tell you what I think you should do," he said grimly. "You should ride out to fight the bluecoats who are coming here from Fort Lyon. The soldiers who follow will not attack until they have been reinforced. If the reinforcements do not come then you have nothing to fear from them."

"This is a trick," said Wolf Chief, glaring at Hawkes. "More of the white man's treachery. He is lying. The soldiers sent him here to deceive us."

"This is the man who once saved your life," replied Black Kettle. "If he is our enemy why did he do that?"

A sullen Wolf Chief did not answer. Hawkes figured Black Kettle was trying to reason with the warrior, but all he had managed to do was stoke Wolf Chief's anger. He did not want to be reminded that the mountain man had saved him from Talbot and the Volunteers. It was too humiliating to owe his life to a white man.

Black Kettle turned to Horse Catcher, his eyes asking a silent question. He valued the pipeholder's opinion, and needed his advice.

"We should consider this man's words carefully," said Horse Catcher gravely.

Black Kettle nodded. "You are free to go," he told Hawkes.

"One last thing," said Bent. "My family—are they well?"

"They are well, Little White Man."

Hawkes studied the chief's face, wondering if Black Kettle knew all the details of what had transpired between Bent and his family. He knew the chief and the white trader were close friends. But Black Kettle's expression betrayed nothing.

As they rode away Bent shook his head. "You sure surprised me with that idea of yours, Gordon."

"It was all I could think of."

"Well, if it works, you might have saved Gunnison's bacon—at least for a time. But if the Wolf Soldiers do attack the reinforcements, and even if they win a victory, it won't change much for the Cheyenne in the long run."

"It might buy them a few more days," said Hawkes. "And at this point what else are we doing, Bill, except trying to stay alive from one day to the next?"

At the council it was decided that the Wolf Soldiers would try to find the bluecoat reinforcements before they could join the soldiers already following the band. There was a risk involved: that they might not be able to locate their quarry, that the reinforcements would slip past them, and if this happened the Cheyenne caravan would be virtually defenseless, for only a handful of warriors would remain behind. But Black Kettle put his faith in Horse Catcher. The pipeholder possessed strong medicine in the sacred bundle that he carried wrapped in a wolf skin. This bundle gave him the ability to see visions that would tell him where to find the enemy. And besides, Black Kettle had given up all hope of peace. The whites had driven his people to this point. Let what happened next be on their head.

Deep in his heart Black Kettle knew the Cheyenne were doomed, though for the sake of his people he maintained that they would succeed in reaching the safety of the Powder River country. One of the most difficult things to do was convincing others of something you did not believe, but he had tried. The only hope for his people had been that the white man had honor and would keep his word as written down on the treaty papers. This had been proven not to be the case. So the old chief was no longer inclined to stand in the way of the Wolf Soldiers. They sought vengeance—and if they were to die they wanted it to be in battle. So be it. There was too much sadness in Black Kettle's own heart to feel the rage that men like Wolf Chief experienced. He did not thirst for revenge for what had been done at Sand Creek. He simply preferred that his people die with honor, rather than perish without it.

Though the Wolf Soldiers relied on Horse Catcher's medicine to guide them to the bluecoats, the pipeholder left nothing to chance. He sent out eight pairs of scouts, with strict instructions on the direction each pair would take and how far they would travel and how many days would elapse before they turned back to rejoin the main group of warriors, which would travel due west from dawn to dusk each day. Most of the pairs were to report back every second day. But a few he sent farther afield. It seemed unlikely that the reinforcements could remain undetected for long, not with so many watchful eyes scanning the sagebrush plains, looking for that telltale dust that would mark the passage of many horses and would be visible from many miles away. Horse Catcher and Black Kettle had agreed that if they had found no sign of the bluecoats in five days the Wolf Soldiers would turn back onto a northeasterly course to rejoin the band.

At the end of the second day of searching, after they had made camp, Horse Catcher walked away into the gathering gloom and built a small fire some distance from the others. He had the wolf bundle with him. He chanted to summon the spirit of the wolf, and when at last the spirit answered he asked for its help. He smoked the pipe and much later in the night, when he was not asleep but not awake, either, he was rewarded with a vision. The next morning he rejoined the others and told them that this very day they would find the bluecoats to the north. The Wolf Soldiers rejoiced. Horse Catcher had had a vision and they knew it was true.

It was nearly midday when Horse Catcher called a halt. He informed the other warriors that in his vision he had been shown how to secure a victory over the bluecoats. The leader of the soldiers was as brave as the bear, but he was reckless. He would not form a defensive square when he saw the Wolf Soldiers and rely on his firepower to keep them at bay. No, he would charge right at them. It was his way—he always charged his enemy. For that reason Horse Catcher sent forty braves led by Yellow Coyote behind a hill to the east and forty braves led by Wolf Chief behind a hill to the west. He and the rest, less than a dozen warriors in all, would continue north until they saw the bluecoats. When the soldiers attacked, Horse Catcher would turn and run away, leading the enemy back to this place, where the Wolf Soldiers would fall upon them and kill them all. Then the massacre at Sand Creek would be avenged. Then the white man would finally understand the magnitude of the mistake he had made by forcing the Cheyenne into a war they had wanted to avoid. The other Wolf Soldiers shouted their approval of Horse Catcher's plan as well as his sentiments.

It happened just as Horse Catcher had said it would. He and the handful of warriors who served as the decoy traveled but a few miles before spotting the telltale dust, and not long after that they saw the column of soldiers, and they rode on, even closer, until they heard a distant bugle and the column surged forward, sunlight flashing off the blade of the saber held high by the officer in the lead. Horse Catcher and his men spun their fleet ponies around and galloped back the way they had come.

The bluecoats had closed to within a quarter of a mile as they passed between the hills concealing the

Wolf Soldiers. Suddenly Horse Catcher checked his pony and turned to face the bluecoats. The warriors with him did likewise. The leader of the bluecoats ordered his troops to halt.

Major Nathan Blalock sensed that something was wrong. Why had the Indians stopped when they were so badly outnumbered, when their only hope was to outdistance his troops? Only one answer came to him. Because they weren't outnumbered at all. Because they had led him into a trap.

Even as this thought occurred to him, Wolf Soldiers suddenly appeared, swarming around the hills and falling on both flanks of his command.

Blalock remembered what Lieutenant Gunnison had told him: Even if the odds were against you, you stood a fair chance of holding off a superior force of Indians—if you could make it too costly for them to try to kill you. But that meant holding a defensive position, and it was too late for that now. Blalock realized he had made a terrible, perhaps fatal, mistake. On the battlefields back East the gallant charge had always served him well. It could break an infantry line, or blunt the advance of enemy cavalry. But this wasn't an Eastern battlefield, and the Cheyenne were not Confederates.

Having left a skeleton crew at Fort Lyon, Blalock had less than fifty soldiers with him. Most of these were armed with carbines, but in this instance that wasn't much of an advantage. The Cheyenne closed with them too quickly. At best the cavalrymen could get off one shot before the fight disintegrated into hand-to-hand combat. And at that point carbines weren't all that useful against the lances, tomahawks and knives wielded by the Wolf Soldiers.

It all happened so quickly. Blalock tried to rally his men to the guidon, but his bugler was down, along with his lieutenants, in a matter of seconds. Then the color sergeant was killed, and as the flag fluttered into the dust Blalock wheeled his horse around and charged straight at Horse Catcher, the first Cheyenne he saw ahead of him, saber raised high. He knew then he was going to die. Most of his men had already fallen, and his moment of truth was at hand. He was determined to die bravely, as befitted a legend.

But the blow that killed Nathan Blalock came from behind, a lance already bloodied plunged into his back by Wolf Chief with such power and such fury that the iron point emerged between his ribs in front. Blalock was dead before he hit the ground.

In a matter of minutes it was over. Fifty soldiers lay dead. Only nineteen Wolf Soldiers had perished with nearly as many wounded.

Some of the warriors wanted to take scalps, and while Horse Catcher disapproved of this he did not try to stop them. For himself, Wolf Chief wanted only the jacket and the saber of the last man he had killed, because he knew that this man had been a chief of the bluecoats. The dead braves were tied to their ponies. Most of the horses belonging to the bluecoats were rounded up and taken as well. Horse Catcher did not want to linger at the site of their triumph for long. They needed to get back to the band as quickly as possible. He was wise enough to know that this victory would not save his people. If anything it would only hasten their end. When the other white men found out what had happened here they would send many more soldiers. Vengeance begat vengeance. That was always the case.

That night Wolf Chief told Horse Catcher that he and some of the others had decided it would be a good idea to attack the bluecoats who were following Black Kettle's band.

Horse Catcher shook his head. "We must go back to our people. Why fight the bluecoats who follow? When the soldiers we killed today do not join them they will probably just go home."

"But we could easily kill them all. Look at what we did today. The bluecoats were easy to kill."

"That is not always so. Today we were fortunate. The soldiers were led by a brave fool. I do not think that is the case with the ones who follow."

"It does not matter," insisted Wolf Chief. "They are few in number. We should kill them now, before they go home."

"No, we will go back and talk to Black Kettle about this."

Wolf Chief fumed. He knew how loyal Horse Catcher was to Black Kettle, so he refrained from speaking his mind about the chief, but he could not understand why so many of his people still depended on such a foolish old man for guidance—the same man who had persisted in believing the white man's lies, and who had depended on the white man's flag to protect him. Wolf Chief was convinced that if only they had fought back at the first sign of white treachery, the tragedy at Sand Creek might have been avoided. But Black Kettle had insisted on peace. Still, there was nothing to be gained by arguing with Horse Catcher.

The following morning, as the Wolf Soldiers broke camp, two dozen warriors led by Wolf Chief rode away in a different direction from that taken by Horse Catcher and the others. Horse Catcher knew what they were going to do, but he didn't try to stop them. The warriors followed him only as long as they wished to, and he had no authority to prevent them from striking out on their own.

Chapter Fifteen

Hawkes didn't tell Gunnison about his visit with the Cheyenne. He was pretty sure that the lieutenant would not understand, and certainly would not approve of his actions. Especially if he knew that the mountain man had suggested that the Cheyenne attack the reinforcements coming from Fort Lyon. Hawkes had a hard enough time dealing with that himself. He didn't need Gunnison's recriminations on top of his own self-doubts. By his agency men would die. That knowledge was a terrible burden, even though he realized that the fight would have occurred anyway—those men would have died sooner or later. He had merely determined the time and the place.

Even though Hawkes kept his mouth shut, Gunnison soon knew that something was going on. The mountain man did report that eighty or ninety Cheyenne had split off from the main body and headed west. Hawkes figured he had to do that because it was likely the lieutenant would see the tracks himself as he followed in the wake of Black Kettle's band. Gunnison asked him what he thought it signified, and Hawkes lied and said he didn't know. The lieutenant couldn't do anything to satisfy his curiosity. He had his orders, and remained on the trail of the band, exactly as Hawkes had been counting on.

The mountain man continued his usual routine—riding out at dawn before the soldiers were on the move, closing up with the Cheyenne but keeping out of sight, paying close attention to the sign and still managing to find some game every other day or so, providing the cavalrymen with fresh meat. And he still kept his distance from the soldiers, even though they had come to accept his presence and even rely on it That included Sergeant Crocker, who went so far as to admit to Gunnison that he might have been dead wrong about Mr. Smith—or whatever his name was after all.

On the sixth day following his visit with the Cheyenne, Hawkes saw where the sign of nearly one hundred horses rejoined Black Kettle's band. It had to be the Wolf Soldiers. But something was odd about the tracks. Around thirty of the horses were iron-shod. Indian ponies didn't wear iron. And not all of the horses carried riders. It looked to him as though twenty or thirty of the warriors were missing. What had happened to them? Had they located the column from Fort Lyon? Had there been a fight? Had the Cheyenne lost twenty men? Even if twenty Cheyenne died, the others would have brought the bodies back, if that were at all possible. Had the Wolf Soldiers won or lost the battle? Hawkes contemplated riding in to find out. But he decided that would be tempting fate.

As it turned out, he did not have to wait long for details. A couple of hours later he spotted a pair of riders approaching. One of them was William Bent. The other one looked Cheyenne, and it wasn't until they had come closer that Hawkes recognized the second man. He was surprised to see that it was Bent's son, Charlie.

"They found the reinforcements, Gordon," said Bent, as they checked their horses alongside one another. "Charlie came out to tell me. And I figured I'd better find you."

"What happened?" asked Hawkes.

Bent was grim. "They wiped them out. Killed every last soldier."

Hawkes didn't say anything. He had made this happen, and it was a responsibility he did not cherish.

"I reckon the Cheyenne losses were heavy," he said, wanting to know just how many men had died due to his actions.

"Nineteen killed," replied Bent. "They say there were about fifty bluecoats."

"Jesus," muttered Hawkes. "Did the Cheyenne bring back their dead?"

"Yes, they did."

"Then where the hell are the rest of them?"

"That's why I had to find you," said Bent. "The others decided to attack Gunnison's command. More than twenty of them, led by your old friend Wolf Chief."

"Damn it," breathed Hawkes. "I've got to get back, warn them."

Bent reached out to grab his arm. "Charlie here says Horse Catcher and the other Wolf Soldiers aren't going to play a hand in this. Not unless the band is attacked."

Hawkes nodded, and glanced at Charlie. "I'm glad to see you're talking to your father again, son."

"Wolf Chief and the ones who follow him will kill any white man they find," said Charlie. "I don't want my father to die. I never wanted that."

"Convince Gunnison to go away, Gordon," urged the elder Bent. "Before it's too late."

"Might already be." Hawkes spun the mountain mustang around and rode south hellbent for leather.

When he saw the way Hawkes was pushing his horse, Gunnison immediately knew that something was amiss—and he had a pretty good idea what it could be. Halting the column, he turned in his saddle and told Sergeant Crocker to make sure the men kept their eyes peeled. All along the line the troopers pulled carbines from saddle scabbards and commenced to scanning the horizon.

Reaching the column, Hawkes checked his horse in a spray of snow.

"Are they coming?" asked Gunnison.

Hawkes nodded. "About twenty of them, led by Wolf Chief."

"When will they get here?"

Hawkes was impressed by how calm Gunnison seemed to be. "I'm not sure," he replied.

"Where did you see them?"

"That's just it. I don't know where they are because I haven't seen them. They rode out with the other Wolf Soldiers but didn't come back. Charlie

Bent told his father what they were aiming to do, and his father told me."

Gunnison nodded, warily scanning the snow-covered plains. "Well, they can't be far. We need to find a place to make our stand."

"There's a dry creekbed about a mile north of here."

"Then let's go."

"There's one other thing you should know, Lieutenant."

"I'm listening."

"Your reinforcements from Fort Lyon—they won't be coming."

"How do you know that?"

"The Wolf Soldiers found them, and killed them all."

Gunnison was stunned. "Are you sure about this?"

"I'm very sure." Hawkes figured he ought to tell Gunnison just how it was that the reinforcements had met their death at the hands of the Cheyenne, but he opted not to. It would have to wait. In time he would tell the whole story. Right now he had to make sure Gunnison survived the imminent attack.

They rode north at a quick pace and reached the dry creekbed Hawkes had mentioned. Gunnison made up his mind that it would do. This country did not offer much to choose from when it came to terrain suitable for defense. He placed his men along a fifty yard stretch and gave four troopers the responsibility of holding the horses at one end of the line. He knew from experience that Indians often tried to run off the horses of their enemy, and he stressed to the four men that they could not under any circumstances allow that to happen.

The creek had steep banks, about four feet high all along the line. The snow in the creek bottom was a couple of feet deep. Gunnison was hoping that when the Indians did come they would not be able to see his men until they were well within range of the carbines. If there were only twenty warriors with Wolf Chief then he was confident that they could hold the Cheyenne at bay.

He was partly right.

Less than two hours later they spotted the Wolf Soldiers, coming up from the south, following their tracks. The iron-shod cavalry horses left distinctive sign in the snow, making it easy to distinguish them in the trail made by Black Kettle's band, which had passed this way previously.

Gunnison didn't have to tell his men to hold their fire. He knew they would await his order, for these soldiers had been with him in a half-dozen scrapes with Arapaho warriors. They were veterans, and not likely to be unnerved by the presence of hostiles. They were aware of what was expected of them by their commanding officer, and they had faith in his judgment. Gunnison waited until the Wolf Soldiers were within a hundred and fifty yards of the dry creekbed before rising up to take aim with his pistol and pull the trigger. The range was long for a side-gun, but the pistol's report was the signal that the cavalrymen crouching in the creekbed had been waiting for. As one they rose up and fired a volley into the oncoming warriors. The results were devastating.

Men and horses went down in a bloody tangle. Exhorted to do so by both Gunnison and Sergeant Crocker, the soldiers continued to fire at will.

Through the drifting gunsmoke Hawkes watched the Wolf Soldiers scatter, and at first he thought the survivors were going to run. But instead they wheeled their ponies toward the dry creekbed and charged straight into a hail of bullets. Hawkes saw that Wolf Chief was in the lead—and he was wearing the blue tunic of an officer in the United States Army. Astonished by the charge, he realized what was happening. Some of the cavalrymen stopped shooting, awed by the bravery of the Wolf Soldiers. Crocker, however, wasn't awed in the least. "Keep shooting, damn it!" he roared, and led by example, until an arrow caught him in the shoulder and hurled him backward. Other carbines spoke. A warrior fell, and another, and then another, and yet the few who remained kept coming. Hawkes glanced at Gunnison, just as the lieutenant looked across at him, disbelief etched on his face. This wasn't bravery as much as it was suicide. The Cheyenne warriors wanted to die.

Only a half-dozen Wolf Soldiers reached the creekbed. The cavalrymen scrambled to get out of the way as the warriors rode their ponies right down into them. In the melee, Hawkes made a move to reach Gunnison's side, trying to keep an eye on the lieutenant. Gunnison crouched against the creek's bank as an Indian pony sailed over his head. The horse stumbled in the deep snow of the creek bottom and the warrior who was riding it jumped clear, whirling to locate Gunnison and then, with his lance held high for a killing blow, lunging at the lieutenant.

Gunnison raised his pistol and pulled the trigger—but nothing happened.

Hawkes had only a split second to act. He hadn't fired his Plains rifle, assuming that the soldiers would make short work of the Indians. Now, though, he had to use the rifle or watch Gunnison die. He wasn't yet close enough to have any other options. Bringing the rifle to his shoulder, he drew a quick bead and squeezed the trigger. The bullet entered the right side of the Cheyenne's skull and blew out the left side. The corpse struck Gunnison, knocking him back against the embankment. The lance fell harmlessly at his feet.

A savage cry made Hawkes turn—just as Wolf Chief hurled himself at the mountain man. The Indian's weight bore Hawkes facedown into the deep, churned snow. Hawkes groped for the knife in his belt, drew it from his sheath and plunged it into Wolf Chief's thigh. The Cheyenne roared at the pain and struck with his own knife, aiming for a spot in the middle of the mountain man's back, but Hawkes was twisting his body violently, trying to throw off his adversary, and Wolf Chief's blade merely cut a deep gash in the mountain man's arm. Try as he might Hawkes could not gain an advantage—Wolf Chief was too strong, too agile. The warrior raised his knife again, and this time Hawkes knew he would find his mark, and there was nothing he could do about it . . .

And then Gunnison drove the war lance he had picked up out of the snow at his feet into Wolf Chief's back with all his might.

Shoving the dead warrior aside, Gunnison helped Hawkes to his feet.

"How bad is that?" asked Gunnison, frowning at the blood from the wound in the mountain man's arm—enough blood to soak the sleeve of his hunting shirt.

"I'll live." Hawkes surveyed the creekbed. There was no more gunfire. The last Cheyenne war cry had been silenced. Gunnison knelt to roll Wolf Chief over and study the blue Army tunic the warrior had worn into battle.

"If I'm not mistaken," he said, "that belonged to Major Blalock. I guess what Bent told you was true."

Hawkes nodded. "His entire command was wiped out. I guess that leaves you in charge. So what next?"

Gunnison stood up, still gazing at the Wolf Soldier he had slain. He knew what Hawkes was really asking. He wanted to know if the killing was going to continue.

"First I'm going to take a look at that arm of yours," he replied.

"Don't worry about my arm."

"You don't understand. You're not the only one who has to answer to Grace."

In spite of everything, Hawkes had to smile.

The next day, when they saw the bluecoat column approaching, the Cheyenne of Black Kettle's band panicked, assuming that an attack was forthcoming. Horse Catcher gathered up the Wolf Soldiers and rode out to fight. But as the warriors drew nearer the bluecoats, Horse Catcher saw that the mountain man who rode at the head of the column with a young officer had tied a strip of white cloth to the barrel of his rifle, which he carried with the stock resting against a thigh. It was a sign of truce. And beyond that, the Indians could see that the soldiers were leading Cheyenne war ponies, with the bodies of Cheyenne braves draped over them. The pipe-holder knew these had to be Wolf Chief and the men who had followed him. Saddened, he wondered if he could trust the white flag. He had little reason to trust anything the white man did or said. Telling his warriors to remain behind, he rode on alone. At a gesture from the young officer the bluecoat column halted, and the officer, accompanied by the mountain man, proceeded on to meet Horse Catcher.

Hawkes made Indian sign language as he spoke; his Cheyenne was passable, but this matter was far too important to leave anything to chance. He could not risk being misunderstood.

"We have brought your brothers back to you," he told Horse Catcher. "We did not want to kill them, but they came to kill us and we defended ourselves."

Horse Catcher nodded gravely. He knew that at least the last part of what the mountain man had said was true. Wolf Chief and those who rode with him had had only one goal in mind.

"They died bravely," continued Hawkes, "and we could not leave such brave men to lie on the ground." He gestured at Gunnison. "The young bluecoat chief wishes to have words with Black Kettle."

Still, Horse Catcher did not say a word. He looked at Gunnison, peering into his eyes as though through them he might see the man's heart, and know whether it harbored treachery. Though uncomfortable under such scrutiny, Gunnison steadfastly met the pipeholder's gaze, and finally, with a curt nod,

Horse Catcher spun his war pony around and rode back to rejoin the other Wolf Soldiers. He dispatched one warrior back to the band, and ten were sent forward to the bluecoat column. Seeing the warriors approach, and sensing the uneasiness among his men, Gunnison told them to keep their hands clear of their weapons. He realized that one wrong move on either side would mean disaster. The Wolf Soldiers silently collected the ponies burdened with their dead brothers. Wary glances passed between soldiers and braves, but no one made a mistake, and as the Indians returned to their caravan Gunnison remembered to breathe again.

Women were wailing their grief throughout the caravan as Black Kettle rode out with William Bent and Horse Catcher on either side. The sound the women made was pure torment for Gunnison. "My God," he muttered. "What have we done to these people?"

Hawkes figured he wasn't just referring to yesterday's fight, but rather the whole sordid scheme hatched by Governor Evans and Colonel Chivington, and an assortment of willing accomplices—all the whites who, for whatever reason, welcomed any excuse to act on their fear and prejudice where Indians were concerned.

As Black Kettle and his companions arrived, Bent gave Hawkes a friendly nod. "Glad to see you're still above snakes. Though it looks like it was a close thing," he added, studying the bloody bandaging on the mountain man's arm.

"The lieutenant here has something he wants to

tell Black Kettle," said Hawkes. "I'll leave you to do the translating."

Bent sighed. "I grow weary of translating bad news, Gordon."

"Just hear him out."

"I believe that I am the acting commander of the garrison at Fort Lyon," said Gunnison. "At least I am going to act on that assumption. And with that authority, I am here to tell Black Kettle that it is my intent to escort his people to the Powder River. I will not permit any harm to come to them. And if the Colorado Volunteers should try anything, I will fight them."

Stunned, Bent stared at Gunnison, not quite sure he had heard correctly.

"It's no trick, Bill," said Hawkes.

Bent translated. Black Kettle and Horse Catcher could not remain inscrutable—they looked as shocked as Bent, and conferred momentarily among themselves.

"What are they saying?" Gunnison asked Hawkes.

"They're discussing whether or not they should believe anything you say."

"I can't blame them for thinking twice about trusting a white man."

Black Kettle spoke to Bent and Bent turned back to Gunnison.

"He says his heart is filled with joy. All he has ever wanted was to live in peace."

Gunnison nodded grimly. "Yes," he said. "I know how he feels."

*   *   *

In the autumn of the following year, during the Drying Grass Moon, Black Kettle of the Southern Cheyenne and Little Raven of the Arapahos reluctantly agreed to meet with representatives of the White Father at the mouth the Little Arkansas River. Present were General John Sanborn and a civilian named James Steele, Sanborn's interpreter, a man the Indians knew was a straight talker. A small cavalry detachment from Fort Lyon was also there, under the command of Lieutenant Gunnison, whom Black Kettle was very happy to see. Gunnison's presence meant that there was a second white man whose words could be relied upon.

Through Steele, Sanborn told Black Kettle that the heart of the White Father was filled with sympathy for the Cheyenne and the Arapaho people. He had been sent from Washington to make a new treaty, one that would forever protect those tribes. One that would guarantee that another tragedy like Sand Creek would never happen again.

Sanborn went on to say that William Bent had tried to convince the White Father to give the land between the Republican and Smoky Hill Rivers to the Cheyenne and the Arapaho because it was very good buffalo country, and the Indians could thrive there. Unfortunately this was a request the White Father found impossible to grant. A railroad was to be built through that area, one that would connect the west coast with the east. Many white people would be traveling that iron road, and the White Father feared there would be more trouble as a consequence. No, the Cheyenne and the Arapaho would have to live south of the Arkansas River, among the Kiowa. But if they would consent to do so, and put their marks on a treaty to that effect, the White Father would guarantee them their new land forever.

"This will be a hard thing for us to do," said Little Raven, "to leave the land that the Great Spirit gave to us. Our friends and families are buried there. Their spirits walk that ground. There is something strong for us there. The soldiers came and killed our women and children at Sand Creek. That was very hard on us. We still do not know why that had to happen. There, at Sand Creek, my friend White Antelope and many others lie. There our lodges were destroyed. There our horses were stolen. And there our hearts remain. I do not want to go away to a new country because we would have to leave all that behind— including our hearts."

Translating for Sanborn, James Steele said, "We fully realize how hard it is for anyone to leave their homeland and the graves of their ancestors. But, unfortunately, gold has been discovered in your country, and many white men have gone there to live, and many more will come in the future, and there is no way to stop them. A lot of these white men are your enemies, and they do not care about your interests. All they care about is getting rich, and they will not let anything stand in the way of that. These men live in all parts of your country. There is no part of it where you could live and not get into trouble with them. That means something like Sand Creek might happen again. It means you would once again have to take up your weapons to defend yourselves. We believe you when you say you wish only to live in peace. But in order to do that you must move south of the Arkansas."

"The White Father cannot keep his people from

taking our land?" asked Black Kettle. "Then what happens if his people decide to take the land south of the Arkansas next? Then where will we be forced to move so that we can live in peace?"

General Sanborn assured him that this would not happen. The whites had no use for the land south of the Arkansas. There was no gold there. But there were enough buffalo there to feed the Cheyenne and the Arapaho for many years.

Black Kettle and Little Raven conferred privately for a few minutes. Watching them, Gunnison wondered why they were even considering the government's new proposal. They had reached the Powder River country and found some measure of security there among the Sioux and the Northern Cheyenne. In the past year an uneasy peace had reigned in the Colorado Territory. Chivington's Volunteers were not strong enough to venture north against such a concentration of Indians; the temporary alliance of the tribes was able to field thousands of warriors. And yet here was Black Kettle, contemplating yet another treaty with the white man. It could only be due to the fact that with the war in the East now over— General Lee had surrendered only a few months ago—word was that the Army's attention might now be turned to crushing that Indian alliance. It was ironic, mused Gunnison, that the alliance was now viewed as a threat by his own race, even though it had been the actions of white men that had forced the tribes to set aside old differences and join together for protection. Perhaps Black Kettle realized that war was coming to the Powder River country, that the sanctuary his people had found there was only temporary. And maybe he had known this all along.

Finally the two chiefs concluded their discussion.

"When our forefathers lived they roamed all over this land, free like the wind," said Black Kettle. "They are dead now, and so are those days. The White Father sent you here with his words, and we have taken them to heart. Although the bluecoats attacked us for no reason we will put all that behind us, and will meet you in peace and friendship. What you propose I will say yes to. The white people can go wherever they want and we will not disturb them. All we ask is that they not disturb us in our new country. We are different nations, but it seems to me that we are but one people, and we should be able to get along." He extended a hand to General Sanborn. "I take you by the hand, as I have done before, and pray that the peace we make here today will last."

"Splendid," said Sanborn enthusiastically. "Splendid."

Gunnison turned away, unable to watch. Now he knew why William Bent had declined an offer to be here. This was just too painful to bear witness to. He pitied Black Kettle. The old chief knew better. This treaty would not last. No treaty ever had. But what else could he do but hope to buy a little more time for his people. He was fighting a delaying action, and knew perfectly well how it would all end.

When the treaty had been signed and the parties were preparing to depart, Sanborn sought the lieutenant out.

"You were right about Black Kettle," said the general. "He is a reasonable man. What was done at Sand Creek was criminal, and I intend to press for a full inquiry."

"I hope you do, sir."

"You did the right thing, Gunnison, escorting Black Kettle and his people up to the Powder River. We did not need another stain such as Sand Creek on our national honor."

"Yes, sir."

"I understand you are to be married soon."

Gunnison smiled—as he always did when the subject of Grace Hawkes came up. "That's right, General."

"Congratulations, son. The girl's father—he's a rather notorious fellow, isn't he? Wanted for several murders. I've even heard a rumor that he was behind the massacre of Major Blalock's command."

"I've heard that rumor, too, General."

"But you give it no credence."

Gunnison looked the general straight in the eye. "If he did that, I don't hold him accountable. And I wouldn't categorize it as a massacre. Major Blalock wanted a fight. He wanted to cover himself with glory. To go down in the history books. Well, he certainly got what he wished for."

"Indeed," said Sanborn. "What happened to him and his men has fired up a lot of resentment toward the Indians."

Gunnison shook his head. "I'm not surprised," he said dryly.

"You know where Hawkes is to be found, don't you, Lieutenant?"

"Yes, sir, I do."

"But you won't tell anyone."

"No, sir, I will not."

Sanborn smiled. "You've put yourself in an unenviable position, Gunnison. I trust she's worth it."

Gunnison thought about her—about her touch, her smile, her voice, the way her golden hair shone in moonlight, and how Grace Hawkes somehow made the world right even when everything else had gone awry. He nodded.

"She's worth it, sir," he said. "She's definitely worth it all."